THE PIRATES BLOOD OATH

Timothy Patrick Means

Book One
Pirates Born of Iron & Blood

Mad Dog Publications

The Pirates Blood Oath
Copyright 2022 by Timothy Patrick Means

ISBN: 978-1-7376017-3-9
All rights reserved
Printed in the United States of America

This book is a work of fiction. Names, characters, places, and incidents are either a product of the author's imagination or are used fictitiously. Any resemblance to actual events, persons, or locales, living or dead, is purely coincidental.

Published by
Mad Dog Publications
Boise, Idaho
www.timothypatrickmeans.com

Printed in the United States of America

To the adventurous among us, I lift my glass and toast to your audacious souls. To those willing to cast fear and worry aside, travel to unknown destinations seeking fame and fortune. Stay hearty, me buckos, and steer a course true to ye compass wherever yer heart takes ye!

Chapter 1

"REDBONE, YOU SON of a bastard pig. I'm not surprised by this betrayal. I have warned the captain not to trust you. No matter the outcome between us, you can never return to the ship."

"Aye, I see you there, Señor Montoya, hoping to have all ye treasure for yourself. No, it shall never be; it's all mine."

"Si Señor Redbone. Again, it was easy to outwit your simple understanding. Never had you suspected me of surviving this day to buffet your attempts to take all the booty for yourself. This treasure is for all our shipmates, not merely one man. Today, I shall cut you down where you stand."

"Come boy, come now and try."

IN THE YEAR OF OUR LORD 1701, before the conception of the Iron Born pirates, two lone buccaneers battled for supremacy upon an isolated stretch of beach in what today is known as the Turks and Caicos Islands. The notorious first mate, Redbone, wanted all the pirate gold for himself. The prize: several wooden chests full of gold and jewels taken from the Spanish. The valuable cache belonged to Captain De Vries and the crew aboard the pirate ship *Triumphant*.

Redbone, driven by tenacity and blind ambition, had rousted his captain, alerting him to a British man-of-war anchored in an inlet nearby. The prudent captain decided to bury the treasure instead of handing it over to the British admiralty, who would keep the prize for themselves.

But De Vries had been fooled by Redbone. There was no British sloop. And now, Redbone stood ready to claim his prize.

Redbone was not alone; he had met with several other pirates in Port Royal, that Jamaican port famous as the most wicked town in the western hemisphere. Unhappy with their current captains, they conspired to bring about a new band of pirates who answered to no one except themselves.

Yes, it is a bold strategy if he could form this new pirate band, more vicious and deadly than before. He had pulled a double-cross upon his shipmates on the *Triumphant* to make his plan successful. The dead bodies in and around the hole in the sand resulted from Redbone's betrayal. Only one man still stood in his way.

As a slicing cutlass came crashing down upon a defending sword, Redbone gritted his teeth at Montoya, who had caught on to his scheme and attempted to thwart him by whatever means necessary.

Montoya, an aspiring navigator and loyal to DeVries and the *Triumphant*, was nobody's fool. Suspecting something was amiss, he had hurried to bring the last chest of gold to the shore. Redbone hadn't had time to hide the bodies of the men he had killed.

Now they were caught in a clash to the death. Both men squared off, hatred flashing from their eyes as they fought. The sharp, deadly edges of the swords were pitted with dents as each buccaneer looked to gain the upper hand. Making any headway in the soft soil was difficult at best. However, Redbone, an experienced pirate and a ruthless killer, knew Montoya's weaknesses. Trained from his youth in combat, Redbone applied all the techniques known to gain supremacy over another. Still, he had just killed two other men and was growing weary.

The two now cursed and grunted in the tropical heat, wearing heavy boots and heavy clothing that were burdensome at best. Still, they fought on. Seeing an opportunity arise, Montoya quickly crossed his arm with a wicked right punch directly into Redbone's eye, sending him backward. He decided to cut his losses and ran back toward the only boat available. Montoya ran for his life, crashing through the underbrush until the distant boom of musket fire stopped him in his tracks. Another musket fired, but this time he didn't hear the report. He had already fallen dead in the sand.

Satisfied his adversary was dead, Redbone placed his musket back into his belt and left Montoya, where he fell. He was late meeting the other pirates waiting for him. But he would take only one chest of gold back to his new ship. The rest of the treasure he was keeping for himself.

He quickly kicked the corpses inside the hole he had dug, guardians over his treasure. Like many of his day's pirates, Redbone was a superstitious man; he believed these men he had killed would guard the chests of gold and jewels until he returned for them.

He didn't plan to return for many years. When he was old and tired of being shot at and hunted, he would return for these chests, reclaim his loot, and retire a wealthy, respected man.

Yes, he knew the chances were slim—he could die at sea, and no one would ever discover his treasure. He imagined his demise on some cold fateful day far into the future. He would expect to meet his end upon Hell's Fury, fighting for his life until, at last, fate intervened, and he died bravely. A smile appeared on his face.

When Redbone arrived in paradise, he planned an eternity in the arms of young virgins doing his bidding. For now, though, all would remain secure until he could reclaim his stolen property—if not in this life, perhaps in the afterlife, when he would have enough left to give to the ferryman of the dead, Charon. The latter would bring him across the river Acheron, which divides the two worlds of the living from the dead.

Refilling the hole, he took note of the surrounding vegetation and rock formations. Hurriedly returning to his rowboat, Redbone pushed off and paddled down the shallow inlet that led to a small cove. A small craft waited to take him to the other side of the island. Waiting patiently to greet him were three pirates.

The largest of the three men spoke aloud. "I was beginning to think you changed your mind, Redbone."

"Not to worry ye selves, men. I has kept my side of the bargain. Now let's be off before that pig De Vries discovers our true intentions. Tell me, men, are yer cannons loaded back aboard the *Hell's Fury*, as I have ordered ye?"

"Yes, Captain Redbone, I saw to it before we left the ship."

"Splendid, Mr. Schmidt, now let's be off."

As the four men got inside the longboat, they paddled to the other side of the island and boarded the pirate ship *Hell's Fury*. Once onboard, Redbone supplied every crew member with swords and muskets to prepare for the fight.

Anchored helplessly in a sheltered cove, De Vries and his crew of pirates continued their daily activities aboard the pirate ship *Triumphant*. None suspected Redbone's betrayal; most were relaxing when the Hell's Fury appeared a short time later, blasting her cannons into the helpless ship. Quickly, fires erupted, and men lay on the decks dying. Without mercy, Redbone's pirates boarded the vulnerable ship and fought mercilessly. Swiftly, the crew aboard the *Triumphant* found themselves outmatched and outgunned. Their first mate, Redbone, had betrayed them all, killing the very men he once served. A hulk of burning embers was all that was left of the once-proud ship. Sailing away, having taken whatever they could of value, the men seemed disappointed at not finding the promised abundance of treasure.

A few days later, a disgruntled crew of pirates gathered together to plot an overthrow of Redbone's command. However, it did not escape the notice of the dreaded first mate Mr. Schmidt, who immediately reported it to Redbone. As an example of what happens to those swashbucklers disloyal to Redbone, the conniving comrades were ceremoniously beheaded and cast overboard for the sharks to feed.

A cloud of resentment fell upon the pirate ship, and Redbone quickly realized he needed to band the men together to prevent them from ever wanting to desert again.

ONE NIGHT AS THEY SAILED the Caribbean, just a hundred miles from Hispaniola, Redbone had a dream. In his dream, he saw a man going through a ritual. A large group of other men stood around in a circle holding torches. The man was strapped to a cold device as a low, rhythmic chanting was heard. Something about the top half crashing down and cutting into the man's wrist. Another scene of a pirate unchaining the man, taking hot irons, and forging them into his wrists.

Waking from his dream, he focused on what mattered most. A ceremony to mark the men as pirate brothers. The symbol they bore would warn whoever crossed such a man, knowing it would bring disastrous consequences. But what to call themselves was the question.

Rising from his berth, he opened a window to experience the fresh ocean breeze against his perspiring body. Staring out into the darkness, he could see the rolling sea as the heavy ship parted the waves, leaving behind a white foaming wake. Suddenly the night watchmen sounded off, "Three bells; all is well."

Then, he remembered seeing the ugly device to which the helpless man was chained. An awful-looking thing, one could imagine, sent from hell. *Wait—yes, that's it, a hag so ugly that men would find themselves repulsed by the very sight! Still, what to call themselves? Perhaps, Pirates born of the Bloody Hag? Pirates Born from Iron and Blood. Curses—no, wait, but then again.*

The swashbuckling captain let out jubilant laughter as he thought of those sailing the Caribbean waters, fearing most of all those pirates bearing the mark of the two swords set against a goblet burned into their wrists. Redbone went back to sleep, feeling pride in his newfound strategies for a bloodthirsty set of pirates, feared most by the emblem they burned in their wrists. He was satisfied with his plans to organize the new brotherhood of pirates.

MEANTIME, BACK AT THE deserted island, a lone body lying in the sand suddenly jerked back to life. Montoya opened his eyes for the first time since he had been shot. He blinked several times. A dark coating of dried blood prevented him from opening both his eyes at once; still, he looked about and saw the pounding waves on the beach. His vision, as hoped, was not damaged from the gunshot. His head pounded mercilessly. Realizing what had happened, he didn't dare flinch or move a muscle. Now all around him, the darkness of the night prevented him from making out any objects. The only thing he heard was the gentle waves lapping the shoreline.

After some time passed, he decided he could no longer lie there. Risking everything, he tilted his head sideways and stared down the beach. Seeing nothing around, he tilted his head to the other side and looked about. It was still dark, sometime before the morning dawn. Montoya felt safe enough to attempt to stand to his feet. As he did, to his horror, he saw the coastline littered with bodies. Not far, wading in the surf, was what remained of the burnt-out hulk of the once proud ship, *Triumphant,* still smoking.

Immediately, Montoya cursed Redbone for being the one responsible for this tragedy. Montoya knew that if anyone had cause for the death of these defenseless pirates aboard the *Triumphant,* it would be Redbone; he had the most to gain.

Glancing over to where the treasure was buried, all that remained was a scattering of foliage and sand, nothing to signify the great wealth hidden out of sight.

Now, there was work to do. Being an honorable man, Montoya would take whatever time was needed to bury the dead. The poor souls floating out into the bay were undoubtedly being fed upon by the sharks already. When he took his first step, he felt weak, like he would collapse. The searing pain never lessened. Montoya felt his head and discovered an extended cut from the back of his hairline to his forehead. No doubt, Redbone was sure he was dead.

No one else had survived the battle except He alone. He went to work burying the bodies. Hours later, using his sword as a shovel, he shoved them down inside a shallow grave one by one. As the morning dawn broke, the carnage left behind was painfully obvious. Poor men's faces looked up. Their eyes were still open to the madness and horror of their deaths.

After burying the dead, Montoya examined the beach and saw no further human remains. The remains of his late captain, De Vries, easily recognizable by the brightly colored red and blue jacket, could still be seen on the coral that extended out into the pounding waves. It was the final body, and he found the head missing when he retrieved it. That bastard brigand Redbone's handiwork, no doubt.

The man's boots remained, however. Few men knew De Vries had always carried a dagger in his boot. Montoya tugged on the man's boot, and the blade slipped free as it loosened on foot. Many men would find it valuable for its gold handle; now, Montoya only saw it as a means of survival. Removing the small sheath clipped at the top of the boot, Montoya took the blade, slipped it inside his boot, and dragged the late captain's remains to the beach.

When he was finished burying his late captain, Montoya sat down upon the heap of sand. Panting to catch his breath, he pondered what to do next. No doubt Redbone's brazen assurance that no one would ever find his treasure must have given him a sigh of relief. However, there it was, not far away. At least Montoya hoped it was still intact. The only way to know was to uncover it—something he wished to do as soon as he ate something.

After filling up on coconuts and bananas, Montoya bathed himself to rinse the dried blood that dripped into his eyes. Stripping down naked, he slowly entered the water and dipped beneath the surface. The cut on his head burned him sorely. Scrubbing his face clean, he took another dip down into the salty water, leaving behind a cloud of reddish fog throughout.

Once he wiped away the water, he noticed something not far away. A fin, decorated with a black tip, coasted by. He exited the water quickly and stood naked on the beach, allowing the hot tropical sun to dry his body. Next, he set out to see what remained of the treasure. Again, using his sword as a shovel, he soon uncovered a boot.

A sense of sorrow overcame him. He sat down suddenly in the soft soil. These were the bodies of Montoya's close friends. Here is where they met their end and were buried as protectors of the hidden treasure. No, not a fitting end to a life of piracy. Regardless, Redbone would never see his ill-gotten gain again. Montoya would see to that! Yes, of course, he could take the treasure and run for his life, but if he were captured, those that saved him would take everything, and he would still die.

Slowly, he devised a plan. He reburied the treasure on the other side of the island, far away from where Redbone imagined it to be. When the traitor returned for his loot, he would only find an empty hole.

When Montoya was done, he sat down and watched the sun disappear. The direction of his life had changed entirely. His dreams of a prosperous future were gone, much like the fading light. He laughed aloud as something uncontrolled ruptured from within his soul.

The question now was simple: how to get off the island? He could always return to retrieve the gold at a later time. For now, he must get away.

Over the next few days, he began a tedious routine of gathering firewood in the morning and coconuts or whatever else seemed edible. One day, in his search for food, he saw an abandoned rowboat floating near the shore.

Overjoyed, he shouted, "Oh, mother of precious angels, I'm saved!" Quickly dropping to his knees, he said a prayer for his liberation.

The following day he began to gather supplies for his journey, a few coconuts, bananas, and mangos. He caught a few crabs and drained several coconut shells to hold water.

Before he left the island, Montoya carefully marked the treasure's location on a whale's tooth he found.

Aboard the ship Triumphant, Montoya was one of the only pirates who was a proficient enough navigator to know where they were by dead reckoning. First, one had to line up the stairs to find the island using astronomical observations. Perhaps he would forget the island's location over time, but he had already taken navigational readings with the ship's navigator the night before they disembarked. He etched these details on the tooth: 21 and -72. Without other marks or letters, only another navigator would understand.

One had to wait until it was low tide to find the first clue to the treasure—the symbol he carved was two sets of waves atop each other. The lower line was more pronounced. At low tide, the coral became exposed. In the lowest part of the coral, Montoya engraved the symbol of a bat as the next clue. High inside a cave where the bats called home, Montoya climbed to the top and etched another clue to the treasurer's location—a lone coconut tree and a heart signifying the sadness of losing his shipmates. These symbols were also meant to represent his sadness at the betrayal he felt. There were hundreds of coconut trees on the island, but only one also had a carving depicting a heart. The bat, a blood-sucking flying creature, signified Redbone's betrayal.

Next, the searcher, having found the tree, would discover a new symbol of a rock formation lining up in front of a tall cliff at the highest peak upon the island itself. When the rock formation lined up correctly with the setting sun, the light would shine through the crevasse down into another rock area. Marking the spot was a set of hands clasped together as if praying. Next, a series of tiny dots etched at the top of the tooth continued around and around, totaling a hundred paces. The prominent "X" was at the end of the dots marking the treasure's location at Montoya's chosen place, where the vegetation ended and the sand began. There, beneath the sand, was the precious gold and jewelry worth a king's ransom. If he didn't survive his journey back to civilization, the discoverer would find a small rock atop the rock, where Montoya engraved the last remaining symbol, a goblet representing the cup of Christ.

Montoya, scattering the sand over the hole, was satisfied with his work. One morning, early before the onshore breeze abated his attempt to leave the island, he paddled hard to get past the rocky coral covering the island's exterior.

Finally free of his island's imprisonment, Montoya hoped never to return except to claim his treasure. *My treasure, not Redbone's, that cursed dog. The prize, worth a king's ransom, is never to be enjoyed by Redbone or any of his crew. Oh, might I be alive to witness the look upon that dastardly pirate's face when he digs up that hole only to find the remains of the poor men he murdered? Perhaps, a fitting end to the betrayer, to have his men cut him down when they are robbed and disappointed that there was nothing except pirate bones to be had! Oh, what a happy day that will be.*

AFTER TEN DAYS AT SEA, he succumbed to the torching tropical heat. He felt the effect of heatstroke as he spent his days baking with no form of protection from the sun's blazing rays.

He stared upward, in and out of consciousness, praying for his misery to end soon. He forgot about time and space and was lost in a world of the unknown. Hope for rescue from a passing ship was his only desire, but after time, the tedious rocking motion of the boat left him with little strength.

While Montoya lay in his boat, he thought of his life and pondered the years wasted. In his youth, he had every opportunity to become a full-fledged silversmith, creating fine jewelry for the wealthy elite. Instead, he squandered his abilities and became a pirate.

Back home, the love of his life had been a pretty young lass named Lucia. They were so much in love and planned on marrying and having a family. Regrettably, Lucia became sick with measles and died, the heartache was too much, and his entire world was changed.

Deciding to become a bloodthirsty pirate wasn't a decision he made quickly. When a pirate band captured his merchant ship, the choice was made for him. His talent was soon discovered when the expensive jewelry he had made for a client was found and seized. Afterward, standing at the end of a saber, he was offered a position with the pirates.

Working for years aboard the *Triumphant* gave him many opportunities to learn sailing. He also befriended a swordsman and learned many skills that aided him in staying alive.

But now, alone inside the small boat, the sun dipped on the horizon, and the passing breeze became cold as he shivered. The last food had disappeared, and he knew his survival chance was limited with nothing to eat. His only choice was to curl himself into the fetal position to stay warm.

As the sun lit up the bluish water the following day, his stomach growled, begging for nourishment. With nothing left to eat, his only recourse was to ignore the stomach pangs as the small boat bounced helplessly about on the waves. One could quickly become seasick from this small craft's constant up-and-down motion.

Something else began to trouble Montoya. Besides the lack of food, his wound had become hot to the touch. He felt a sickness invading his body. The infection would soon progress to gangrene. Nothing could be done for him at that point. He had no option but to endure the long days and nights adrift at sea with little hope of rescue.

Time had slowly passed, the measurement of which couldn't be counted. Meantime sailing through the Caribbean, a lone cargo ship returned home from a week at sea. Standing at the taffrail, two crewmen discussed their plans for when they returned home to Santo Domingo and how they would spend their money on their wives and children.

Suddenly one of the men, Javier, saw something a distance away and excitedly pointed to a floating lifeboat. "What is that? Mario, I see something out there floating."

"It's probably a seagull or something, maybe a shark; who knows?" Mario said, discounting the sighting as nothing but his friend's imagination.

"No, I see something; I must alert your father." Javier shouted, running to the bridge, "Manuel, I see something off our starboard. It looks to be a small boat of some type."

"If there is a survivor, we must rescue him at once," Mario's father, the captain shouted. Immediately, the sails were dropped, and the boat slowed to a crawl. A lifeboat was lowered into the water to retrieve any survivors. It took some time to reach the small boat. When the *Hermosa Angelina* crew finally got to the rowboat, they saw inside one man, barely alive, curled up at the bow of the small boat.

Jumping inside, Javier checked on the man. He was burning up with fever, barely alive. Calling his friend Mario to tie a line to Montoya's boat, Javier quickly got back inside their small boat and, taking ahold of both the oars, began to heave hard to bring them back to the *Angelina,* pulling the rowboat behind.

When they arrived, they struggled to bring Montoya aboard. A younger crew boy, all of 14, tried to help. As he tried to join in, Mario quickly ordered the boy to get out of the way, saying, "Bastian, let the men care for the stranger. You should return to the small boat and clean it thoroughly; it might still be worth something of value."

Angered by the older man's comments, Bastian returned to the small boat and stepped inside. Soon he began throwing coconut husks and banana peelings over the side. Besides the garbage, nothing much remained of the stranger's existence but an old sword he claimed for himself.

Having brought along a small bucket, Bastian filled it with seawater and splashed it inside the boat's interior. More garbage floated to the lowest part of the boat. Something not seen before, apparently hidden someplace out of sight, dislodged when he dumped the bucket of water about the boat's interior. It was the whale's tooth.

He picked it up and examined the scrimshaw details. Twisting it around, what he saw was hard to understand. Still young and inexperienced, a lot in his life didn't make sense. Suddenly out of nowhere, he heard his name being called.

He slipped the tooth into his pocket and turned to see who was calling. Mario came toward him, complaining, "Haven't you finished cleaning out that boat yet? Bastian, I swear, I don't know why my father keeps you around!"

In response, Bastian shouted back, "Here, look what I found. It's a sword!"

"Give it to me, now."

"Yes, of course, take it—it's yours."

"You are right for saying that; anything you find, I keep. You are not yet old enough to have anything of great value; you must leave that up to the older ones."

"Of course, I understand; here, take it."

Quickly grabbing the sword, Mario turned to leave. Stopping in his tracks, he turned back and said, "Is that all you have found, Bastian?"

"Well, if you must know, there was something else."

"Tell me at once what else you have found!" Mario

responded excitedly.

"Old banana peelings and coconuts husks."

"Pequeño niño estúpido," Mario shouted and walked away.

Bastian smile back, saying, *"Si, Pequeño niño estúpido."* Stupid little boy.

When Bastian was finished, he walked to the galley to check on the stranger. He found him with a wet cloth over his face. Bastian could tell that the man's face had most of his skin peeled away, and his lips were cracked and bleeding from the sun's rays. The cook, Alessandro, was attending to the man's wounds.

Looking up at the elderly man with concern, Bastian asked, "Do you believe he will survive?"

"It does not look good for the man, I'm afraid. You see, not only is there the possibility he could die of dehydration, but I have discovered that he has a nasty infection that requires medicine we don't have onboard. No, I'm afraid it's not looking good for the man."

"Is it all right with you if I stay with him through the night?"

"Yes, by all means. I want you to promise me that if there are any changes and the man's fever breaks, alert me immediately."

"I shall. Sadly, I feel somehow in my heart that this man has suffered much. Perhaps it's God's way to test him."

"We cannot pretend to know God's heart or plans he made for our lives. Tell me again if his fever breaks."

"I will keep watch."

"Oh, there is something else now. Where did I put it?" Alessandro whispered and began searching through the man's belongings. "Oh, here it is." He announced, handing Bastian a strange object wrapped in an old cloth, "I know how the captain's son mistreats you. Here, I want you to have this. Such valuable items are wasted on the unappreciative. Keep it hidden inside your boot, or else Mario will find it and take it himself."

Holding the costly object in his hand, he examined the dagger briefly. The handle was made of pure gold and encrusted with many jewels. Bastian pulled the blade from its sheath; its sharp edge glistened in the dim light. Looking back at Alessandro, the lad announced, "I don't know what to say, Alessandro. Except, thank you. No one else has shown me the kindness you have. I am most grateful."

"Yes, well, you remind me of myself when I was your age. Do as I say; if the man's fever breaks, wake me at once."

"Of course." Slipping the dagger inside his boot, Bastian quickly pulled his pant leg down to conceal the expensive item. As he sat with the man, Bastian would hear the man calling out names of people he had known or mumbling words. However, sometime in the early morning hours, he grew quiet, no longer restless.

Regrettably, it wasn't long before Bastian fell asleep. When he awoke, he quickly checked on the man to see how he was doing. The stranger no longer breathed. When he took ahold of his hand, it felt cold. The sad outcome of the man's life had reached its pinnacle. Nothing more could be done except a burial at sea—the honorable sendoff for a seagoing sailor.

Bastian walked over to the transom and stared out at the horizon. A small burial, a body dumped overboard, never seen again. There he thought of the man whose life had ended only a few hours ago. He wondered if anyone back home would miss the man. Was his mother or wife back home praying for his safe return? Now, never to return home, his fate would be that of all sailors who die at sea.

Removing the tooth from his pocket, Bastian stared down at the mysterious writings and thought, *what does it all mean?*

Chapter 2

SEVERAL DAYS PASSED BEFORE they returned to their homeport of Santo Domingo. After docking the ship along the pier, it took several hours to empty the hull of fish. After that, the crew was paid, and everyone returned to their homes and family. For Bastian, however, the homecoming was not happy; he was ceremonially greeted by his father, Lucas Fuentes, eager to take what wages the young lad had earned so that he could spend it at the local tavern. Several sudden slaps across his face retorted Bastian's hesitation by his half-drunken father.

Bastian had hoped to give his earnings to his mother, but it was not to be. After his father left him and hurried away to continue drinking, Bastian felt miserable; all of his hard work and nothing to show for it except the painful remnant of his father's abuse.

This exploitation was not unnoticed by the ship's captain, Manuel Rodríguez, who called Bastian back to the boat and surprised him by giving him a much more significant sum of money than before, saying that he suspected this would happen anytime they returned home. He would provide Bastian with only half of his wages. Then, once his father had gone off to drink, Bastian could return for the other half. That morning, Bastian received the other half of his pay and a bonus for being such a hard worker.

Thrilled and excited, Bastian ran home to greet his

mother and there, again, saw the result of his father's handiwork. His mother's black eye. *Enough of this,* Bastian thought. He understood at that moment that the abuse wouldn't stop. Not unless he ended it.

The oldest child, he felt responsible for the lives of his family. His eyes were opened completely, and he decided that his father's abuse had reached its climactic end. Tonight, when his father returned home, Bastian would be waiting for him.

Pushing his plans aside, he surprised his mother with his earnings, telling her that her son had returned home and now was a time for celebration. His mother, Valentina, took her son into her arms and hugged him tenderly, noticing that Bastian suddenly stood taller than herself.

She went to work making his favorite meal and ordered his younger brother Nicolás to race to the butcher to buy two chickens. His two younger sisters, Maya and Gabriella, were handed some money, ran to the market, and returned with vegetables. Older sister Maria helped their mother prepare the dinner. Soon, a delicious smell filled the house.

LUCAS RETURNED HOME TO FIND A FESTIVE PARTY. Bastian played the guitar while Maria sang a happy song. When their father burst through the door, drunk as usual, he shouted, "Where did you get the money for a party? I barely had enough to buy a drink!"

Ignoring his father's comments, Bastian confronted him. "You, father, shall never abuse mother again."

"Oh, I see. The big man returns home from the sea and wants to be the hero. Come, big man, let Poppa show the pup who's the big man in this family." He grabbed Bastian by the collar, and his fist found its mark on the boy's chin. Bastian flew backward into the wall.

This abuse was nothing new; for years, the family

had endured the father's cruelty, especially when he was drunk. But today, that would end. Bastian grabbed the dagger in his boot and plunged the knife into his father's throat. Lucas pulled the blade free from his neck and angrily threw it across the room, where it landed on the floor with a distinct metallic clink. Blood gushed outward down his neck. With surprise and horror, he understood he was about to die. He stumbled across the room, heading to the door, when Valentina stopped him with the crash of a pottery jar against his skull. He lay there, blood spilling out, gurgling sounds escaping from his neck. A few minutes later, it was over. The abuse for so many years had ended.

Putting things back in order with the help of her children, Valentina placed Lucas's body down in the cellar until she could figure out a plan to rid them of his remains. The family felt relieved knowing the abuse had ended and were eager to get on with their lives.

Their father's violent death had hampered the mood in the tiny home, so Maria, seeing the sad faces, picked up the guitar and began singing as though nothing had happened. Valentina reached over, grabbed ahold of her younger son Nicolás and started dancing to the music. This night would be remembered as an awakening from the pain and hardship they had endured for many years.

The festivities continued late into the evening. Everyone fell asleep without being hungry—something they rarely experienced. The following day, Bastian decided to discard his father's body away from home. He struggled to drag his father's corpse upstairs through the back door and place it inside a cart used to gather firewood.

When he returned to close the back door, something caught his eye. The weapon he used to murder his father was lying on the kitchen counter. It was the forgotten item that brought deliverance to the family. Taking it and placing it back in his boot, he returned outside.

Walking to the front of the horseless wagon, he grabbed hold of the cart and dragged it back to the place his father loved most: the pubs filled with whores, and a particular establishment where he loved to spend all the family's money. As he struggled with his father's body, the man's old straw hat, marked with a blue feather in the brim, fell from his head. Picking it up, Bastian carelessly tossed it in the cart. He noticed his father's lifeless expression, his eyes staring back as if begging for forgiveness. Bastian ignored the pitiful sight and placed the hat over the dead man's face.

In the still early hours of dawn, he quickly discarded his father's body in the back alley of his favorite tavern. Bastian thought whoever found the body would assume a desperate bar patron had robbed and killed Lucas. These things happened often, and the authorities, he was sure, would consider Lucas's demise the end of a wasted whoremonger's life.

Unfortunately, the best plans are often foiled by an unsuspecting glance. Bastian had no way of knowing that he was being watched by his fellow crewman Mario, who was aboard the cargo ship *Angelina*, retrieving some personal items he'd left behind. As Mario watched, he noticed Bastian stop just outside the back door of *Los Cuervos Anidan*. He saw young Bastian grab hold of a pair of legs and pull hard, and a man's body flopped out of the cart. The man was dragged to the back door and left behind as Bastian disappeared into the shadows.

Hum, what to do about our young Bastian? It seems he's taking a new hobby of murder and mayhem. As a law-abiding citizen, I have no choice but to report this to the constabularies, Mario thought.

Returning home, all seemed well to Bastian. Soon it was daylight, and Bastian helped his mother wash away the last remnants of the blood from the floor. When they were finished, they rested at the small dining table.

"Son, I see upon your face that what you've done to your father bothers you greatly."

Staring up at his mother, Bastian said, "In all my life, I never thought that I was capable of murdering anyone, especially Father! Although I often dreamed of murdering the cowardly dog for how he treated you, I never thought I could do it."

"You had no choice, son. Your father was drunk, and I had never seen him so furious as when he came through that door and saw all the festivities. He was hell-bent on killing someone! The truth be told, you saved my life, Bastian!"

"Tell me, Mother, why do I feel so miserable if that's true?"

Suddenly, a loud pounding noise was heard at the front door, "Open up, by order of the Governor!"

Staring at his mother, Bastian announced, "It's too late for me, Mother; they've found me. I cannot tell you why, but I felt like I was being watched when I dumped my father's body in the alley. I haven't much time before the guards burst through the door. Take this, please. I cannot say what it is, but I feel it's more valuable than you can imagine. Please, mother, take it before someone discovers it."

She took the small whale tooth from her son and placed it inside a flour jar.

Just as Valentina took a step toward her son, the front door burst open, and a flood of guards entered the tiny home, waking the children with the loud crashing noise. To everyone's horror, the guards took hold of Bastian and escorted him away.

WITHIN A FEW DAYS, Bastian was brought before the local magistrate. He was convicted of murder and sentenced to hard labor aboard a galley ship. His mother cried out to the judge for mercy, but her pleas were ignored.

The day he was taken to the galley ship, his entire family met him. His siblings cried out for his release, saying Bastian was innocent of the crime. Someone else had murdered their father. The cries were, in fact, so disruptive that the ship's captain ordered the guards to remove the family from the pier.

Unfortunately, Mario had testified that he witnessed Bastian dumping his father's body. And, of course, there was the murder weapon found in his boot. A priest was brought to hear Bastian's confession, but none of it changed the fact that he had murdered his father. Although the Jesuits claimed that patricide was not a sin if committed in the service of God, the shackles around his ankles said otherwise. His fate was sealed.

As his ship caught the morning tide and sailed away, Bastian said goodbye to the only place he had ever called home. The quiet, sleepy port of Santo Domingo seemed not to notice its native son's departure. Instead, business continued as if nothing had changed.

A final glance toward the harbor gave Bastian a last glimpse of his younger brother standing on the rocky breakwater as Nicolás watched the ship sail out to sea. He knelt and cupped his hands to his face, crying.

"I shall return," Bastian screamed out. He felt a hard tug near his legs as a group of men were escorted down into the ship's hull to be locked away inside their cells. One final look back at the small harbor, and a single word fell across his lips: "return." Bastian's sentence had begun.

His voice was silenced as a series of curses echoed deep in the ship's bowels, and Bastian was led down into the abyss, not knowing if he would ever see home again or survive this ordeal. *What of my family? Who will care for them?* Sorrow pierced his soul as the chains were locked into place. His fate was sealed; he could do nothing else but worry about what would happen to his family.

Chapter 3

IT WAS NOT LONG BEFORE REDBONE'S desire for a device to perform the Iron Born ceremony became a reality. Now, the search for a particular sculptor skilled in carving and others to work in iron and bronze. Arriving in Barcelona, Spain, Mr. Schmidt, the *Hells Fury's* first mate, had precise specifications for creating the Bloody Hag. He was equipped with drawings from one of the crew members who once made his living as an artist: the sketches drawn on paper were a derivative of Redbone's imagination.

Mr. Schmidt, with long blonde hair and a fair complexion, disguised himself as a wealthy Scandinavian traveler. Disembarking from the ship, he eyed his surroundings and saw several inns near the port. Hiring a coachman, he soon arrived at one of the inns, a young man carrying his bags behind him.

Later that evening, he took in a symphony orchestra performance and enjoyed a fine lady's company. The following day, he undertook the daunting task of finding a skilled artist. He considered visiting some of the art dealers in town but thought it best to start at one of the universities that taught art. There he hoped to discover a rising star whose talents had not yet been revealed.

Schmidt was fluent in four languages, Spanish being one of them. A young secretary met him upon his arrival at the university.

"*Buenos Dias Señor.* May I help you?"

"Oh, you speak English!"

She carefully eyed the large man. His appearance seemed unique; he stood taller than most men she encountered. His broad shoulders, muscular build, long flowing blonde hair, and light complexion gave the appearance of an ancient Greek god visiting the earth amongst mortals. Adjusting her glasses, Isla replied, "Yes, of course, most of our students here at our college have studied the language in one form or another. So, tell me, what brings you here, *Señor?*"

"Simply put, I'm mostly a traveler in search of art and sculpture, and I'm astonished by all the examples of creativity I've seen throughout your fair city. Tell me, have any of the art pieces I have seen proudly displayed in churches and town squares derived from your college?"

"Why yes! If you have time and your schedule allows it, please don't forget to visit the Conquering Hero Statue in the town square near the Blessed Saint's Church. It was completed nearly five years ago by a student of ours."

"I remember seeing the piece of which of you speak. The artist's use of bronze and iron seemed technically brilliant. Tell me about this student who created such a magnificent piece."

"Oh, I must not say anything, you understand."

"Oh, where are my manners? My name is Señor Schmidt. Please allow me to introduce myself. I understand that this situation is awkward at best, but let me ask you, where would I begin my search if I were to seek out the artist?"

"The responsibility of making such a wonderful depiction of our country's most decorated general is too much for some. In response, they find themselves using alcohol to relieve the pressure. It would be safe to say that you could find Antonio Alvarez in any tavern, although there were rumors that he traveled west to Madrid. His father seemed gravely ill, and he wanted to see him before he passed."

"I thank you, my lady, for your time; if it's all right, I want to see what art pieces are available to purchase."

"Certainly, if you walk down the hallway behind me, you'll see a class taught by one of our famed teachers, *Señor* Cordova."

"Thank you again for your help. Have a pleasant day, *Señorita.*" Tipping his hat, Mr. Schmidt was off. As he traveled down the decorative hallway, the rich marble floor reflected light against the white marble columns that lined the long hallway with many decorated doorways. Walking toward one particular opening, Schmidt could hear voices. Stepping inside, he saw several students busily painting. The girl near the door was painting a landscape scene. Her pastels gave the painting a vibrant, rich shade, as if one was standing on a hill overlooking the countryside. The colorful swaying grass perched up on the hillside gave the illusion of a brisk day. The fluffy clouds overhead seemed to be pushed along by the breeze.

A man called out. "*Señor,* may I help you?"

Turning back toward him, Schmidt responded, "Hello, yes, please allow me to introduce myself. My name is Schmidt, and I have traveled far and wide to discover new talents. I have recently arrived in your fair city. I am a lover of art and searching for new pieces to add to my collection. It seems I have come to the right place."

"Splendid. On behalf of our college, I would like to welcome you. You are free to examine any art you see. Besides these pieces, I have works from past students in my office that you might find interesting. I can make arrangements through my office if you wish to purchase any pieces. Just ask for Cordova; everyone knows me."

"Thank you, *Señor*. I have no doubt I shall enjoy my time here. If I may, I would like to inquire if any of your students are skillful in sculpting?"

"Hum—well, most works in marble or iron and bronze are taught in *Señor* Vega's class. You can find him in the room at the end of the hallway."

"Thank you again." With customary tipping of his hat, Mr. Schmidt examined each piece of art the students were painting, several pieces he imagined would look attractive hanging over his mantel. A question struck him at that moment: retire from piracy? That is, of course, if he ever gave up his pirate ways and retired as a proper gentleman. Instantly he thought, *no, never!*

As he continued his tour, something caught his eye. Something more refined than he'd seen thus far. A young girl near a window was adding finishing touches to a painting. She had painted a flotilla of French ships blasting their cannons into a burning English man-of-war. Instantly, Mr. Schmidt recognized it as a famous sea battle. The choppy seas and dead bodies floating in the water were so life-like that he found himself mesmerized; this particular sea battle had a significant meaning to him.

The British and the French fleets fought the naval Battle of Lizard Point; the British lost. One particular ship lost all her men except three hearty souls. Schmidt was one of the survivors aboard the 80-gun *Devonshire*. She defended herself for several hours against seven French ships until she caught fire and blew up.

Schmidt loathed the French and took pleasure in killing as many of them as possible, even to the point that Redbone understood never to question Schmidt's mercilessness, even if some of the men they conquered wanted to join the pirate band.

"May I say, a brilliant choice of colors? Tell me, how did you choose this particular subject matter?"

The girl's French accent was unmistakable. "It was

one of my country's finest hours, the defeat of the English near Lizard Point. My brother served with dignity aboard a French battleship and was awarded the medal of valor for his bravery. Tell me, *Monsieur,* are you familiar with this battle?"

"Oh, yes, indeed, I am. I visited my dear mother back in Bristol when the news reached England. I'm half English and half Scandinavian on my father's side."

"I'm sorry to say, *Monsieur*, but to me, all Englishman are dogs, and they deserve what they got that day. Who said the English could conquer the world and take whatever they wanted? No, I'm afraid the English got what they deserved. Now, if it's all the same to you, I would like to be left alone to continue my painting."

"Hum, such a rude child to speak to strangers freely without a care in the world. I would still like to buy your painting regardless of your opinion on the English monarchy. Tell me, how much for the painting?"

"To you, Monsieur, it is not for sale. I already do not like you and wish you to leave." Her shout alerted the class, and soon everyone was watching the exchange.

"Nicolette, is there a problem?" Cordova asked.

"This man has tried to get fresh. I asked him to leave, but he refused."

Schmidt's expression turned cold. A sinister smile appeared on his face, frightening Nicolette. There was more to this stranger than she first realized.

Turning back to the teacher, Schmidt responded, "Nothing could be further from the truth, *Señor* Cordova, but regardless, I shall be on my way. I want to thank you for your kindness."

Turning to Nicolette, he said plainly, "Oh, the foolishness of youth. To boldly broadcast one's disdain without regard for a stranger's feelings is common rudeness in your compatriots. It can only mean that you have been raised without proper correction. Perhaps there is still time for you to learn before it's too late."

Gathering courage, Nicolette responded, "Are you the one to teach me these lessons? No. I'm afraid that I have grown tired of our conversation. *Señor* Cordova, could you please make this man leave?"

Schmidt waved his hand, stopping the teacher from approaching. "I'm leaving; good day, *mademoiselle*, until we meet again."

"Never shall we meet, Englishman. I am done speaking to you."

Schmidt shook his head in disgust and left the classroom. As quickly as it arrived, the benevolence shown by the stranger had disappeared, rolled up as if a welcoming carpet had been jerked away. Schmidt passed Isla at her desk, continued out the door, and descended the stone steps. Stopping in the middle of the street, he turned back and shouted, "Obviously, *Mademoiselle,* there is much for you to learn. I shall enjoy being your teacher."

Looking up at the sun, he surmised it was close to four in the afternoon. Feeling hungry, he looked for a bite to eat, saw a nearby tavern, and walked inside. He ignored the patrons' unwelcome stares and took a table next to a window toward the back. There were too many chairs, and he felt crowded. Moving them, he got comfortable and decided this was an excellent place to rest his worries.

A robust woman appeared a short time later, wearing an apron across her shoulder. Her black hair was tied in a braid. Her large breasts were barely confined within her blouse.

"*Buenas tardes, Señor.*"

"*Buenas tardes,* do you speak English?"

A strange look came over the woman's face. Without hesitation, she called out to a young girl behind the bar, "*Maria, ven aqui ahora.*"

Appearing at the table, the girl quickly bowed and

said, "Hello, sir. May I help you?"

"I speak Spanish, I was simply asking if the madam spoke English, but no matter, I would like a bottle of rum. Tell me, how's the salted pork?"

"Excellent, *Señor*."

"Very well, that shall do nicely. Please hurry; I'm famished."

"Si, I shall be right back with your meal."

It didn't take long before Schmidt was satisfied and delightfully full. The rum kept coming as though he had a personal servant at his table. Feeling the effects of the alcohol, he decided to take a break from drinking and refused another glass. As the evening wore on, a young man appeared with a guitar and began singing love songs.

The pleasant atmosphere, combined with the conversation with his waitress Maria, led to a genuine liking for the girl. As they spoke throughout the evening, she discussed her life and hopes for the future. After some time, she asked the reason for his visit. "I'm looking for a sculptor," he explained.

Wanting to know who it was, she encouraged Schmidt to give her the individual's name. Still unsure if this artist would agree or if he could build this project, Schmidt explained to the girl.

Maria knew Antonio Alvarez, who had frequented the tavern but had not been seen for many months. The latest news she'd heard about him was the same as Isla's; Antonio traveled to Madrid to care for his sick father.

Schmidt heard the news with regret. As he pondered his next move, a small group of young men appeared, sat in the opposite corner of the room, and stared at Schmidt as they whispered amongst themselves. The other waitress took their orders and soon brought two bottles of wine and glasses to their table.

Schmidt's features were unmistakable, and he stood out like a piece of rice in a bag of pinto beans. Regardless, no one would ever guess that the stranger to their city was a pirate—the first mate of the infamous Iron Born Pirates.

Schmidt's disdain became apparent as he made eye contact with one of the men at the table. However, he grew suspicious of the three men and decided it was time to leave. Reaching into his bag, he dumped out several gold escudos onto the table and stood to leave. As he approached the door, he overheard one of the strangers saying something to his friends. The words were French.

One of the men, Raphael, looked at the giant and didn't move. Schmidt's full size, now recognized as a force to consider, Raphael and his friends stared back and said nothing. They watched Schmidt leave the establishment and disappear down the street in silence.

It was raining, but no matter, Schmidt's inn was not far, and he hurried across the cobblestone street until he reached the lodging house. It was close to midnight when he entered his room—and immediately sensed trouble.

The girl from the school was French; the young men in the tavern were also. Perhaps it was best to leave Barcelona as quickly as possible. He would rise early in the morning and visit the stables, buy himself a horse, and travel to Madrid. He only had two full moons to complete his task. Then he was to meet Redbone back in Tortuga.

Crawling into bed caused the bedsprings to strain under his weight, but exhaustion overcame him, and soon the sounds of heavy rain droplets hitting the window were the only sounds he heard, then nothing. Sometime later, the morning's announcements from a distant rooster caused him to stir.

Barely opening his eyes, he quickly dressed and left the small room. After paying for his lodging and enjoying a quick breakfast at the inn's kitchen, he asked the waitress for the location of the stables. He was directed to visit a family farm named *"Los Encabritado Caballos."*

At the stable, Schmidt asked for a large animal big

enough to handle his weight and added a saddle and bridle for more *pesos*. Before noon, he departed for Madrid.

The horse was black as midnight, and Schmidt thought of a pirate back aboard the *Hell's Fury* named Hondo. Originally from Africa, the son of a warrior and a close friend to Schmidt, Hondo was dark-skinned, and Schmidt decided to call his new horse in the man's honor. On any given night, Hondo was known to sneak up on him and growl, "Schmidt, you old salt, good thing we are friends, or else it would be easy for me to slit your throat without you knowing I was here." Schmidt petted his horse and whispered, "Your name shall be Hondo, a friend."

Equipped with directions to Madrid, Schmidt was finally on his way. He had only ridden half a day's journey when he came to a deserted crossroads. Waiting there to meet him were the three young men he'd seen back in the tavern. Without any plausible reason, the eldest-looking man raced over and took hold of the horse bridle, halting him.

"What is the meaning of this?" Schmidt demanded.

"I'm here to teach you a lesson, *Monsieur*. You have dishonored Nicolette, my fiancé," the highwayman announced, his French accent unmistakable.

Schmidt smiled. He stared down at the man holding onto his horse's bridle. "Oh, I shall enjoy this lesson you speak of, but I must warn you that it will not be me that's schooled but you young fools. Stop this charade at once or else I draw my sword and bring a disastrous end to all of you." Grabbing his sword handle, he added, "I must tell you that my blade has a particular taste for French blood."

In a foolhardy move, young Raphael drew his sword and slashed at the giant. His sharp blade cut Schmidt's right cheek. The giant's brute force was released. He kicked young Raphael in the face and knocked him to the ground.

"You fool! Now tell me, what profit is there in sacrificing your life for love? Is it worth the deplorable nights your young mistress will spend alone pining for you or perhaps the brutal rape she will receive at my hands? No matter, when I'm done with your Nicolette, no one will want her."

Raphael struggled to speak as the Iron Born pirate began to exact his revenge. The screams of pain soon quieted, and the shining blade beheaded the young man with such force that his head landed some thirty paces away in a layer of scrubs. Within minutes, his friends lay dead nearby.

Schmidt lifted his sleeve to his cheek to wipe off the blood and took a moment to see the carnage before him. In a final assault, the other bodies, too, were beheaded. Discarding the headless bodies behind a group of trees and covering them with branches, Schmidt turned his attention to the men's horses he found tied to a tree. After removing the saddles and discarding them a distance away, Schmidt cut the mounts loose and watched the horses disappear.

Then, the injured pirate traveled some distance with the heads of his victims in a leather bag tied to his saddle. He continued his journey until the following morning when he discovered a stream following the road. Finding a grassy spot next to a tree, he stopped to rest. He surveyed the surrounding area until he was sure no one lurked in the woods. Feeling exhausted, he led his horse to an oak tree and tied it securely to a branch.

Before he could get comfortable, Schmidt had matters to address. Taking the heads, he walked a short way until he found another clearing next to the stream. He dug a hole in the soft soil with his sword and deposited the skulls of his victims inside. Next, he covered the hole and packed the ground tightly. Later, he did something odd and out of character, even for him. Taking a beaded leather strap from his wrist, he fashioned a small cross from surrounding twigs, knelt, and placed it atop the grave.

Standing to his feet, he cursed aloud. "You fools, I tried to warn you but look at you now at the end of your lives. What great things have you accomplished? Nothing now but food for the worms. You should have heeded my warning, but you refused. Now a forgotten memory. No doubt my fate will match your own. I fear it will not be long before I join you all as food for the worms."

Leaving the gravesite behind, he walked over to his horse and removed the saddle and blanket, carrying them to a spot under the tree. He removed his boots and heavy jacket, reached for a jug of rum secured to his saddle, and walked down into the cold water.

There he began washing the blood off his body, giving special attention to the gash upon his cheek. When he cleaned that area, the burn was quickly realized but not as painful as when he splashed some rum across it.

Afterward, he returned to his saddle, downed several long gulps of rum, and enjoyed some smoked fish he bought from the wife of a nearby farmer. The instant searing pain from the alcohol made him curse loudly. Satisfied, he lay down and slept.

Chapter 4

HOURS LATER, HE AWOKE TO the sounds of hoofs galloping nearby. As Schmidt opened his eyes, it was nearly sundown, and he could barely see a lone rider barreling down the road, seeming to be in a bit of a hurry. No doubt a messenger was traveling between cities. Once awake, Schmidt's wound ached dreadfully. Reaching over, he grabbed his rum and took a long swig. Still feeling exhausted, his body resisted waking, and instead, he lay back down and fell fast asleep.

Sometime the following day, he awoke to the sound of birds singing in the nearby trees and the sun piercing through the morning clouds. Moaning like a bear waking from his winter nap, he slowly stood and surveyed his surroundings. The horrid act he'd done recently was still fresh in his mind. Pirates, by nature, were religious men, and Schmidt was no exception. After making the Sign of the Cross to appease God, he understood that self-preservation had driven the killings—a basic instinct to stay alive. Besides, he had warned the youths not to cross him. Pushing the remembrance aside, he returned to the stream and washed. Bringing along his stained jacket, he attempted to wash out the blood.

Leaving the cold water and now partly naked, Schmidt stood for some time in the sun and took in the morning rays. The warmth felt both pleasing and comforting. The cut upon his cheek ached terribly, but nothing more could be done. The constant annoying pain, however, put him in a grumpy mood. Afterward, satisfied with the results, he felt the jacket looked better than before.

After a short time, he mounted his horse and continued to Madrid. Passing a sign that pointed the way, he noticed that other small settlement distances were posted beneath it. Still determined, he galloped onward, ignoring the invitation to visit other towns.

Hours later, toward evening, he entered a small metropolis and saw what he desired, a tavern, a most suitable place to get some refreshment and bed for the night. Stopping at the stables, he paid the man to board his steed, requesting special attention to be given out to sweet oats and grain. Schmidt, taking his personal belongings with him, couldn't help but notice the man eyeing the wound on his face.

After depositing some coins in the man's hands for his services, Schmidt turned to walk away. Before he had traveled very far, the man announced, "You need to see a doctor; please wait here while I go get him."

The pirate's first mate was led into a small room adjoining the stables and was somewhat annoyed by the delay. He was asked to sit there while the stableman ran off to fetch the doctor. A short time later, an older man carrying a small black bag appeared.

Examining the wound on Schmidt's face, the doctor began whispering something under his breath while reaching into his bag to remove a brownish bottle and a clean cloth. The doctor opened the bottle, poured the contents into the fabric, and turned to Schmidt, saying, "My name is Alejandro. I need you to understand that this will burn like hell, but it must be done, sorry."

Schmidt braced himself to receive the burning liquid upon his face and grimaced at the pain as the wound was cleaned.

He was already numb from the attention, and when the doctor reached for another cloth and dipped it into the bottle of pure grain alcohol, the smell seemed familiar to him from his time aboard the ship. It didn't seem to bother him as much. However, when the doctor was done cleaning, reached for a needle, threaded it with catgut—a fine thread woven from sheep intestines—and began to sew the wound closed, Schmidt lifted his right arm and made a tight fist as if he would strike the poor man. Nonetheless, the doctor continued his treatment until he was finally finished.

Receiving orders to keep the wound clean for at least a week, Schmidt was told nothing could be done about the scar. Unconcerned about his appearance, he grinned at the thought. After paying the doctor and being most grateful for his care, Schmidt invited the man to dinner.

They retired to the tavern, where they could hear the locals discussing the realities of the war between Spain and England, grumbling about the cost of taxes they had to pay to support the effort. Seeing Schmidt's fair complexion and blonde hair, many in the small gathering began to scowl and hiss.

Ignoring their rudeness, the doctor escorted Schmidt to a small table and called a waitress to come over. After the doctor placed his order, Schmidt said, *"Ich werde eine Flasche Rum haben."* Ordering his rum in German seemed to relieve everyone's worries.

The waitress, however, looked confused and so translated for the girl. She then introduced himself to Schmidt and Alejandro, and a short time later, both men were brought a piping hot bowl of stew, along with a piece of bread. A young boy soon appeared with the rum. The evening was passing pleasantly when Alejandro, having downed several glasses of rum, asked, "Tell me, who was it that struck your cheek?"

"Unfortunately for them, I met highwaymen on the

road who mistakenly took me for a fatted goose and easy pickings; sadly, none survived."

"Oh, I see."

"These are dangerous times in which we live, Alejandro. I realized that hazards exist everywhere. Spain is no exception, my friend."

"True, it is sad to say, but you are right; please take precautions on your journey to Madrid."

"I'm no stranger to danger. It seems that in my travels, it's a constant companion."

"Yes, that is something that I wanted to ask you; what exactly is your occupation?"

"Let me see, how I can say this, exactly? My business involves shipping and commodities."

"Oh, I see; for a moment, I half expected you to say that you were a pirate or perhaps some raider."

"Hm, yes, well, in my line of work, there are hazards, to be sure, but none that cost me my appearance as you see me today. Still, you do not need to fear me. The kindness you have shown will not be forgotten. In the same way, the cowards who attacked me on the roadside will not be forgotten either."

"I understand your meaning only too clearly, my friend. Look, your rum has run out; please, allow me to have it refilled."

"Spoken like a true gentleman. I thank you."

Alejandro talked about his life. He was a widower and lost his wife many years ago during childbirth. Although many opportunities were allotted to him, he decided never to remarry. The doctor had studied medicine abroad and only returned to Spain to be near family. Truthfully, after hearing about Schmidt's exploits, it seemed that he still carried some regret for his decisions.

The evening passed quickly, and soon it was time to retire. With Alejandro's help, Schmidt could acquire a room for the night. Promising to meet again before leaving in the morning, they parted ways, and soon Schmidt was fast asleep.

The following day he enjoyed breakfast with the doctor before heading to Madrid. Three days later, he reached the city's outskirts and began searching for the artist Antonio Alvarez.

Schmidt visited the many taverns in the city, asking barmaids and bartenders if any had ever heard of the man. The answers were all the same. No one knew of an artist by that name. Besides this, another reality soon became apparent; Schmidt's fair complexion seemed to offend most residents in the city, and some even refused to talk to him.

Utter frustration clouded him, and he considered abandoning his quest. But as luck would have it, as he busied himself with his inquiries on his last day, a vagrant appeared begging for a drink. Annoyed by the man's intrusion, the bartender set loose his displeasure and shouted out curses, saying, "*Señor* Alvarez, you have been warned to stay away and cease your begging; now, perhaps a lesson is in order?"

Schmidt assisted Alvarez to his feet. The beggar did nothing to resist the punch to his face and fell to the floor. The tavern's patrons enjoyed the abuse and watched as the owner positioned himself to strike again. Realizing that this man could be the artist he had been searching for, Mr. Schmidt stepped up, stopping the artist from receiving any further abuse. The tavern owner looked at the giant with surprise.

Ordering a bottle of rum, the pirate assisted the homeless man over to his table. Across from him sat the hopeful resolution to his problems. However, the man's smell filled his nostrils, making him queasy. *Señor* Alvarez, still dazed from the bartender's punch to his face, sat at the table, swaying side to side.

When the bottle of rum appeared, Schmidt poured two glasses full. Alvarez took the glass in hand, saying, *"Gracias, Señor,"* and slowly slurped down the alcohol, some dripping down his chin.

"Tell me, *Señor*, are you the man that created the Conquering Hero Statue, located in the town square back in the city of Barcelona?"

The man's eyes brightened as he announced, "Oh, you have seen my work, *Señor*."

"Yes, it is the very reason I have traveled to Madrid."

"Perhaps another glass, my friend; what say you, *Señor*?"

"Yes, of course, all of that in due time. Listen to me; time is of the essence. I need your services and want to hire you to make a device that is also a statue resembling a witch."

The drunken smile plastered across the man's face gave little indication if he understood what Schmidt was asking. Still undeterred, the pirate yelled out to the waitress to bring a container full of black coffee. Hearing Schmidt's request, the man became angered, shouting, "No, no, *Señor*, I do not want any coffee. You promised me another drink—rum; I shall have rum instead of coffee."

Schmidt leaned in close and whispered, "No, *Señor*, you shall have coffee and sober up. I need your artistic services, and it would not be wise to disappoint me." Sitting across the small table, a brief moment of clear-headedness struck Antonio Alvarez, and he thought, *He's just a man, but considering his size, I shouldn't upset this Señor Schmidt!* The man's expression made the artist's blood run cold.

By the following morning, the statue's creator lay on the floor of Schmidt's room, snoring.

Later that morning, two older women appeared at the door to bathe the stinking artist. Antonio fought all attempts to return to the living and get a wash and shave. Again, a scowl from Schmidt, now tired of the whining, changed the artist's view. Afterward, the two women were paid handsomely for their work. However, with his desire for more alcohol going unanswered, the artist remained in a foul mood, eventually falling asleep on the floor.

Over the following days, a metalworking studio was found suitable for crafting the iron device. Working hand in hand, Schmidt discovered why the artist was in such a sad, depressed state. His father owed much and could not pay his debts, had been thrown into debtor's prison, and his family's estate sold off. The inheritance Antonio hoped for was lost forever.

Over the following days, with everything assembled to make the horrid device, the pirate and artist sat down to discuss the project. After studying Redbone's sketches, a smile appeared on Antonio's face as he came to understand the real reason why this stranger wanted the object built. Especially the unique elements of the two slots on the hip of the witch. What else could it be except two openings for swords? The intersecting angles and the precise space needed to hold a blade in place left little doubt.

The ghastly facial features of the woman, meant to frighten those who looked upon the creature, were also a tell-tale sign that whoever was attached to the cold iron would have made a pact with the devil himself.

After many days, Schmidt appeared in the studio and gazed upon the gory hag creation. Before him, the solid hunk of iron and bronze symbolized a laughing witch. The work that went into making this monstrosity was nothing short of miraculous. Somehow, fused with vigorous creativity, the artist seemed connected to the Bloody Hag. The forgotten part of his soul was the missing piece to complete the project.

Mr. Schmidt never described her silent laughter,

never heard but imagined, as she stared down at the fools hearty enough to join the secret organization. That was left up to its creator. For now, it was complete, including the long guide poles to hoist up the upper half and the adjustable base, plus the strange-looking branding irons, with the strange symbols of crossing swords over a goblet.

The hard work exceeded Schmidt's expectations, and that evening after dinner, he and the artist celebrated the completion of the strange device with wine and song. Ladies were invited to the festive affair, and the party went on throughout the night. Still, something about Antonio's behavior seemed off, as though he were somehow troubled.

The last evening before his return to the Caribbean, Schmidt and the artist dined together one final time. The following day, men were hired to crate up the device for shipping. Antonio grudgingly approached, saying, "*Señor* Schmidt, soon you shall depart, and there is something that I must ask you before you leave."

"Go on, Antonio, we have no secrets between us. You have performed your task beyond all my expectations. For that, I am most grateful. What is it you want to ask me?"

"One does not need to be of superior intelligence to figure out that the device you now refer to as the Bloody Hag is nothing less than a way to torture those foolish individuals that have crossed you in some way. Your enemies will no doubt fear what is about to happen to them and beg you for mercy as their lives slowly end from bleeding to death."

"No, I'm afraid that you have it all wrong. Although the Bloody Hag will involve blood flowing, that choice will be up to the ones who decided to join a particular band of brothers, whose only requirement will be a steadfast heart and strong moral fibers needed to survive the ritual."

"If it is as you say, and there are no secrets between us, tell me, what ritual is it of which you speak? What type of induction will require such a costly sacrifice? Already, I recognize that you are not a simple art dealer looking for objects to sell abroad. No, *Señor*, there is something about how you carry yourself, always suspicious and on guard. Besides that, you are marked with a scar from a sword fight. I feel that you are nothing short of a buccaneer."

"Tell me, why would it matter what type of business I have in Madrid? I have hired you for a service, and you fulfilled our bargain and have been paid handsomely. Now, it is time for me to leave."

"Fine, but still, there is something that you're not telling me. Please, I have nothing here and want to ask if I could accompany you on your journey."

"Antonio, you have been honest and forthright with me this entire time. Where I go is paved with dangerous exploits. I cannot know what I will encounter, but I have chosen this life for myself. I cannot, in all honesty, ask you to join me. I expect to die at any moment."

"Why, the horrid device? You owe me that much, *Señor* Schmidt!"

"Fine, it is for a pirate known by reputation. The device you have fashioned will be used by numerous men wanting to join the brotherhood. My captain and I intend for those inductees who survive the ritual to become members of our crew. As of yet, it is only a dream that will soon become a reality."

"According to your expectations and the mere fact that I installed certain details into the design that will guarantee it a success, I feel I should be the first to try the ghastly object."

"Antonio, don't speak like a fool. You have no idea what you're asking me. This dreadful thing you have shaped and twisted is to be used for one reason alone. That purpose is to put a man in peril and close to death. Afterward, the man is marked with irons you have made, burned into his wrist. Forever scarred, the one bearing the mark will be hunted above all other pirates. Pirates not by name alone but by the marks upon their bodies. Tell me now, are you sure you will want this life instead of being an artist?"

"An artist, yes. I have been born with certain talents you have seen for yourself. Sadly, now with my father disgraced, what life will I have? Scratching out a living as a drunkard and beggar makes me depressed, with no prospects of having a normal life here in Spain. I feel as though there is a bleak future ahead of me. Tell me, what is better, to try the device later and discover that your captain will be disappointed for whatever reason or to allow me to be the first one chained to the Bloody Hag and see for yourself that it will perform flawlessly?"

A brief pause of contemplation. Schmidt thought about what Antonio had said. He looked at the man; his expression was one of excitement, and he seemed thrilled by the prospect of becoming the first Iron Born pirate. Turning to look away, Schmidt said, "For whatever reason, I always thought I would be the first to take the blade. Perhaps you are right; we should have a test to see how it performs. All right, the ceremony will be performed tonight at midnight. One last time I will ask, Antonio, are you sure?"

"I have given this much thought; yes, I'm sure, more than any other time in my life."

"You do realize that there is a chance that you could die!"

"All things considered, it would be better than living the life I was given."

"Enough talk. Go prepare yourself, it will soon be midnight, and I must prepare the device."

Chapter 5

"I MUST ASK, ARE YOU SURE about lifting the weight of the upper piece? Are you sure that you can lift it by yourself?"

"Rather easily; I had already tested that when you went for supplies. No, no need to worry. I am quite strong, you know! Tell me, Antonio, the irons, where are they? I must place them in the fire."

"Oh, you will find them next to the woodpile you ordered for the shipping containers. They are in a small box near the door."

"Fine, I'm going to prepare everything for the ceremony. I do not want to see you again until it begins."

"I understand, Señor Schmidt! Before you go, please tell me, do you believe I will survive the ritual?"

"Truly, I'm not sure. Because your wrists are cut asunder, and you're bleeding to death, there is a chance you'll perish from the loss of blood! All daring enough to join the brotherhood, myself included, will face death. You will feel disconnected from your body. You will travel between heaven and earth. Close to death, your past life will disappear. Antonio, while you're in that special place, listen to the sound of my voice. I will be there calling to you in quest of you returning to the living."

"I cannot say why our paths have crossed, but regardless, I find your company pleasant. The simple promise of friendship seems to have sprouted. *Señor*

Schmidt, I trust you. I trust you with my life; please do not allow my faith in you to fade and leave me dead!"

With nothing else to be said, both men departed. A short time later, they met in the large studio. There, a fire was glowing hot in the large fireplace. Knowing what would be needed for the ceremony, Antonio gathered long chains. He also had the foresight to visit a local blacksmith earlier and bought two long stilettos and fitted them to the small slots beside the witch's hips. Later, the owner might want to use swords; either way, both would work.

It was time for the ceremony to begin. Antonio looked upon the horrid device he had created. Truthfully, he couldn't have made the facial features ghastlier. The long nose and protruding jawline resembled a woman that would repulse or cause fear in most people that saw her repulse.

In the roaring fire, two irons set in the red-hot coals. Their tips were burning red. Appearing shirtless into the room, Antonio eyed Mr. Schmidt carefully. Schmidt seemed preoccupied, busily writing thoughts down on paper.

"That's it; yes, that will do nicely for now," the large man blurted out. Taking a long drink from a glass, he set it down with a thud and turned to Antonio. "I have finished the oath! Of course, there must be an oath, or we are nothing but ordinary pirates."

"Yes, you are right." Antonio's fear was unmistakable. Stopping in front of the cold iron creation, he gently rubbed its surface, saying, "I am anxious. Tell me, how soon can we begin?"

A smile crossed the pirate's face as he took another drink and said, "That depends on you; tell me, are you ready to proceed?"

"Yes, I am ready to laugh in the face of death, as ready as I will ever be."

"Follow me; we must prepare you for the ceremony."
Appearing at the Bloody Hag with chains in hand, Mr.
Schmidt set about securing Antonio to the cold device.
When he was finished, he looked about, saying, "Tell me,
I don't see the blades; where are they? I don't see them
anywhere. I thought there was supposed to be a goblet to
catch the blood,"

Straining to look around the room, Antonio said,
"Look behind me, next to the woodpile; I set them there
for the men to crate up for the journey, never imagining
that I would agree to be the first inductee."

"Are you having second thoughts?"

"Yes, of course I am. Who in their right mind
wouldn't? Regardless, I am determined to continue this
journey to the end."

Putting up the oath he had written, Schmidt read it
aloud. "Antonio Alvarez, are you ready to embark on the
greatest adventure of your life? Do you swear to be fully
dedicated to the Iron Born Brotherhood, having agreed to
become loyal in your resolve and never to leave your
pirate brothers behind, no matter the cost of life or limb?
Can you honestly say that you will abide by all the laws
constituted by our Captain Redbone without question,
even if you disagree with these orders? Do you swear
never to steal or betray your pirate brothers, even if you
are tortured?"

"I swear to all these with my dying breath that I shall
remain faithful in my pledge."

"Let us begin." The behemoth weighed around 300
kilos. He was ignoring the heavy chains wrapped around
his chest. Antonio instead fixed upon the Hag's face. She
stared down at him; her sinister smile was gruesome at
best, created by his own hands.

A metallic sound broke Antonio's concentration as
Mr. Schmidt began hoisting up the upper half of the
woman's body and locking it into place with two pins.

Next, he disappeared for a few minutes and returned with the two sharp blades. Taking them, he shoved each of them into the narrow spaces on the witch's hips.

Returning, Mr. Schmidt admired the contraption and pondered what to do next. Antonio, twisting his head around, asked, "What is it, Señor Schmidt, tell me?"

"Something is amiss. There in the fire, I have the irons, red hot. You are chained to the Hag. If the two blades were inserted properly, your blood would run into——what? A bucket, a goblet. No, that doesn't seem correct at all. The red liquid must be measured, "The true worth of a man!"

"Measured? How, *Señor* Schmidt?"

"In weight, if nothing else."

"Oh, I see; this is a fine time to think of this, is it not?"

"I'm unaware of any known buccaneers trying something this bold in my lifetime. Its conception was never imagined until now. We are standing at a great precipice, and this must be done correctly, or else we look to be fools and nothing more."

"Fine, if it's a way to measure a man's value in life, why not search the small room within my studio—there you will find a brass scale for measuring compounds used to descale iron. Wash the basin clean and return. Together, we had never figured that part out; it was assumed that the man's blood would coat the deck of your ship, I suppose. No, you are right; I agree with your assessment. There should be some way to measure the amount of blood loss. The average adult male has around five liters. If half of his blood is gone, the heart will stop pumping, and his organs will shut down. Death will soon follow."

"Tell me, Antonio, did you study medicine?"

"Only the muscles of the human body for my sculpting. Hurry before I lose my nerve and change my mind."

"Yes, of course," A short time later, Mr. Schmidt reappeared with the large scale and went to work arranging the measure between two narrow troughs that joined at the base of the statue. He stepped back when he was finished, ensuring everything was in place.

"A reality from my time at sea: Alcohol will thin your blood and cause it to run swiftly into the scale. I brought you a goblet filled with rum; you should drink your fill, my friend."

Turning his head to position himself closer, Antonio gulped down the entire glass until it was empty. Feeling the effects, he closed his eyes and waited. A few minutes later, he could hear Schmidt grabbing ahold of the ropes that raised the upper half.

"I shall see you on the other side."

With that, the pins were pulled, and the heavy metallic piece came crashing down with a heavy thud, locking the witch's upper half into place with a metallic claw, preventing it from bouncing up and down. The pain was instantaneous. The sharp blades, completing their work flawlessly, had sliced Antonio's wrists.

Now, the moment had begun when he was to bleed out. All his worries knotted up into this moment, and time slowed to a crawl. Unexpectedly, Mr. Schmidt jerked away both blades, and hot blood ran down Antonio's wrists, making him aware that his life was ending.

He could do nothing but wait…wait for the unexpected to happen. Perhaps it would be a simple lightheaded feeling and nothing more. Gratefully, he never felt queasy at seeing his blood. He had known some people who fainted at the sight of their blood while others were unaffected. These thoughts invaded his mind, diverting him from the reality that he was now becoming a pirate. He grew concerned about when Mr. Schmidt would take action and plunge the hot iron into his wrist to stop the bleeding.

As an afterthought, he considered this fact of becoming the first Iron Born Pirate ever, even though that thought did not ease his concerns about whether or not he was going to die. As of yet, no one had ever heard of The Iron Born. What did that mean anyway? He supposed that he was the first sacrifice upon the iron creation he had made from his own hands.

Being an Iron Born could only be as profitable as their captain could make them. A pirate captain…it all seemed strange… Now, there was someone responsible for controlling all his deeds…Something seemed amiss…He felt a sickness invading his body, affecting his thoughts. His vision became blurry; he looked at Schmidt, trying to understand the reasons for it all.

He knew the blood loss was affecting him and braced himself for more of the same harsh fatigue and weakness. Coming near, the large man kneeled in front of him and removed the goblet full of his warm blood, blood both dark and red.

Feeling light as a feather, he didn't care in the world. He became aware of his heartbeat slowing. In the silence of the large room, it was as though he could hear each beat in procession, one after another, steadily declining. Time itself mattered very little, and he couldn't tell how long it had been since the blades came cutting down into his wrists. None of it mattered any longer.

A feeling of pleasantness overcame him, putting him in such a relaxed state that he wished to remain there, feeling free, without concern for his fate. That was why he didn't understand why this pirate sought to disturb him with such harsh jerking movements, pulling his body free of the lady's embrace and thrusting him to the ground.

Antonio's screams of searing pain grew quiet, and he fell into a state of unconsciousness. He didn't hear Schmidt instructing him on what would occur next. He missed seeing the hot irons arrive. In an instant, the whole affair was over.

Days later, Antonio slowly opened his eyes. His senses picked up the sound of men shouting at one another. Next, a gentle rocking motion followed by the smell of salt air. As he slowly rose from his bunk, he experienced a stinging pain in his wrists. Eyeing them carefully, he saw them both wrapped with clean bandages.

Suddenly, it all came back to him, the ritual of becoming an Iron Born Pirate and the fact that he had danced with the devil and come close to death in the process. Now, apart from the soreness that rocked his body, he felt decent. Dropping his legs over the side of the bed, he set up from his bunk and stood for a moment, gripping ahold of the wooden rail on the bed. He felt queasy and thought it best to sit back down.

As he eyed his surroundings, he noticed a large painting in the corner. It was a painting of a sea battle. One could see dead men floating in the water and hulks of burning ships in the distance. The boat in the forefront flew the French flag, the captain directing cannon fire into a ship that bore the British flag. The artist had captured such detail that Antonio could imagine playing a part in the battle.

Examining it more closely, Antonio thought *none could appreciate a piece of art like a fellow artist.* Unexpectedly, the cabin door opened, and in walked Mr. Schmidt. "I see you're finally awake. Tell me, how do you feel, Antonio?"

"Hmmm, that is the question. It is sad to say; I feel like a horse and buggy had run over me; sadly, the horses returned for a second turn and dropped feces on my head."

Jovial laughter erupted from the large man, and he remarked, "Man, you're alive and were able to survive the ritual of the Bloody Hag. You are the first to be born of Iron and Blood. I'm delighted to see what our captain will say when he examines the marks on your wrists. Tell me, are you feeling hungry?"

"Yes, strangely enough, I am."

"Say no more; I shall have the ship's cook bring you some stew. Why, in no time, you will be right as rain, my friend."

"Tell me, are we at sea then? When? How was it possible?"

"All I can say is that it took you over a week to recover from your ordeal. I suppose you recall the evening of the ceremony? I had prearranged for the Bloody Hag to be shipped the next morning on a horse-driven wagon to the port city of Barcelona. I hired ten men to guard the precious cargo on our journey. Upon our arrival, I booked passage aboard this ship destined for Tortuga. There we will meet Redbone and begin our new brotherhood."

"You know, on second thought, instead of having that stew, could you have them bring me some beef broth? I'm afraid I won't be much of a pirate, after all. I'm sad to tell you that I'm prone to seasickness."

"Nonsense, you haven't found your sea legs yet."

"Yes, this fateful decision could still come with consequences yet realized. Mr. Schmidt, before you go, tell me who belongs to this magnificent painting. I should like to acquire it!"

Mr. Schmidt chuckled. "The painting is mine. I'm afraid it is not for sale. It cost me too much to obtain, and I could never sell it at any price."

"What of the artist? Tell me about her. At least I can hunt for future works by this artist. A woman named Nicolette, whose signature is on the painting. Her brush strokes and use of color are so refined and lifelike that I see her going far."

"I'm afraid that this particular artist won't be painting anymore. It is sad that she had an accident and lost sight."

"That is horrible news. To be so gifted and lose this talent because of an accident would be maddening in the least."

"Yes, very true, how sad, indeed. Now please allow me to get that broth for you. Before you know it, you'll be on the main deck admiring the view."

"Oh, I'm a bit thirsty too; please bring me some rum. Will you be so kind?"

"Rum, you say! Spoken like a true artist or a pirate, could it be?"

"You know, one day, I should like to visit this Nicolette, I think. Tell me, where do you think I shall look for her?"

"I think the best place to search for her would be the insane asylum. As you said, losing such a talent would be enough to drive anyone mad. I did hear a bit of news before leaving Spain. Reliable sources informed me that going blind and losing her fiancé was too much for the girl, and she attempted suicide."

"A sad tale, Mr. Schmidt."

"No. For the artist, to spend the remainder of her days at a nunnery alone would be the best solution."

"Since you put it that way, perhaps. Still, such talent should have never gone wasted."

Schmidt smirked and said, "Perhaps, she was cursed by God for some sin she committed in her past. Ultimately, all of us will face certain damnation of one sort or another. I know I have mine to contend with, but don't we all?" He walked away, leaving Antonio alone to consider his remarks.

Antonio contemplated his sins in life and whispered aloud, "Yes, don't we all."

Chapter 6

A NEW COURSE SET, the *Hell's Fury* traveled under full sail toward an unknown island. The pirate captain kept their destination a secret. Soon, rumors began circulating among the crew about Redbone's strange behavior and the mysterious cargo they would pick up when they landed. Nothing about the voyage seemed right, especially when they passed by promising ships to plunder. Their captain seemed hell-bent on arriving at the unknown destination before the next full moon.

Once back in Tortuga, the ship took on supplies and met up with its first mate, Mr. Schmidt. Accompanying him was a man called only "Artist."

Before they sailed, the crew met in a deserted cave on the island's far side. Redbone and Mr. Schmidt stood at the back of the cave. Next to them was a large object hidden under a tarp. Lit candles illuminated the dark space. As the men piled into the damp place, they were handed goblets full of rum by several barmaids attending the event.

Once all the men were accounted for, the barmaids were swiftly dismissed.

"Ye fellow brothers, it has long been me ambition to see ye formation of a brotherhood of pirates," Redbone intoned, "bonded together not by mere birth. No, something greater than family, something much greater. Free choice of those wishing to bear my mark on their wrists, signifying something bigger than themselves.

"Ye have all met the man that goes by the name of "Artist." Under me direction, he has fashioned ye object that all of ye will soon see. This instrument will enable us to become a new band of pirates, ye most feared to sail ye Caribbean waters."

"I want ye all to know that when ye see thee next full moon appearing in ye night sky, it will signify the time when I shall take me turn to dance with The Bloody Hag me self. Not only me but also yer first mate Mr. Schmidt, who will have his turn after me." Redbone reached over and jerked the canvass off. Gasps echoed throughout the cave. Then, afterward, silence.

The would-be crew gazed upon the hideous device, the unique facial features of the metallic creature, crooked jawline, and sunken cheekbones. The Hag stared downward toward whoever would be chained to her cold, uncaring body. Her smile exposed crooked and rotting teeth; her chin narrowed to a point where a hairy mole rested near her lip. The creature's nose was sharp and long. Her balding forehead and receding hairline exposed her tiny head. From the back, metallic hair swept across her shoulders. Her body was crooked and distorted, with hands that reached outward as if to capture the foolhardy in her grasp.

Mr. Connelly, the ship's doctor, yelled, "Redbone, let me get this straight. You want all your men to endure this torturous device and have their wrists cut asunder? Do you not realize the dangers of infection or some tropical diseases? Why, a man could die from any number of dangers, not merely blood loss."

"Aye, it is as ye have said. Not only all these men but me self as well. Ye, too, will take a turn, doctor."

Next, Mr. Arness, the master gunner, a ruddy man in his thirties and barely five feet high, shouted out, "Tell us, Captain, what if any man here refuses your command?"

Other crew members began shouting all at once. "This is madness!" "We need a new captain!"

Redbone, able to yell the loudest, soon quieted the crowd as Mr. Schmidt stood poised for action, gripping his sword tightly if any man was foolish enough to attack.

At the mouth of the cave, two men stood with glowing torches. Next to them were large barrels of rum. Waiting for word from Redbone, they were to be ignited and rolled against the cave entrance to block any attempt to escape from any unwilling pirate who did not want to join.

After the grumbling quieted down, Redbone addressed his men again. "Arrrr, ye best listen and listen closely. I realize that some of ye are not wanting to be joining thee brotherhood. If it is yer lack of courage, I says, to hell with thee! If it be out of a desire to have a new captain or whatever yer other arguments, yer complaints have fallen upon deaf ears.

"Choose for yerself whom ye shall follow. Nevertheless, know that all who agree to continue sailing under me command will have to endure this trial of thee Bloody Hag. It will mark yer devotion and bravery to all the world. Those others stand to me left, no longer me brothers in arms but something far worse."

Confusion and chaos erupted from the group of pirates. Soon. Mr. Hornby, the ship's navigator, stepped forward, saying, "Redbone, this time, you have gone too far. No one here agrees with this madness. I shall take over command of the *Hell's Fury* myself. No longer will you be captain; you have been replaced."

"Aye, I see, thee truth be exposed. Very well, men, all who deem Mr. Hornby for the job, take yer place to me left. Still, me devoted crewmen, stay where ye are."

Altogether, the men gathered at the cave that day totaled ninety-six souls serving under Redbone's authority. After his announcement, only seventy-three stayed. Reviewing the turncoats, Redbone's expression changed and became crooked and vile. He screamed out, "The Hell with all ye traitorous bastards!"

Redbone signaled the men at the cave's opening to perform their tasks. They ignited the rum barrels and rolled them toward the cave's exit, blocking anyone from escaping.

Redbone gave the order to attack, and the men under his command drew their weapons and fought their brothers to the death. Over twenty men lost their lives that day by choosing the wrong side.

It was a bitter victory for Redbone, who had expected more men to join his cause. Still, he realized that once the reputation of the Iron Born was revealed to the world, hundreds of men would join the pirate band and bear the mark of the Iron Born Brotherhood rather than face the sword.

The pirates agreeing to be marred upon their flesh, followed their captain to the *Hell's Fury*. Soon after, Redbone and his men left Tortuga to sail to an unknown, unclaimed island. They knew that if the ship were caught off-guard by a foreign military vessel, it would be disastrous for Redbone and his remaining crew.

Surveying the horizons for any sign of sails approaching, everyone onboard kept a strict vigil until the day they arrived at the mysterious island of shipwrecks, sinking keels, and torn sailcloth.

The island was surrounded by a dense fog that hung just above the hilltops, giving the impression that something sinister lived within its confines. Arriving at the island, all the men aboard looked at one another with eyes of wonder, bewilderment, and concern. They imagined it as one of the most dangerous places a sailor would ever visit: the island bore the name "Dragon Song."

Once, a young maiden was deeply in love whose fiancé drowned in the turbulent waters. Her songs to her lover brought death to those that heard them rippling upon the still waters. Her songs brought listeners closer to the rocky coral and their imminent doom and destruction, much like the sirens that sat on the rocks in the Mediterranean, luring sailors to their deaths. Here, in this dreadful place, it was said, lived a witch.

Redbone ordered his men to assemble a makeshift raft. They lowered the wooden object into the dark waters and maneuvered to the ship's port side. The three remaining lifeboats were lowered alongside and positioned next to the raft. Next, the heavy crate was swung over the side with block and tackle, lowered upon the wooden raft, and secured tightly. The smaller items for the ceremony were carried to the rowboats.

Leaving the ship undefended, everyone, including the captain and first mate, rowed to shore; with them was a small chest of gold to appease the witch, whose taste for the yellow ore was legendary.

Once they arrived on the strange island, a group of men went to work to bring the heavy crate safely onshore. The men strapped the box with ropes and inserted long poles through metal grommets. They struggled to lift the heavy weight, walked a few feet, and quickly set the strange object onto the soft sand.

Redbone took the small chest of gold from the longboats and handed it to Mr. Schmidt. "Follow me, men; I'd be thinking the witch's lair is this way."

The caravan of pirates followed a small rocky path from the beach up toward a rocky cliff that overlooked the water. They could see the remains of a wrecked ship scattered across the shoreline from the top. The most significant part, the hull, complete with its rudder still intact, lay against what appeared to be a cave. At the entrance was a stack of human and shark skulls. Atop them, a torch burned as if to bid welcome to any visitor foolish enough to step foot on these rocky shores.

The pirate captain advanced inside the ship's hull and to the quarterdeck, from where he could see deep inside the cave. Burning torches lit the way down into the unknown. Fearlessly, Redbone called out to his crew, "Follow me, boys; it can't be much farther."

Grunts and groans echoed in the cramped space from the crew members responsible for carrying the heavy crate. Ahead of them was the mysterious and unknown. Not one pirate had any idea of what to expect. Still, they followed their captain.

Of course, they heard tales of an Asian girl shipwrecked and left to die on this island. Her fiancé, a merchant captain by trade, had met her, and they traveled together to meet his family and receive their blessings. Sadly, a great storm arose, and everyone but the couple drowned or was lost at sea. Although the girl and her new fiancé made it to shore, he was lifeless and unresponsive.

The girl's ability to use mystic spells and incantations was unknown at the time. Her grandmother, a powerful witch, had taught her magic.

With only moments before her fiancé was to depart into the afterlife, this young woman had defiled all that she was taught and was able to capture the man's life essence inside a glass medicine container that had washed ashore. She would have him by her side for the rest of her days and never be alone. All of this, of course, was superstition and stories.

Up ahead of the crew, the remnants of sail cloth were draped over a shadowy opening. Inside were several candles glowing brightly and the image of someone sitting at a table.

"Stop here and wait for me," Redbone ordered his men. Walking to Schmidt, he took the small chest of gold and advanced toward the tent covering. Once inside the space, the smell of incense gave off a sweet, pleasant aroma. Several lit candles around the room gave off a soft glow as they flickered.

Alone in the middle of the room sat a young, attractive Asian woman. She was dressed in fine silks of various colors, her long jet-black hair with a brightly jeweled comb behind her. Her delicate fingers with gold, pointed, long nails cupped a crystal ball that sat in the middle of the table. Inside, the crystal swirled blackness that flowed like a thunderous cloud during a storm.

She clicked her fingernails against the round glass and, in a soft voice, asked, "Who is it that dare disturb my solitude?"

Advancing closer, Redbone put down the chest full of gold near the crystal ball and opened the lid. Stepping backward, he somberly said, "Arrrr, it is I, Redbone, the pirate captain, who requests your indulgence."

"Bold indeed, Redbone. Tell me, is it not known throughout the seven seas that this particular island is hazardous and should be avoided at all costs? Many ships have run aground, and all their crewmen have perished upon this rocky shoreline."

"Aye, it is, as ye say. Written upon all thee sailing charts is an image of a dragon on this rocky coast, a place to be avoided."

"Tell me, man, what brings you to my door?"

"Merely stated, I need yer unique talents. It is rumored that ye possess certain abilities that will aid me and me crew if ever we hope to sail these warm waters unopposed."

"I see."

"Forgive me for my rudeness, but you must understand that there is no other way to approach ye; unless one does it without fear! I must ask ye for indulgences. Ye see, I have too much at stake and traveled a great distance to seek yer audience."

"Tell me, Captain, what is this thing you wish me to do for you?"

"If I has found favor in yer eyes and me request is not offensive, then please allow me to ask help in protecting me men from death itself, as they take an oath to become an Iron Born pirate. Starting with meself."

"I see; this thing that you ask is great. The gold you offer me is not enough for such a great request. Besides, you must realize that I cannot save anyone from death. I cannot bring anyone back to life. Forget the fairytales you have heard, Captain."

"With me, I has brought a device that will be used to perform the rites to become a member of me crew. It be formed in the shape of an old hag. Thee inductees, agreeing to become crew members, must spill thee blood on this monstrosity. Afterward, bearing the marks of such an agreement on thee wrists. I ask ye to provide a way for me crewmen to not bleed to death but endure the ritual and not perish in the process."

"Tell me, Captain, who amongst you is braver than the rest? What pirate is there who is strong in their soul, without fearing death?"

"I believe that no one knows ye courage of a man until it has been forged in combat."

"That is correct. I can offer you a test for your measly payment, beginning with you, their captain. You, Redbone, will be the first; then everyone will be tested in worthiness, down to the lowest young cabin boys, to see if they can stand the test, "The Kiss of the Dragon." Those failing such a test will forever bear the mark upon their forehead, showing the weakness in their character, and they will serve me for the rest of their days."

"Arrrr, let it be as ye have said. All ye pirates sailing aboard thee *Hell's Fury* will be tested, including meself. Afterward, any crewmen not found worthy will be left here on this godforsaken island to serve ye for the rest of their days. I agree to ye terms."

"Again, I want you to understand; this offer begins with you, Redbone. If you fail in your character, then there is no need to continue with your men."

"Already, I have given orders to me first mate, Mr. Schmidt, to expect something like this. Me men will follow behind. I realize that begging the favor of a mysterious creature like ye self would require more than gold and jewels to bring me pirate band to greatness. Obedience is a requirement that all who sail aboard ye *Hell's Fury* are accustomed to. Tell me, witch, what should I expect?"

"For the ritual to be a success, I will first deal with the crew; then, I will attend to the object you have referred to as the Old Hag. Afterward, I will call your men inside, one after another. As I said earlier, there is no sense in any crewman enduring the ceremony of becoming a pirate if they have been deemed weak in moral fiber. Again, you must be the first to lead your men, Captain."

"Be it as ye says, but know this, I has no fear of God or man; why should I fear a Dragon of all things?"

"Fine, let us begin." The petit woman skirted across the room to where a broken-down-looking cabinet lay partly on its side. She pulled open the doors and removed a small, black stone mortar and pestle. On it was decorations depicting a dragon. She slowly added ingredients and set the pot on the small table that held the crystal ball. Walking over to a cupboard where she stored her incense burners, she withdrew a long hollow tubular object with dragons engraved on it.

Taking a knife from her skirt, she lifted her arm over the small bowl and sliced her hand. Immediately, blood spilled into the bowl. She removed a silk scarf from her shoulders and wrapped her hand several times to stop the bleeding. Afterward, she walked over to one of the incense burners, picked it up, and carried it to the table. Unaffected by the heat, she removed the lid, pulled out a smoking incense stick, and dropped it into the bowl. The smoke from the bowl immediately changed from grey to a dark, thick green plume.

"Come closer, Captain; let's dance with the dragon, shall we?"

Taking a step forward and removing his hat, Redbone yelled, "Aye, I let us dance with this dragon, says me!"

Turning back, the witch inserted the tube into the rising smoke and inhaled it into her lungs. Next, she approached Redbone, leaned close, and blew the smoke above his head. The smoke formed into the shape of a dragon and floated briefly just above the captain's head; then, it changed in size, becoming smaller and shrinking to the size of a pencil. It circled Redbone's head and entered his nasal cavity.

Redbone felt lightheaded and dizzy. The world around him became a dark place. He heard voices coming from the shadows, strange and uncommon, but as he focused on them, he recognized them as men he'd killed or double-crossed. Most recognizable were those from the "*Triumphant.*" Most of them cursed him before their deaths, particularly the pirate Montoya, whom he had left for dead on a solitary beach.

The vision changed, and he was at the beach where he and Montoya fought. A flashing light and the image changed again. Montoya's body rotted on the beach. But now, it rose from the sand. Redbone cursed at the vision as his head cleared and saw the witch before him smirking.

"As expected, Captain, I see that you survived the dragon's kiss. But tell me, man, who is it that has so disturbed and troubled your thoughts?"

"Arrr, just a man it be, whose corpse should be

rotting away in the hot sun, but instead, I sees him alive. I thought I had killed him for sure, but he lived on in this dream ye dragon have caused me. Tell me now, what does it mean? Is Montoya alive?"

"I cannot tell what men will see when the dragon's breath caresses them. It did not bother you to hear men's dying curses; instead, you are troubled by a deed you thought was finished, only to discover that the man you thought you killed has survived."

"Then tell me, witch, is it time to call me first, mate?"

"Yes, let it be so; we together will soon see who survives the dragon's kiss amongst your crew."

"I, we shall."

Once all his men were tested, only thirteen souls were lost to the dragon's kiss. Although Redbone couldn't explain the half-smiling expressions on their faces, the thirteen seemed to be in a happier place. These unfortunate souls would remain behind to serve the witch.

Some pirates regretted becoming Iron Born during the ceremony but still surrendered their wills to taste the steel's kiss on their wrists. Somehow, the process was made easier than it had been for the Artist because of a special potion that the witch fashioned to slow the pirates' blood flow.

Over the next few days, every crew member experienced the taste of the blade, and when it was done, all remaining pirates bore the marks on their wrists. Except, that is, the two cabin boys. They proved to be courageous, with sturdy attributes of moral character, but in Redbone's eyes, they were too young to bear the mark.

Now and forever, a new brotherhood of pirates would sail the seven seas in search of treasure. Soon they would become ruthless and unforgiving, and all who crossed their paths would remember the experience.

Once the Bloody Hag was back aboard the *Hell's Fury,* Redbone charted a new course known only to him and his first mate. A few men short, they sailed away from the horrible place. Still, the thirteen would not be missed or spoken of again. Their weakness exposed by the dragon was considered a blessing in disguise. It was better for everyone aboard the *Hell's Fury* to see the weakness of their shipmates rather than have it be exposed in battle. They were weak links in the chain that were cut clean and tossed away.

Nonetheless, a secret kept deep in Captain Redbone's soul was that the youngest crew member left behind to serve the witch was a young Danish boy named Baggi. Not a pirate like his father, who had just abandoned the boy to a life of service. Truth be told, Redbone's only child was to live out the remainder of his days as nothing but a brainless servant of the witch. It's a sad tale, one of many regrets Redbone would take with him to his grave.

It has long been known that one should never strike a bargain with a witch; there is always a higher price to pay than one expects. Redbone had not thought about losing his only son. But he had paid the ultimate price when he decided to accept the witch's terms. Yes, his band of pirates would become the most feared sailing the Caribbean waters, but he would have no heir to whom to pass his legacy.

The realization of what he'd done caused bitterness to swell up in his soul. As he stood alone in his cabin, he began to curse aloud. Reaching for his sword, he withdrew it from its sheath and thrust it high, vowing a curse upon the witch. Sometime after he had filled all his desires for gold and blood, he would return to this despicable island and behead this witch.

He swore an oath, running his hand across the blade. Blood dripped onto the floor. Gripping his hand closed, Redbone made a fist, pointed it back toward the island, and shouted, "I swear on me soul to return and have me revenge on this witch, or else me spirit never rests. Aye, says I, Redbone, swear, to me last dying breath."

Chapter 7

ALONE IN HIS CABIN, reviewing the maps on his table, Redbone took a long swig of rum as he carefully studied the sailing charts and graphs. A moment later, he called out to Abisai, the cabin boy.

"Sir, you called me?" came a distant reply.

"Arrr, Abisai, come here; ye needs to go tell Mr. Sneed that I needs to see him at once."

"Right away, sir."

A short time later, Redbone heard a knock on the door and called out in response, "Come in, Mr. Sneed."

Opening the door, the old sailor hurried in, removed his hat, and stood at attention. "You want to see me, Captain?"

"Arrr, hear me now, Ye, be changing course, and I, wants ye to travel on a new route heading to yonder Turks and Caicos Islands."

"The Turks, Captain? Why there's nothing there but sand and crabs, sir."

"True, Mr. Sneed, but I has me reasons. Come here and let me show ye." Staring at the map on the table, Redbone pointed at a group of islands. "According to me calculations, ye need to set a new course 21 degrees north."

"Yes, sir, will do right away, Captain. Will there be anything else, sir?"

"Nay, not at this time. I believe that will be all, Mr.

Sneed, or perhaps you prefer Harv-Dog as ye shipmates so endearingly call thee?"

"Mr. Sneed will work nicely; thank you, Captain." With nothing else to say, the navigator turned and walked out. Redbone sat on the small, feathered mattress, removed his boots, and lay back on his bed. He thought of the treasure he'd lost, a king's ransom of precious jewels and gold coins. He gritted his teeth and cursed Montoya and the witch who had stolen his son.

NAVIGATING THE SHIP on its new heading took several weeks. While maneuvering the vessel toward the distant shore, one day, the lookout in the crow's nest shouted, "Sails approaching off the port side!"

It was most likely a merchant ship. Still, at this stage in the game, no one would know for sure, not until the captain took to the spyglass to search out the features of the approaching vessel.

On edge, each crew member quickly imagined a Spanish ship full of gold, jewels, and little else. In contrast, Redbone considered the sails belonged to a British man-of-war searching for pirates. The only way to know for sure was to sail on a course intersecting the unknown, either to a golden treasure or possibly destruction. Redbone shouted to his first mate, "Prime the cannons; we're in for a fight."

Mr. Schmidt took control and shouted out the order to load the cannons. The entire crew felt exhilarated. This test of their fighting abilities was the first test of combat since the formation of the pirate band. No one knew for sure what this fight's outcome would be, but one thing was sure. It would be a fight to the death.

As they continued their course, Redbone had time to survey his men. A hearty bunch of pirates, perhaps not as ruthless and desperate a group of cutthroats as some of the men he'd sailed with in his past, but still, each man was devoted to a single cause, to become the wealthiest and most famous men sailing these waters. Why else become a pirate unless there was a treasure to be had? Treasure the likes that mortal men only dreamed of possessing. As a pirate, one man could make his fortune and retire a wealthy nobleman. Retire, what a noble idea, one he fancied. On the other hand, one could be just as easily hung on the end of a noose.

Now, with this strange vision of Montoya the witch had conjured up, Redbone was unsure if his nest egg was still intact. He wanted to see the hole in the sand for himself. There had not been a time so far, but by commanding this pirate crew, he would soon have to prove himself worthy of being their captain.

Presently, all of Redbone's hopes and dreams seem to have come to fruition. At no other time in his life had he felt so alive. He thought of his childhood in Bristol. His father struggled to support all ten children. As the youngest child, Redbone witnessed his brothers and sisters scratching a living. By the time he came of age, he had found himself enjoying the taverns and brothels rather than working as a butcher like his father.

He had preferred the sea, where the salty aroma of the deep ocean and the rocking motion of a ship made him feel alive. The fierce battles he fought were often skirmishes to the death. On more than one occasion, his opponents met their end not by the edge of his sword but rather by a shot fired from any musket pistols hanging from a thick black belt strapped across his chest.

First and foremost, Redbone was a pirate, a damn good one! A seasoned sailor and privateer. He believed in his plan to form an Iron Born brotherhood, and nothing would stop him.

Today, his crew would be tested to their limits. Gratefully, the weakest among his crew members were abandoned at the witch's island. What remained was something to behold. Fearless and determined, these men were joined together for a single cause sailing aboard the *Hell's Fury*, and soon their mettle would be tested.

They were still too far off to discover the type of ship about to cross the blood pirates' path, but one thing was sure, the approaching sails hadn't altered course. Ahead of them was the unknown. Were his men ready to face the challenge? Would they survive the burning and exploding cannonballs blasted at them? All would be lost if a blazing fire reached the powder stores at any time during a sea battle. These facts alone would worry the weary heart, but the reality of being pierced with a sword would make the faint-hearted cringe in fear.

Redbone eyed his navigator while he struggled to hold the steering wheel. They maintained their heading, and the course set true. Redbone glanced down at his first mate and saw the man standing at the ready. This orchestrated battle couldn't commence until Redbone was confident of his opponent. There was always a chance to get away if these sails belonged to a British man-of-war or another type of fierce battleship. They were not equipped to face such a powerful opponent, not yet, not until his crew grew in size.

With spyglass in hand, Redbone could see that the ship looked small in size, no doubt a brigantine or even East Indiaman, but not a man-of-war. He studied the vessel and saw a black flag through his spyglass. The circumstances had changed.

Harv gripped the giant wheel and focused on maintaining course, heading directly toward the oncoming vessel. The ship's navigator, one-eyed Harv-Dog, heard a chuckle from his captain and turned to look at what amused him. Redbone shaking his head, announced, "Arrrr, Mr. Sneed, it seems that our daring privateers are buccaneers themselves."

"Steady as she goes, Mr. Sneed; it seems we have

fellows who might want a scuffle," Redbone announced. Redbone thought, *why show one's colors unless you want to frighten your prey into submission? Regardless of the outcome, we'll show these rabble-rousers a thing or two. A daring move in these waters with every Spanish ship hunting pirates.*

Seeing his first mate standing by, Redbone yelled, "Mr. Schmidt, it seems our prey are pirates much like ourselves; however, ready thee cannons. I be in the mood for a fight."

"Aye, aye, Captain." Mr. Schmidt yelled into the darkness of the hatch to the gun crew, "Load your cannons with a shot, men. We are in for a fight."

Time slowed to a crawl. Staring at the steel base of his saber, Redbone could see the forged work of the hammer, the steel wrought into something firm and dependable, a weapon of death.

He heard the cries aboard the ship as men prepared themselves for a fight. Redbone considered. *Could these be my final hours before I rests with Davey Jones? A life, his life, taking satisfaction when he could. Nothing in me future seems feasible; now me treasure is gone, and someone else is thee owner.*

Redbone needed to taste blood. What was most important was a genuine concern for the ship's superstructure. Would it hold up in an actual sea battle, or had it been battered enough in previous skirmishes to become useless? What did it matter if the ship's design was attractive to the eye? Could it survive when unknown forces bombarded the hardened oak timbers with cannon fire?

None could ever guess how this ship had changed from its original purpose, initially built by the Dutch to hunt pirates. Who would have expected to see a black flag flying from her transom?

Redbone finally recognized the oncoming ship; he

had sailed with it under a different captain many years ago in a daring raid. This De Vries, a ruthless pirate himself, had gathered a group of men and mutinied, taking the ship and treasure for themselves.

Mr. Bisset appeared in a colorful silk display, saying, "Captain, still waiting for your order to hoist the black flag. I've embroidered the new design onto the flag as you directed; look here and see the two swords crossing behind the goblet as you wanted, both the swords and goblet in red against the black fabric."

Redbone rubbed his hairy chin, lost in thought, as he stared at the white sails approaching. He hesitated. A moment later, he screamed to his first mate, "Mr. Schmidt, tell ye gun crew to keep thee gun ports closed until I give thee the order to draw out thee irons. Make sure ye master gunner, Mr. Andrews, understands. Otherwise, thee trap will be sprung!"

"Captain Redbone, sir, what shall I do?" Mr. Bisset inquired.

"Very good, Mr. Bisset; return to the transom and await me orders." Turning back to his navigator, Redbone shouted, "Mr. Sneed, turn thee ship starboard to these pirate dogs!"

Sailing under full sail, the approaching ship seemed determined to intersect the *Hell's Fury*. A few minutes later, as was customary for pirates and other military vessels of the day, cannon fire erupted in white plumes. Whistling through the air and ending in two distinct splashes near their bow, the cannon fire was intended as a warning shot to announce their need to surrender or be blown out of the water. A tactic Redbone himself has used in times past. However, these pirates had not realized their mistake in thinking that the *Hell's Fury* was a helpless merchant ship or even a Dutch pirate hunter.

Redbone laughed; his diversion was working perfectly. Mr. Schmidt appeared. "The cannons are loaded and ready to fire."

"Very good; now have the men lower the main topsail, fore-topsail, and mizzen topsail but keep the forecourse sail and main course sail in place, along with the flying jib and jib sails. Stay under enough sail power to give us some maneuverability to turn and fire a broadside when the time comes. Keep the men aloft; they must remain standing on the yardarms, ready to unfurl ye sails at a moment's notice." Placing his hand on Mr. Schmidt's shoulder, Redbone announced, "I want ye to fasten ropes to both the fore-yard and main yard, long enough to make it easy for men to swing across."

"Captain, what of the boarding planks, sir? We're not using them?"

"Curses, no, not at this time. To me, thee men lost to arrange boarding planks are not worth ye lives we will lose; besides, this is a new day, me friend. Today will be a test to see how our pirate brothers fight to win. If worthy, few men will be lost. However, if me faith has been misplaced, then it will be a fight to thee death for us all. Now, sir, ye have ye orders; see to it."

A simple nod from the large man and Mr. Schmidt hurried away, shouting orders to the waiting crew. Soon, a frenzy erupted topside, and buccaneers hurriedly began climbing the three different masts, lowering the sails as ordered. The *Hell's Fury* started to slow, plowing through the choppy sea as Redbone remained focused on the other vessel. He wasn't the least bit surprised to see its gunport doors open. Considering his next move carefully, he yelled to Mr. Bisset, "Hoist the Black Flag."

Mr. Bisset quickly went into action, unfurled the giant flag, and hung it over the stern, snapping the cleats into place.

Gratefully, the other ship's cannons remained in their stays as the *Hell's Fury* continued to slow while exposed to a broadside and turn hard to starboard as it approached the other ship. This ploy was a chance Redbone was willing to take. After all, he planned to cause some diversion, and he knew that when the captain of the other pirate ship spotted their black flag, a parley would be attempted, setting their weapons aside.

While observing the other pirate vessel, Redbone discovered that its mainsails were being lowered. As the craft got closer, Redbone recognized its shape as a brigantine, somewhat smaller than their boat. Changes to its superstructure had allowed more cannons to be added to the main deck.

Glancing down at his first mate, Redbone shouted, "Mr. Schmidt, stands ready."

Maintaining course fifteen degrees North, the *Hell's Fury* slowed to about four knots. At the same time, the other ship continued approaching from the South. Redbone shouted for his quartermaster, Mr. Toner, who ran up the stairs to the poop deck and said, "Yes, Captain, you wanted to see me?"

"Ye have the boarding party armed with muskets and swords and be quick about it before our intentions are known. Afterward, keep ye men stowed below decks until ye hear me command to attack. At that time, ye will see ropes hanging from thee yardarm, specially arranged for ye men to swing across the two ships and bring thee fight to our unsuspecting pirates."

"Consider it done, sir."

Lifting his spyglass, Redbone stared at his adversary. There he saw the pirate captain directing his men, pointing to the sails as the fabric was stowed. For his plan to work successfully, Redbone would have one chance to take his prey by surprise. The betrayal of his kind was ruthless and desperate. Still, there was no other way to mark oneself as the most dreaded and feared pirates sailing the Caribbean except by treachery, even to their kind. After today, there would be no safe harbor or sanctuary. After today, they would become the most hated and feared pirates, known as The Iron Born, second to none!

The other pirates and their captain were now visible on their bridge. The man was wearing a red jacket and powdered black wig, similar to Redbones. What wasn't known was the fight in the man's soul; what resistance would he or his men give?

Never taking his gaze from the pirate bridge, Redbone whispered, "Mr. Sneed, steady as she goes."

The other ship closed the gap between them, just a hundred yards away. Redbone saw his opportunity as the pirate ship turned to starboard to come alongside.

Below the musky ship's hull, no less than forty men handled a row of cannons poised to pounce when the word came. No one understood this more than the master gunner, Mr. Andrews, who eased the anxious hearts of his men by saying, "Wait, wait for it, boys, until we get the word, do not fire yer cannons until Redbone gives us the order. Trust me, boys, he knows what he's doing good and well!"

Apprehensively, the men waited to hear the one word from their captain that would release a barrage of destruction. One could hear a pin drop. The only sounds came from the lapping waves against the hull, occasionally seagulls screeching above, but all else remained quiet and still.

Then as if none could hold on any longer, they heard from above the command, "Fire—ye sons of bitches. Fire—curse ye hides! Men, give 'em all ye iron ye have!" Redbone screamed out. Immediately, the gunport hatches flew open, and all the cannons ran out from their guns and burst outwardly in a blazing array of smoke and fire. The damage was instantaneous, causing the bow and jib sails of the other ship to burst apart in a fiery plume of wood splinters.

"Now——Mr. Schmidt, unfurl ye topsails!" Redbone shouted. Never taking his eyes off the other ship, Redbone yelled out to his navigator, "Turn ye——hard to port, Mr. Sneed, do it now, sir!" Gripping the large wheel, the old pirate spun the large wheel over and over, causing *Hell's Fury* to tilt hard to port, exposing their stern to their enemy.

Fires erupted on the other pirate ship that never saw the betrayal coming. Their captain, Lawrence Blackburne, withdrew his sword and cursed the men aboard the *Hell's Fury*, screaming out the command to fire a broadside into the departing vessel.

Now gaining momentum, the Hell's Fury began to pull away with all her sails unfurled. The gunners below struggled to withdraw their cannons and prepare their guns to fire another salvo as quickly as possible. What mattered most was who would make the necessary adjustments to their armament first.

On Mr. Andrews, the master gunner's command, the touch holes were closed off, preventing the gases from eroding the cannons' vent holes. Next, the guns were swabbed out and loaded all over again. As the crew lowered the ship's sails, the passing trade winds filled the white fabric and surged the *Hell's Fury* forward, out of danger, as it struggled to get underway.

What happened next came as no surprise to Redbone as he watched the other vessel turn hard to port and unleash a bombardment of cannon fire toward the *Hell's Fury,* ripping into her stern. The damage couldn't be ascertained at that moment.

Quicker than he ever thought possible and ignoring the damage to his ship, Redbone watched as another salvo blasted outward from the *Hell's Fury* into their enemy. He didn't need to shout orders to the gun crew; his master gunner had taken command of the firing and directed the cannon fire's bombardment.

Appearing next to his captain, Mr. Schmidt said, "Captain, we need to win the day; all depends on the master gunner, Mr. Andrews, to give a good account of himself."

"Arrrr, believe me when I says Mr. Andrews will perform his work brilliantly; I have no doubt! Tell me, are thee men prepared for boarding?"

"Standing by, waiting for your orders, sir."

"Very well, still too early to distinguish thee outcome of this battle, but come hell or damnation, we will fight to the death. Hard to starboard, Mr. Sneed, be quick, man."

The *Hells Fury's* hull lifted out of the water as its rudder was cocked hard against the keel in a desperate attempt to outflank its opponent. The two seasoned commanders shouted orders to gain the upper hand in this fight. All the men could do for now was hang on as the two ships waged war against each other in a desperate attempt to gain any advantage.

The damage to the other ship was most noticeable; jib sails and forecastle were torn away, exposing the two lower decks where fires raged out of control. Black billowing smoke rose above the waterline. Still, the pirates fought on. Shortly after the other ship fired another salvo at the *Hell's Fury*, Redbone noticed the number of shots dispersed was smaller than before. The enemy ship was diminished in its ability to fight. Still, the battle raged on.

Although the *Hell's Fury* had fires burning onboard, the powder magazines remained protected as the main deck rocked from the outpouring of exploding cannons beneath Redbone's feet. The destruction of both ships seemed inevitable, but Redbone discovered a gleaming ray of hope as the enemy's remaining main mast came tumbling down into the sea.

Redbone ordered his navigator to come alongside the burning ship. Turning to look at his first mate, Redbone announced, "Mr. Schmidt, ye know what must be done, sir."

"Aye, aye, Captain." Running to the taffrail, Mr. Schmidt was met by Mr. Toner and the rest of the boarding party, armed with muskets and swords. The *Hell's Fury* crashed into the other ship, narrowly bouncing off the hardened surface and floating past without coming to a complete stop.

Both sides were eager for a fight and cast boarding lines with metal hooks toward their enemy, drawing the two ships together.

Grabbing hold of one of the ropes, Mr. Schmidt was the first to swing across the gap. On the other side, he was met by a pirate of similar stature. The man's eyes glowed red with hatred as he swung at Schmidt with a double-edged ax. Blocking the man's maneuver with his saber, Schmidt heaved him backward.

As the behemoth stumbled back, waving his arms wildly to catch himself from falling, Schmidt advanced and swung at him with his sword. His blade bounced off the metal handle. Schmidt moved with determination and took another swing. This time his blade slid down the ax handle and stopped short of the ax head.

The two men snarled at one another. Schmidt took a step forward, punched the man in his face, and laughed aloud. The pirate wiped away the trickle of blood from his lip and heckled back.

Dropping his saber, Schmidt struggled for dominance, placed his hands on the ax handle, and jerked it sideways to free the weapon. The pirate lifted his heavy ax and swung it madly at Schmidt's head; Schmidt struck the man in his face, and instantly, the man's right eye swelled twice its size. The pirate's killing weapon was temporarily blocked, so he head-butted Schmidt in his face and broke his nose.

The man's spit splattered across Schmidt's face as he

shouted curses mingled with his blood and sweat. Pain ignored and broken nose forgotten, Schmidt pushed hard against his opponent. The man drove back with equal tenacity and brute strength, matching Schmidt's own. As they fought to the death, both men were oblivious to the world around them until two other pirates slammed into them and engaged in a swordfight.

Schmidt reached down as their attention was diverted, took his stiletto from his belt, and plunged it deep into his opponent's neck. Over and over, Schmidt drove his blade into the man's carotid arteries until his fist was coated in red.

Still, the man resisted and fought to stay alive with all his might. However weakened, he lowered his ax, and Schmidt jerked it from his grasp. He twirled the heavy object in his hand; a worthy prize won in combat. He'd carry it with him throughout his pirating adventures. Looking at his adversary, inspiration struck him. *Perhaps, I should test this weapon for effect. It will be no use carrying the damn thing if it doesn't perform.* Schmidt lifted the ax in the air, crashing down with a heaving motion, splitting the man's head asunder; the big man fell over dead.

Now, searching the bloody deck, Schmidt went on a killing spree, killing many pirates with just one swing from his newly acquired ax. When it was over, men lay scattered about the deck, many missing body parts or with gaping holes through their heads from large-caliber musket balls.

The stench of death was everywhere, but only six Iron Born lost their lives in the conflict. The pirates fought with such vigor that it overwhelmed the other crew. Eighteen men surrendered and threw down their weapons before Redbone.

Their captain, Lawrence Blackburne, met his end in a sword fight with Redbone. However, Redbone was shot in the leg by a desperate pirate wanting to end the battle. The musket ball needed to be removed, nothing that Mr. Connelly, the ship's doctor, and some rum couldn't fix.

The eighteen remaining pirates were brought to their knees when the fight ended. Bound with their hands behind their backs and displayed as prizes won in battle, they awaited their fate. One pirate, however, gained Redbone's notice. He claimed to be the master gunner.

The victors took their time plundering the ship of all its valuables. Then it was time for Redbone to decide if these swashbucklers were worthy of bearing his mark. If not, they would be thrown overboard. That night under a crescent moon, those remaining pirates would be given a chance to dance with the Bloody Hag.

The other boat, the *Calico,* was scuttled and slipped beneath the waves, none wiser for the Iron Born betrayal except Davy Jones himself. While the ship's doctor was mending his wound, Redbone had time to consider his actions. He felt the betrayal of his kind as something of a necessity; otherwise, the Iron Born would be just another desperate band of cutthroats, scratching out a living on the Spanish Main.

As the doctor dug out the wad of cotton and musket ball from Redbone's leg, Schmidt appeared with Mr. Sneed, carrying a treasure chest of gold and jewels. "Ah, Mr. Schmidt, tell me, what ye have there?"

"Captain, it be all the booty was taken from the *Calico,* sir."

"Arrrr, it be now, I see. Tell me, Mr. Schmidt, how many brave souls we've lost, sir?"

"Only five, including our Master Gunner, Mr. Andrews, who was blown apart by the last bombardment."

"I see," Redbone said, then yelled in pain as the doctor applied a bandage to his leg and snuggly tied it off. "Curse ye, Doctor Connelly, is it necessary to pain me so?

Fetch me some more rum and be quick about it, lads."

"Brendon!" Schmidt shouted. "Where is that boy when you want him?"

"I'm here, sir; yes, what is it?" the other young cabin boy announced, running into the room.

"Get our captain some more rum, lad, and be quick about it," the first mate demanded.

Grabbing Redbone's heavy mug, **Brendon** was off and returned shortly with the rum, slopping it everywhere. "Here you go, Captain, will there be anything else, sir?"

"Aye, yes, lad, be a help to Doctor **Connelly**, who needs to attend to the wounded. When ye are done there, ask Mr. Toner if he needs ye help to store the weapons and gunpowder we've taken from thee, *Calico*."

"Right away, sir."

"Mr. Schmidt, go and store the treasure chest in me cabin; ye know thee location. This night, we shall dine like kings and send our fallen heroes to thee afterlife in style befitting ye Iron Born."

"Aye, Captain, but concerning your cabin, sir, it was destroyed, along with the officers' quarters."

"Ahh, blasted pirate dogs. Mr. Schmidt, go and take thee survivors and cast them overboard! No, wait, something better for these men; tonight, we shall perform the Bloody Hag ceremony. We shall allow fate to intervene; if any should survive, they can take their place as Iron Born brothers. Once ye formality is complete, we shall divide thee treasure amongst our original Iron Born, a fair share, based on rank. For now, store thee treasure in me cabin, under lock and key. We wouldn't want any temptation, now, would we?"

Schmidt and the old sea dog Harv scuffled away, carrying the heavy chest of gold.

"Mr. Conner, check on thee prisoners after ye doctor up our men. I doubt that they escaped unscathed."

Standing, Redbone eyed the three-masted *Calico* sinking beneath the waves.

Sometime later, Redbone appeared on deck to eye his catch. Still in chains, they remained on their knees. Time for a speech. Redbone gathered all Iron Born on deck.

Looking over his captives, Redbone scrutinized the men. Slowly moving past each one, he announced, "Men, ye have a choice before thee. An alternative, better than most of us ever receives as brigands. Today, as thee captain aboard the *Hell's Fury,* I offers ye a chance to become a crew member. Don't think me foolish or take this opportunity lightly. To become a member of this pirate band, ye must survive the dance with the Bloody Hag."

"Bloody Hag, you call it, sounds like an invitation to become a cowardly traitor to your kind! Curse you and your crew for flying the black flag; it was the only reason our captain didn't blow your ship out of the water."

Redbone turned back to see who was addressing him in such a rude fashion. A man leaned forward, looking at him with hate in his eyes. Stopping in front of the man, Redbone had little doubt he was a seasoned pirate. The man bore tattoos upon his face and neck, besides the markings on his body. In his ear was a gold ring.

"What be that you say? Cowards, ye call us?"

"I cannot think of a better title for you and your men."

"Tell me, man, am I to take it that ye do not want to be a part of this crew?"

"Bastardly cowards, the whole lot of you."

It was the last thing the man said. Redbone removed his blade from his belt and sliced the man's throat open wide without hesitation. Next, he shoved his fist into the man's neck, pulled his tongue out, and laid it against his chest. The man could only gurgle out a bubbling sound.

"Mr. Schmidt, please set our little birdie loose, will

ye?"

"Right away, Captain," The man was unchained, carried over to the railing, and tossed into the sea.

"Now, where were we?" Redbone announced loudly.

"Captain, I'm honored to be a member of your crew, sir," a faint voice spoke out from the end of the row.

"Tell me, lads, who be the bravest amongst yer crew so eager to dance with the Bloody Hag?"

Redbone saw a small, ruddy pirate stand upright and step forward.

At last, a brave soul to be the first, Redbone thought. Walking over, Redbone eyed the volunteer carefully. "Mr. Schmidt, come ye here at once."

When the large man arrived, he too saw something peculiar about this pirate, something he hadn't noticed before.

"Mr. Schmidt, tell me, sir, have ye seen this ruddy pirate before me?"

"Ay, Captain."

"Could you please explain why thee pirate is not a man but a woman?"

Standing to her feet, the woman declared, "My name is Mary Wolseley Scott, a gunner aboard the *Calico*, sir. I would be honored to take a dance with the Bloody Hag if for no other reason than to show your crew that she's nothing to fear, just a bitch in disguise, sir."

Rubbing his chin, Redbone wasn't sure how to respond. *Never in his imagination had he considered a female pirate. What of the men, the dangers, what of— ahh hell.* "Lass, if ye want to become an Iron Born, then ye too will have yer turn; all of you shall dance with the Hag this night."

Nothing was left to say; Redbone had other preparations to attend to and walked away.

Still, the idea was unsettling, and a short time before the ceremony began, Mr. Schmidt unchained Mary from the rest of the pirates and brought her to see Redbone. Alone in the remains of his cabin, opened to the outside world, Redbone stood, drinking rum. Still shackled, Mary appeared and was ordered to sit on a small stool.

"You wanted to see me, Captain?"

"If indeed I becomes yer captain. Tell me, this volunteering to become an Iron Born was not a ploy to save yer skin?"

"No, Captain, I saw the way your crew fought. None could match the tenacity or resilience they displayed today. I saw something more noteworthy than simply being a pirate; I saw a brotherhood."

"Would ye care for some rum, Mary?"

"Aye, Captain, I would love to share a drink with ye."

"Mr. Schmidt, come and remove these cursed bracelets, sir."

Stepping inside the small space, the first mate unlocked Mary and vanished out of the room.

Redbone handed her a glass and toasted it to her health. Downing the drink in one gulp, Mary thanked him and handed the empty glass back.

Redbone, chuckling, said, "Here, now, I must say, ye drink like a pirate! Now, listen, this dancing business with thee Bloody Hag is unsettling. Perhaps ye should change yer mind and return home?"

"Captain, there is no home for me. That is a story in itself, sir."

"Do tell; we have a little time before this evening's trials begin; go on. First more rum, to steady ye nerves."

"Yes, please." As Mary told her tale, Redbone listened intently to her life story.

"I have not always been a pirate, as you may guess. Circumstances out of my control have brought me here. Call it fate. I was once happily married, but that didn't last long. The Sovereign's tax collector, Wilford Barrow, had an infatuation with me. Although he knew I was married, it didn't deter him in the least. When I told my husband about the unwanted flirtations, he punched that tax collector in the nose. Thinking about it now, we should have left our farm and moved away."

"Hmmm, yer tale is an old one. A pretty young lass, a frail old man of power, wanting something that didn't belong to him, that scurvy dog."

"Aye, captain, it is so, but why throw my Robert into debtors' prison, that cowardly arse? I never saw my husband again. The taxes came due that spring, and I had no money to pay. A gleaming light of hope came from the fact that we had no children. None to experience the desperate situation of two parents. Then came the news I feared most. Robert had died in prison; the guards claimed he was shot while escaping. I knew better; it was that cursed Wilford Barrow. No surprise, the man showed up on my doorstep, offering his help."

"Here, now, lass, drink up; it will quicken yer blood flow. Already, lass, I decided that ye shall be the first to dance with thee Hag if nothing more than to prove she's a bitch as ye say so smartly." Filling Mary's glass a third time, Redbone looked her in the eye and said, "See now, Madam, it be not too late to change yer mind. None here will think any different if yer did. I see the fear in yer crew's eyes. They all recognize that death could come for them this very night! Why not return home and start again with a new family?"

"Captain, I have no home. I was guaranteed that when I accepted Wilford Barrow's invitation to dine with him. I understood he was the cause of all my troubles.

"With the promise of a sexual conquest before his eyes, the man followed me into his bed-chamber. He quickly undressed and approached me. I told him to be patient. As I undressed, he hungered after my body, never knowing it would never be his. There, straddled atop the man, I took my revenge. He never saw the small blade in my hair; he only felt the searing pain as my knife jabbed out his eyes. When it was over, I was coated in the man's blood, grabbed my clothes, and ran out of the house crying."

"No, not always what we hope for, this revenge, lass!"

"No, you're wrong, Captain, it was all I hoped for and more, but sadly Wilford's servant informed the authorities. I was a wanted woman and ran for my life.

"Sometime later, while taking refuge in a tavern, there was an argument between two pirates over a prostitute. As I observed, they drew swords and were about to fight to the death. The older pirate was outmaneuvered and was about to die. Seeing his distress, I intervened, took a stool, and slammed it into the head of the other pirate, knocking him unconscious. The man I saved, Godfrey, brought me aboard his pirate ship *Calico* and taught me everything there was to know about aiming cannons. He was the one chained next to me."

"Aye, I see now. I have heard ye enough, Mary; please finish yer drink and be gone. Soon, fate will play its part in yer future. None can tell whether it be death or a life of piracy, but for me, I be happy to have ye aboard me ship."

Downing her glass, Mary walked only a few steps when she turned and said, "Captain, what of my shackles?"

"There be no need of them, is there, Mary? If ye throw a fuss aboard this ship, I slit ye throat meself and throw yer carcass overboard; now be gone with ye."

"Thank you, sir," With that, Mary walked out of the cabin and made herself useful for the rest of the day, helping store gunpowder and cannonballs below.

That night, Redbone gathered all the men on deck, each with a mug in his hand filled with rum. Redbone eyed his crew and, raising his sword, said, "Men and fellow Iron Born brothers. Today ye have met thee enemy and fought bravely. I could not be prouder than I be now. As a fighting force, ye have exceeded all me expectations, not only mine but yer first mate Mr. Schmidt's as well. It was regrettable that five of our comrades lost their lives in today's skirmish, but tonight we will toast their voyage into the afterlife with song and merriment. But first, there are a few matters we must attend to, one being paid a man's wages for a job well done. Mr. Schmidt, will ye please?"

Cheers and shouts erupted on deck as Mr. Schmidt and Abisai appeared carrying a treasure chest. Soon, equal shares of the loot were distributed to every crew member, including pieces of eight and gold doubloons. The high-ranking officers mainly received jewels and gold necklaces as a form of gratitude from their captain.

After some time, the evening's entertainment was about to begin. Redbone called on the artist Antonio Alvarez to arrange a different set of blades for Mary. Redbone realized that a miscalculation could result in the woman having her hands cut off, and then she'd be no use to anyone.

In the end, all but two survived the dance with the Bloody Hag. Mary was one of the fortunate souls. With the ship's need for repairs and the crew's pockets full of coins, Redbone charted a new course for the famed port of call, Tortuga.

Chapter 8

THE PASSAGE TOOK ANOTHER ten days before Tortuga appeared on the horizon. Captain Redbone ordered the Hell's Fury to anchor close to the port as the crew lowered the ship's sails and prepared for arrival. Afterward, he ordered a few men to remain on board as the others paddled their longboats ashore. The suspicious stares were not a welcome sight for Redbone and his men. Although few people practiced piracy as their stock and trade, these buccaneers in Tortuga were different, mainly because the French Governor offered Marque letters to any pirate who would attack Spanish ships and split the booty.

When the rowing party arrived at the waterfront, several merchantmen were unloading supplies from a three-masted sailing ship. Regardless of the suspicious looks, the newcomers' party had one thing in mind: the brothels, then the taverns. In Tortuga, a man had several entertainment choices, but most had their favorite haunts. Those younger men would have to taste for themselves the delicious delicacies of a promiscuous woman to discover which satisfied their particular palate best.

The Governor's mansion was always the first stop of all pirate captains and their first mates on visits to the island. Redbone had just one stop in mind to see the French Governor and arrange repairs for his ship. The entertainment could wait; he was the captain, responsible for everything and everyone aboard his ship. Although he never had dealings with this particular administrator, he knew that an appearance was in order. Otherwise, he and his men could be considered trespassers. Redbone would be no exception.

The Governor's house was on the top of the hill, where the man had a grand view of the harbor. It was not hard to find; follow the booty, and you'd see the extravagant results of plundering the high seas. Redbone pounded on the front door. A negro answered and pleasantly ushered them inside; the Governor was already alerted that visitors had arrived in port. They followed the steward to a drawing-room and were asked to have a seat. As Redbone eyed the elaborate decor, he wasn't amazed to see fine works of art hanging on the walls, no doubt meant for a Spanish royal estate but deemed as booty raided from the Spanish galleons. Next, they were poured a glass of brandy and left alone.

Mr. Schmidt, seeing something of interest, walked over to the bookshelf, picked up Shakespeare's First Folio, and thumbed through it as a flamboyantly attired man walked into the room.

"Gentlemen, welcome to Tortuga. Please allow me to introduce myself; my name is Jean-Francois de La Rocque de Roberval. I'm the Governor here in Tortuga. Please make yourselves comfortable; I see that my steward has poured you some refreshments."

"Aye, indeed, Governor," Redbone replied.

"Gentleman, there are just a few matters we must discuss."

"Aye, I see; it comes as no surprise to me. Ye be talking about thee port tax, now would ye?"

"Somehow, Captain, you, sir, seem familiar to me; tell me, have we met before?"

"I, perhaps, one cannot say," Redbone announced, downing his brandy. Slamming down a bag of gold coins on the table, he turned to the Governor. "I needs some repairs to me ship, sir."

"No, worries, Captain, we have some of the finest craftsmen around; I'll be happy to make the proper arrangements for you."

"Aye, our business be finished, then, sir," Redbone announced and stood to leave.

"Captain, a word of caution. Although I cannot place you, I'm still certain we've had dealings in the past. Here, in Tortuga, we have a respectful armistice that all pirates must oblige. Inform your men that we will not tolerate any unnecessary killing. If a man's life is threatened, that's another matter altogether, you understand?"

"Aye, aye ye be coming through clear enough, Governor. However, I must inform ye, sir, that if any of me men are threatened or murdered, I will hold ye responsible! An Iron Born is unlike any swashbuckler yer run into in ye past. Each of me men has vowed himself to his shipmates. Kill one, and death and destruction will follow thee."

"Understood, Captain, although Iron Born is a name I'm unfamiliar. Nevertheless, we accommodate all pirates here. Especially those attacking the Spanish; they must remain unharmed, sir! Please, you and your men, have a pleasant stay here in Tortuga, and if I can be of any further service, don't hesitate to knock on my door."

"Good day, Governor." With that, Redbone and Mr. Schmidt walked out.

The following morning, alone on the poop deck, Redbone eyed the sleepy town slowly coming to life. After a night of carousing, he understood that most of his men would be sleeping below in their bunks or still in bed with the prostitutes back in town. Mr. Toner, the quartermaster, appeared at his elbow.

"Captain Redbone, sir, we have a bit of a problem."

"Aye, tell me, quick, what be the problem, man?"

"It seems that some of our scallywags have run into their old shipmates. When they inquired of the whereabouts of their previous captain Lawrence Blackburne, a fight broke out."

"Yes, a problem, surely it be. I expected this sooner or later. Where be our men now?"

Apprehensively, the quartermaster continued, "Captain, that be the problem itself, sir."

"Mr. Toner! Curse your carcass to hell, man! Tell me quickly," Redbone shouted.

"Those old shipmates took five of our Iron Born hostage, including Mary. They drug them up to an encampment on the island's far side!"

Redbone called for his first mate. Soon, Mr. Schmidt appeared on the poop deck, looking as if he had just crawled out of bed.

"Mr. Schmidt, it be time to gather the men. I have just received news that our brothers have been taken, hostage. We cannot allow these cowards to take an Iron Born. These buffoons chose to take our comrades in arms hostage and will pay for their foolishness with their blood."

Mr. Schmidt, smirking, responded, "It's a good thing I sharpened my ax when I did. I'll gather our men from the brothels and meet you back at the ship, Captain. It will take a little time to collect all the men; after all, many will still be drunk. But after hearing that their shipmates were abducted, they'll see it as an insult, the same as us, sir."

"Very well, ye know what must be done." Looking back toward the Governor's mansion, Redbone proclaimed, "This insult could not have gone unapproved. Perhaps our Governor Jean-Francois de La Rocque played a part. This treason will be his undoing, I assure ye. For now, we must rescue our companions."

Redbone's eyes glowed red as he strutted off toward the *Hell's Fury* armor. He was determined to save his men and quickly gathered what firepower he could from the assortment of black powder muskets and pistols. A dismal gathering of men appeared on the main deck a short time later, looking ragged and shabby. Still, one common thread united them all, the desire to avenge those Iron Born taken captive.

Appearing on the quarterdeck, Redbone addressed his men, "Ye Iron Born brothers, no doubt ye heard from Mr. Schmidt of the kidnapping of yer pirate comrades by some former shipmates. From what I be told, they're held up in an encampment not far from Tortuga. From this time onward, all those sailing throughout these Caribbean waters will understand we Iron Born pirates never leave a brother behind. Thee foolhardy souls crossing paths with a blood pirate will pay for this mistake with their lives!"

Loud cheers erupted aboard the *Hell's Fury*, more boisterous than in previous times. Today, the battle would be played on land instead of the sea. The Iron Born would play the role of invaders, not **swashbucklers**. To plan such an event took time they didn't have, but the overall consensus was they'd invade the pirate camp with guns blazing.

Redbone's plan? Well, frankly, there wasn't one. The captain understood that when they rushed the camp, the first ones to die would be his men held prisoner, not to mention Mary, who he was sure was being violated repeatedly.

Brendon, the cabin boy, appeared with a young girl, saying, "Captain Redbone, sir, I have news that you must hear!"

"Aye, ye do. Tell it, boy, and be quick."

"Sir, this girl, Matilda, works at the brothel where the fight broke out. She has told me that a couple of whores are staying at the encampment where our crew members are being held hostage."

"Hum, I see. Unfortunately, these prostitutes have chosen to put themselves in a dangerous position. There will be no mercy for those within thee camp, nor will anyone be spared."

Turning to Matilda, Brendon announced, "You have heard my captain. It is the way of things, I'm sorry. You best be going."

"No, I be afraid that's impossible," Redbone explained. Calling out to Mr. Toner, standing by, the captain ordered Matilda to be held temporarily in the small jail below decks. Turning to Brendon, Redbone clarified, "Ye must understand, lad, we cannot allow anyone to know of our plans. I assure ye she'll be released unharmed when thee fight is over."

Mr. Schmidt eyed the distress in young Brendon and gripped his shoulder as he was leaving.

Redbone inquired, "Mr. Schmidt, tell me, where be Mr. Clements?"

"The last I saw him, he was at the bow, sharpening his blade."

"Ye tell the man I needs to see him."

"Right away, Captain."

When the first mate appeared at the bow, Mr. Clements was deep in thought. His shipmates called him Hunter because of his ability to hunt wild animals. Approaching the man with caution, Schmidt said, "The captain wants to see you."

Looking up, Clement spat on the sharpening stone. "Aye, he does now?"

"See to it, sir. Redbone is not a man to keep waiting."

"I imagine ye be sharp enough, little sticker." Clements gave his knife one last rub, grinned, and headed toward Redbone, who was talking with Mr. Connelly, the ship's doctor.

"See that ye have plenty of bandages and ointment, doctor, especially alcohol," Redbone ordered.

"Already taken care of, sir."

Redbone turned around. "Oh, Hunter, I need a word."

"Aye, aye, captain. What be on your mind, sir."

Redbone turned back to the doctor. "That be all, man, for now." As the doctor left, Redbone addressed Hunter, saying, "I want ye to scout out yonder pirate encampment. Take with ye three men that have similar stealth abilities as yerself. These cursed dogs will be expecting us, and I cannot say what type of opposition ye will encounter but know that yer not to give any quarter to these bastard dogs. Unfortunately, I heard reports that these men are not alone and have some whores with them."

"Prostitutes, Captain?"

"Aye, it be a sad truth these women have decided to join thee, foolhardy buccaneers, instead of comprehending thee danger involved. No, we cannot be hindered from ye mission. We cannot promise safe passage to thee women inside the camp. Do what ye must, Hunter; I want ye to spearhead this mission. Now listen closely. There be a leader among the group, someone giving orders. Find this man, whoever he be, and keep him alive."

"Alive, sir?"

"I realize a man with yer stealth will have no problems scouting out thee troublemakers but know this; we'll leave no survivors. In our wake, we'll leave such destruction that all sailing these Caribbean waters will realize that hell will follow if ye mistreat an Iron Born. Hunter, we're sending a message, man."

"Aye, indeed you are, a clear message, Captain."

Mr. Schmidt appeared at that moment with his ax over his shoulder. "Captain, the men are ready."

"Very well, thank you, Mr. Schmidt."

"Captain Redbone, wouldn't it be wiser to attack at dawn? When there is an element of surprise?" Hunter asked.

"No, these bilge-sucking cowards took our men in broad daylight without fear of reprisal, and that arrogance will cost them dearly. Hunter, we must kill them! I promise they'll not see ye coming; do yer duty, man."

"Aye, Aye, Captain, I have my orders. I have already decided which three men will accompany me; they are more cunning and ruthless than me."

"Good, see to it; thee rest of us will soon be on yer heels."

Chapter 9

THE BATTLE PLANS WERE CLEAR, and Hunter and the three brigands left the *Hell's Fury*. With Hunter were André, Cadmael, and Ryker, each equipped with daggers or similar small weapons. There was no need for swords or other fighting arsenals; these weapons were light to carry and effective in killing.

Banana plants and mangroves often grew along the estuaries, disappearing through a thicket of coconut palms and banyan trees. The small band made their way to the island's top of the hill. Soon they approached the ruins of Fort de Rocher, a pirate fortress destroyed by the Spanish some years earlier. Stopping to rest, Hunter examined his three companions for signs of weakness. All had been tested in battle. Still, his thinking was haunted by the harsh reality that one or more of them, himself included, could be killed this day. Who could predict the outcome? Regardless of his doubts, the Iron Born needed to be liberated.

As they took time to rest, no one spoke out of fear of giving away their position. After a quick break, the small group silently moved up the hillside through the thick overgrowth. Arriving at the topmost part of the island, they took a moment to admire the view. The dark blue waters and lush green vegetation against the clear blue sky gave the impression of an island paradise. But from this time forward, buccaneers choosing this island as a place of refuge would remember the slaughter that occurred this day.

Not far ahead stood the pirate encampment—no defensive barriers were visible around the camp, nothing but a cabin and a scattering of small tents. But the beheaded remains of two Iron Born pirates were displayed on spikes near a burning campfire. As Hunter examined the remains, he could see the Iron Born mark on the deceased's wrists. As another symbol of disrespect, a set of arms cut off at the elbow were ritualistically mounted above the cabin door.

Nearby, stakes held the surviving pirates, but Mary was not visible anywhere. Just then, a commotion came from inside one of the tents. Hunter saw a pirate exit. The man stood erect, pulled up his trousers, and began buttoning his fly. His gratified expression said it all.

Hunter moved in behind the man while the pirates with him glanced one last time around the compound. No one was in sight. The man, still busy with his britches, turned toward them. Had he heard something? Hunter snuck up from behind, covered his mouth, and slit his throat clean, dragging him to the bushes and discarding him on the ground to die. Still seeing no other signs of life, Hunter returned to the tent. Inside, he saw Mary tied over a log, her bare backside in the air. Gagged and unable to talk, she tried to kick at her new attacker, half-expecting another round of humiliating assaults upon her body.

"Shhh," whispered Hunter, cutting away the bonds that held her captive. Placing his hand over her mouth, he motioned for her to remain quiet as she pulled her clothes over her body and followed him to the nearby scrub. When Mary saw the man who had ravished her on the ground, she spat on him and kicked his dying carcass.

The Iron Born brotherhood was armed with black powder muskets and swords to the hilt. Suddenly, voices came from behind them. Hunter turned to see Redbone sneaking up to their position.

"Aye, Mary, it be good to see ye alive," Redbone whispered.

"Yes, Captain, sad to say, not without regret for what those cowardly bastards have done to me. Please, Captain, give me a weapon or something I can use to kill them all."

"Mary, ye promise thee, by the setting sun, ye will have your revenge this day." Turning to his scout, Redbone said, "Hunter, what have you discovered thus far?"

Pointing to the dying man on the ground, Hunter remarked, "Other than this brigand, all is quiet. No doubt the remainder of these pirates are in the cabin, celebrating their latest kills."

"Aye, but those will be their last. Have ye discovered thee, pirate leader?"

"No, Captain, I heard cheering from inside the cabin, as if they're involved in a game of chance."

"Mark me words; this day will be their last. Poor Alfred Tate and Oliver Reese deserved a proper death upon the roaring seas, not here in this dreadful, miserable place. No, today, thee Iron Born will have their fill of blood revenge."

Without warning, Mary removed a blade from Hunter's belt and cried, "No, Captain, now I shall take my revenge on the coward who raped me." As the pirates watched, Mary stooped down and ripped off the dying man's trousers. Unable to scream out——barely alive, this man experienced all of Mary's fury as she slowly castrated him. Muffled sounds gurgled from his throat as the sensitive nerves felt the sharp blade cut away at his manhood. Afterward, in a final humiliation, Mary sliced off his penis as well. When it was over, no one spoke a word.

Their attention returned to the cabin when laughter erupted inside. Three pirates appeared from the house, drunk and passing a jug of rum between them. The oldest of the three looked across the compound at his companions' tent, shouting, "Godfread, where you be?" They stopped, surprised when they saw the Iron Born, ready for battle, in front of the cabin.

Two of Hunter's scouts silently appeared behind the bushes and cut down the two men as if in unison. Godfread watched stupidly as his fellow pirates fell to the ground dead.

The rest of the Iron Born sprang from the bushes and surrounded the camp. Two Iron Born appeared and cut their injured companions free while others searched the cabin, finding two half-naked prostitutes sleeping but no one else in sight. Pierre, the only survivor, dropped his jug of rum and looked about, surprised by the show of force that appeared from nowhere. Taking Pierre by the scruff of the neck, a scout dragged him to see Redbone.

Knowing his life was short, the enemy pirate was thrown down at Redbone's feet. Looking up at his captor's captain, Pierre shouted, "Aye, it be, Captain Redbone in the flesh! Tell me, man, how do you like our camp decorations? There be one thing sure about yer men; they died bravely."

"While ye still breathe, tell me, man, where be yer captain and the rest of yer party? Or else, I slit ye throat before ye take another breath!"

"My captain asked me if I'd stay in the camp while they did their business. I understood there was a chance that you and your men would stage a rescue. I'm dying of syphilis and wish for a quick death and volunteered to stay behind."

Redbone withdrew his sword, saying, "Aye, ye are ready to meet yer maker, then. Tell me what I want to know, and I give ye a quick death. If not…"

"They've gone to burn your ship where she lies anchored in the harbor and kill any man bearing the mark of the Iron Born on their wrists!"

Redbone looked in the direction of the harbor. He could see a small plume of smoke rising near the docks. Suspecting a cowardly act like this, he had left Schmidt and hand-picked crew members behind to guard the ship; they'd be enough to ward off any would-be attackers. Hearing deck guns erupting from *Hell's Fury,* Redbone turned to his men and ordered everyone back to the ship.

Mr. Harper turned to Redbone. "What of the coward, Captain?"

"My name is Pierre; I certainly am no coward, ye fool!"

Looking down at the man, Redbone remarked, "His death will not be as painless as ye had hoped; we have no time; take Pierre and throw him inside the cabin and set it ablaze. But first, lest we forget how he and his companions treated our Iron Born brothers with cruelty and death. Mr. Harper takes the coward to the nearby stake and pins him hard against the log. Extend his arms out from his body with ropes. I, too, would like to decorate me ship as these bastards have adorned their camp. Hurry, man, we haven't much time!" Instantly, panic glazed over Pierre's face as he realized what was about to happen.

Redbone followed the accused to where his men met their end, the bloody log in the middle of the camp. The man kicked and screamed insults and spat on his captors as ropes were tied securely around his wrists and pulled hard. His face was smashed against the hardwood. No time to waste, Redbone approached while gripping his sword tightly. No words were spoken; he took a heaving downward swing and severed the man's arms just above his elbows.

The man's screams filled the camp as he was dragged

to the hut, bleeding. Watching the whole affair, the two whores, who had awakened and stood inside the doorway, cried out for mercy, looks of terror on their faces.

No mercy or pity was offered as the enemy pirate was thrown inside the small hut. Kerosene was splashed about the cabin, leaving a path that led to the outside. The two whores cried out to Redbone for compassion.

"Here me now, ye wenches, and tell me honestly, what mercy was given to me men when their heads were severed from their bodies and parts of them cut clean off? What kindness did they receive as ye women prostituted yourselves for silver?"

Redbone, eager to leave, ordered the entrance boarded up. Before the final plank was nailed in place, he approached the two women and said, "Although ye did not realize the consequence, both of ye chose to cast yer lots with these cowardly bastards. Despite yer stupidity, I will offer ye quick death instead of suffering pain from the flaming fire. Here me now, make yer choice; expose yer wrists to me!"

Their choices for dying were limited, and both the ladies extended their arms. Redbone's sword sliced across their wrists. They returned to the cabin's interior and collapsed on the worn mattress, awaiting the flames of hell's fire.

From outside, a burning log ignited the kerosene. Flames followed a path leading to a puddle of lamp oil inside the cabin, erupting all around.

The whore, Marie, could hear shouting outside from inside the cabin from the pirate captain, shouting orders to his men to get to the harbor. Her escape was blocked; there was nothing she could do but wait to be cooked alive. She began to feel lightheaded from blood loss but regained enough of her senses to comprehend the reality that if she could stop the blood flow and escape from the burning cabin, perhaps, there was hope that both she and

Deborah would survive.

She watched as the flames built. Ignoring the dying man close by, she looked about the cabin for something she could use to pry open the doorway. Marie quickly rummaged through the assortment of swords and muskets the pirates had left near the door, all the while coughing from the billowing smoke.

There, already burning hot, was a small sword. Marie gripped it tightly; the tip glowed red; it would be enough to stop the blood flow. Without a second thought, she pressed the hot metal against her wrist, where the pirate captain had cut into an artery. Moaning in pain, she caught the attention of Deborah, lying on the mattress, surrendering to the inevitable death that was coming fast. Marie reached for Deborah through thick smoke. Grabbing hold of her friend, she cried out, "Deborah, hear me, we must escape at once!"

"Escape, you foolish woman; I've accepted my fate and am waiting for the flaming hellfire to cook me alive."

"No, damn you, listen, extend your wrist, the one the pirate captain cut. I must cauterize it before you lose too much blood."

Coughing from the smoke, Deborah screamed, "It's too late for us; we're nothing but whores; let us meet our maker and be done with it."

"Not today, damn you," Marie answered and slapped Deborah across the face. "Now awake, you fool, we must save ourselves; no one else will!"

"If you insist." Extending her arm, Deborah never predicted the pain of the burning hot steel across her wrist; when it was over, she felt lightheaded, and breathing was becoming increasingly difficult.

The chances of survival were fading fast, but a quick, hard kick against the barrier holding them captive collapsed quickly, and the women ran outside.

The rotting timbers ignited in minutes, and the cabin

collapsed in flames. Still coughing out smoke from their lungs, the women thanked God for the deliverance.

Meanwhile, as Redbone and his band of cutthroats rushed back to the harbor, they saw their ship under attack. As pirates attempted to board the *Hell's Fury*, Mr. Schmidt swung his heavy ax wildly. The *Hell's Fury's* deck guns killed the pirates in their longboats.

Redbone surveyed the battle scene. The combat fought in the small Tortuga port would mark a time in history that could never be forgotten. Here, they would prove themselves the most courageous pirates sailing the Caribbean waters. Here is where their name would be remembered throughout history as the most feared and dreaded buccaneers of all time.

"Arrrr ye, men, to the longboats and carry ye fight to our enemies," Redbone ordered. The remaining Iron Born pirates hurried into their longboats and paddled over to the enemy, still attempting to board their ship. Musket fire erupted between the two pirate bands, killing some instantly. Soon, floating dead pirates littered the bay.

Perceiving who was giving orders to the raiding party, Redbone recognized him as a man with whom he had once sailed. Although they had no previous contention, this man was destined to die at the end of Redbone's sword. The boarding party fought with tenacity but was soon overwhelmed by the Iron Born. The survivors threw their weapons into the sea, hoping for clemency.

That day, the Iron Born lost eight men, including those taken as prisoners at the camp. Everyone appeared on the quarterdeck by that evening, waiting for Captain Redbone. Every Iron-Born pirate present realized that if, by chance, all the pirates within the small harbor port of Tortuga had taken sides and fought against them, none of the Iron-Born would have survived to tell the tale.

Redbone esteemed everyone who swore an oath to

the Iron Born brotherhood. These cowardly bastards kneeling and secured by ropes would not be given a chance to join the pirate band. These men had beheaded the Iron Born brothers and set their skulls on a spike. It was an insult that wouldn't be forgotten.

As the evening grew dark, the assembly of pirates stood quiet, the still deathly quietness present at all executions. Redbone ordered Hunter to take on a special mission in a courageous move that none expected. A single rowboat appeared alongside the *Hell's Fury,* and a gagged Governor was brought aboard. Jean-Francois de La Rocque de Roberval, the Governor of Tortuga, was set down on a wooden stool and ordered to remain quiet, warning that if he resisted, he too would share the same fate as the men about to die.

A small drum began pounding out a military cadence. When the drum stopped, Redbone appeared on the quarterdeck, dressed in his finest apparel. He stood above everyone, eyeing his crew members from his perch and feeling proud of their accomplishments in winning the day.

Seeing everyone gathered, including the infamous Governor, he said, "Men, born of steel and grit, we stand here on hallowed planks, proving ourselves worthy of being called Iron Born—blood pirates. Today ye have met thee challenge headlong and come out thee victors. Thee weaklings before ye who have chosen to surrender will suffer a coward's death. In killing a man tied to a post, there is no fame or honor, yet they beheaded our fellow blood brothers." Condemning the eleven by name, he finished. "Today, you men will meet yer end."

The crew of *Hell's Fury* erupted in loud cheering. Feeling sheepish, the governor squatted in his chair, unsure of the outcome.

Continuing his speech, Redbone announced, "Today, these deserters shall suffer the ritual of a thousand knives.

All of ye shall play a part. Hear me now, all of ye Iron Born pirates, each of ye shall cut out thee cowardice of these men; they will die slowly, without decorum. Refrain from thrusting yer blades into their bodies but allow them to feel thee sting of steel, as yer brothers experienced. Today, we have a special guest, one I believe orchestrated thee killing of yer pirate brothers. This betrayal could not have happened without thee knowledge of this man ye see before thee!"

"No, no, Captain Redbone, you're wrong, sir. I beg you to listen. I was only told that they wanted to have words with your men, not murder them!"

"Oh, I see." Looking down at Matthew Higgins, his old shipmate, Redbone shouted, "tell me truly, Mr. Higgins, is what thee Governor said thee truth, man?"

Spitting out the last remnants of tobacco from his mouth onto the main deck, Mr. Higgins replied, "Redbone, you have known me, sir, many a year now! You know me, an honest man. Today I shall die bravely and spit in the face of the devil himself. This day, you inquired about the Governor's responsibility in killing your men. I will give a full account of his involvement!"

"He's a liar, Captain, don't believe a word he's telling you. He's a true pirate in all ways of lying!"

"No, ye be mistaken, Governor," said Redbone. "I believe thee real pirate is yerself. Go on, Mr. Higgins. Tell yer tale! A warning to you, Governor, don't interrupt again if ye know what's good for thee!"

"We had the Governor's blessing. Before attempting a hijacking on your shipmates, we sought permission from the Governor. For a small fee, we can have anything here; all is for sale. We wanted revenge for the murder of our previous captain and nothing more. The Governor had other plans—to take your ship as booty once you were dead. What the esteemed Governor never realized was the ferocity of your men. We lost everything."

Descending the stairs, Redbone approached Mr. Higgins. He thrust his dagger through his right eye into his brain as the man struggled in his death throes. Redbone gazed back at the Governor with vile hatred.

Next, Redbone approached the Governor. Ceremoniously shitting himself, the aristocrat looked up at the pirate captain for the first time, fully understanding the danger he now faced. The captain could kill randomly in the blink of an eye, and none would stop him on his killing spree. As Redbone wiped his blade clean on the Governor's expensive silk jacket, he turned to his men, shouting, "Arrrr, let thee festivities begin."

Soon, goblets of rum were filled to overflowing throughout the ship. All those aboard bearing the mark on their wrist had their fill of what pleasure they sought most. Screams of torture and singing punctuated the evening's entertainment as each of the pirates who played a part in killing their comrades bled out from the cuts across their bare bodies.

THE FOLLOWING DAY, still sitting on the stool, the Governor hadn't moved from his spot. He eyed the carnage left behind, thinking it better to hide in plain sight and remain still. As the ship rocked about, the oak timbers of the deck were coated in red. The dead were tossed overboard, where the patient sharks waited to strip their bones.

Still, the Governor, unsure of his fate, questioned what would become of him now that his plans to steal the pirate ship were spoiled. Yesterday, while attending to his garden, he had been taken from his mansion; none would have predicted these brash privateers to be so bold as to take him, the royal administrator, hostage. It was unheard of! He still had a company of soldiers at his disposal. Yet, since he's gone missing, his captain of the guard had only dismissed his wife's worries by saying he'd spent the night at a brothel.

A commotion diverted Jean-Francois's attention. Coming up the rope ladder on the port side was a pirate he remembered belonging to the French pirate ship *Le Loup*. Behind him was another man from the English pirate ship, *Revenge*, and still another, until five men were brought aboard and ordered to sit down on the hard planks. Behind them was the man called Hunter and his four companions, each pointing muskets at the men they brought aboard.

As the Governor sat upon his stool, he recognized the hostages as master gunners from the other pirates' ship anchored in the bay. What possible reason would the Iron Born Captain have for bringing these men aboard his ship?

Soon afterward, Redbone reappeared on deck and, scrutinizing the men, turned to Hunter. "What say ye, Hunter? Did these men give thee any difficulties?"

"A musket pointing at their head was the best persuader possible, Captain; none of them resisted."

"Aye, that be a fine job indeed. Soon, thee other pirate Captains will be joining. Make them comfortable, Hunter, comfortable as expected for their stay."

Shortly afterward, another group of visitors arrived. The Governor recognized the eldest man as Tortuga's only shipwright, Paul Matthews, with his son, Henry, behind him. They, too, were brought aboard and made to sit down on the wooden deck.

None could guess the plans of this ruthless Captain Redbone, but what was made clear was that he was not finished executing his vengeance on the small sleepy port of Tortuga.

Soon, the other pirate captains arrived under a flag of truce. On deck, surrounding them, stood the remaining Iron Born, disparaging and sneering at the pirate captains for their betrayal.

Redbone ordered rum to be given to his guests and stood by as the captains nervously filled their glasses. When everyone was comfortable, Redbone stood in the middle of the assembly and said, "Hear me, ye famous Captains of ye Caribbean. I stand before ye today a desperate man. Distressed by betrayal and treachery! Yee sees me honored guest, yer Governor of Tortuga, whom I discovered had hatched a plan to capture me ship."

The French captain, Guiot Jacque Osmont, shouted, "Monsieur Redbone, none here today have been involved in capturing your men. None here have any case against you and wish for nothing more than sailing the seven seas searching for booty. Why have you taken our master gunners? What possible reason?"

"Aye, what reason indeed?"

"I say, there are no reasons at all. To us, ye be looking for a scapegoat to blame for yer troubles, Captain Redbone!" The English pirate captain, Howard Smith, argued.

"Hum, perhaps ye be right there, Captain Smith; perhaps we Iron Born are weak in nature and seek to blame others for our troubles, incapable of any accurate determination of our own. If ye are true captains, please allow yerselves to dismiss thee ritual played out before ye this day!"

"What ye be you talking about, Captain Red-Arse? What ritual?" An Irish captain named Patrick O'Kelly shouted back. Redbone answered calmly, "Trust—I be talking about thee conviction between pirate brothers. To us, every day is an adventure. None can tell whether it be our last day that we'll see thee beautiful sunset upon ye salty seas or thee last time we'll taste ye pleasurable sultry lips of a lady. No, today, ye gentlemen will see something never imagined. Today, ye will experience thee ritual of yer master gunners becoming Iron Born brigands. It is an honor I do not bestow upon everyone!"

"Redbone, you're mad," Howard Smith argued.

"Ye could be right in yer estimation, Captain. Nevertheless, as we soon depart thee beloved port of Tortuga, we'll not be giving ye cowardly bastards thee occasion to blast us out of thee water. Listen to me, all of ye brigand captains. Yer master gunners will be given a chance to become an Iron Born pirate in body and soul and be welcomed aboard me ship."

Before Redbone finished his speech, a group of his men positioned themselves behind each master gunner, swords in hand, waiting for the order to kill the man before them.

Standing to his feet, Henry White, an African man from Jamaica, began cursing at Redbone. "You, man, must be crazy with tropical fever and talking foolishly, you goat's arse. I refuse to allow Mr. Billie Humphries, my most trusted marksman, to join your crew. Enough of this nonsense. Redbone, you have gone too far, away with you, man!"

Appearing suddenly in their midst, a shining steel blade of a double-bladed ax unexpectedly penetrated the oak deck. Gripping its shaft was none other than Mr. Schmidt, the first mate of the Iron Born. Seeing the man sent shivers down their spines—a big man standing over six feet five inches tall and weighing over three hundred pounds. The fresh scar across his face gave the impression of someone accustomed to combat.

Mr. White looked up at the giant and nervously returned to his seat.

"Ye tell me now, ye pirates, what say ye? Are we to have a celebration or a slaughter? It makes no mind to me or me first mate's trusty ax. Are ye ready to give in to me demands, or is it thee game of blood?" Turning to the master gunners, Redbone withdrew his sword and pointed his weapon at each of them, saying, "What say ye, men? Are ye ready to serve under me command, much like thee men I've lost? Those brave Iron Born gave their lives to save their fellow crewmen."

What is life when you face certain death each day, either at the hand of a country bent on eradicating all of your kind from the seven seas or fellow buccaneers feeling cheated when playing a game of dice? There were many ways to die aboard a pirate ship, but receiving a slit throat was no choice.

In the end, all but one of the master gunners survived the dance with the Bloody Hag. The once-proud Governor had a front-row seat to all the events. When the ceremony was over, he still occupied his chair as he pondered his future, feeling a decision was arriving momentarily. All he could do was sit on his tiny stool, regretting his decision to attempt to steal the pirate ship.

Two more visitors arrived as the pirate captains stood drinking their rum—they could do nothing else. Tortuga's only doctor crawled up the rope ladders, followed by a young man around nineteen. The governor recognized his only son Patrick instantly. He stood to his feet and began protesting.

Redbone heard the cowardly peacock flapping his wings, shouting at the top of his lungs. Approaching the distraught father, Redbone laughed, "No, Governor, there's been no mistake. Patrick, yer only son, me new inductee as an Iron Born pirate!"

"This cannot be happening. No, tell me this is not happening. Patrick is my only son; he's no pirate!"

Redbone gripped the Governor by the collar, looked him in the eye, and said, "Ye foolish bastard. Did ye possibly think that ye would not pay for yer treachery? No longer to live thee life of a proud aristocrat, today, if yer son survives a dance with thee Hag, he'll be our latest member to sail thee boundless seas in search of adventure. He'll face all kinds of peril. If he's a stout sort of fellow, his future will be as bright as the Caribbean sun that blinds ye this day!"

"No, not Patrick," the Governor sobbed.

The lad was taken to the Bloody Hag, coated in blood from the previous volunteers. The boy had no chance to resist his captors. His arms were shoved through the metal slots, the swords still in place, waiting for the command. Two pirates stood by, holding onto the upper half of the Bloody Hag, waiting for the order from their captain.

Redbone broke out in joyful laughter, seeing the proud Governor weeping for his son. No longer the high and mighty administrator who demanded port tax from the would-be pirate crew, he was now broken and looking on with tears flowing down his eyes. Governor Jean-Francois de La Rocque powerlessly watched as Redbone commanded, "Let loose thee ropes!" The Bloody Hag's upper half crashed with a thud.

After Patrick's blood filled the golden goblet to overflowing, he received the branding marks on his wrist and was taken below decks to recover, much like the master gunners.

All pressing business concluded, Redbone noticed Tortuga's only shipwrights, Paul Matthews and his son Henry, still on deck. His plan to repair his ship here in Tortuga was no longer possible; few options were left. Approaching the frighted pair, Redbone returned his sword to its sheath and said, "Ye have seen for yerselves what manner of ship and crew ye be in the company of this day. Ye understand I'm not a man to trouble with pleasantries. I need me ship repaired, and ye are thee men I need."

Not surprising, especially to Redbone, a line of excuses about the father's ill health and the son's inability to perform the work of a true craftsman began in earnest. "Enough of yer apologies. This day, choose whom it shall be, or else ye'll see both yer heads hanging from thee yardarm," Redbone shouted angrily.

Paul, a seasoned shipwright, had had many dealings with ruthless men in the past. Why should this be any different, except that it involved his son? There would be no arguing with this captain. He had seen Redbone's ruthlessness. He would give everything to fulfill the man's wishes. To argue at the expense of their lives was foolish.

"Aye, Captain, I'll bear the mark," the seasoned shipwright announced. "Leave my son Henry at home with his mother."

"Father, no—your health. Think of the family! No, you're needed at home." Henry announced to Redbone, "I will bear the Iron Born mark proudly. Leave my father at home; he will not last a sea voyage, no matter how long that be; besides, I'm skilled at using a sword, my father not so much."

"Aye, it's settled. Young Henry, take yer place at thee Bloody Hag; we'll see if ye be worthy and survive thee test."

Their business concluded, and Redbone ordered all the pirate captains escorted off his ship. But there was still the business of Governor Jean-Francois de La Rocque. The *Hell's Fury* pulled up its heavy anchor and unfurled the fabric sails while slowly getting underway. Her port side cannons released a barrage of cannon fire into many of the helpless ships, setting off fires down below decks that the remaining crewman struggled to get under control.

The port city of Tortuga was blasted with heavy steel cannonballs that exploded on contact, sending plumes of damaging fire throughout the wooden structures.

When the *Hell's Fury* finally reached the open water, the Governor of Tortuga didn't fare well. He was taken to a plank and ordered to take a walk. If he were a good swimmer, he'd make it back to his home port. Doubtful as it was, still, the man had a chance of survival by a passing fishing boat or some merchant ship, more than any Iron Born tied to a stake ever was given.

Chapter 10

ALWAYS AND FOREVER, Tortuga will be a place where the hearty pirate crew will be most unwelcome. Still, it wasn't the Blood pirates who betrayed their kind but others who flew the black flag but never honored their pirate brothers. No, to Redbone, justice was served to all who played a part in his crew's deaths; they had either died or become new members of the Iron Born.

The pirate captains in Tortuga offered a reward for Redbone's head. The real question was, who was brave enough to try to take it off?

The proud pirate ship, *Hell's Fury,* cut through the warm salty waves of the Caribbean, pushed by a tropical trade wind. The damage to the vessel and the men's morale caused a dark mood to follow everyone headlong. None were affected more than the scallywags. To them, having no choice but to become Iron Born pirates meant they had to abandon their previous lives and live on the run. All would hunt them, searching for those who bore the mark upon their wrists. Still, there was a bright side to this new life, the promise of boundless treasure.

Back in his cabin, Redbone plotted his new course for Barbados. Surviving yesterday's encounter with the other pirate captains had been a risk he was forced to take. Losing eight crew members meant they were stretched thin to perform the most mundane everyday jobs. However, things were looking up with another doctor on board and extra master gunners who had little choice but to join the brotherhood.

The dark, menacing clouds and choppy seas could only mean one thing; they were sailing into a hurricane, something that plagued most sailors leaving Hispaniola this time of year. The logical decision would be to seek sanctuary, but where?

The fierceness of the howling winds and crashing waves kept increasing, leaving Redbone little choice. There was Castillo San Felipe del Morro to contend with if he chose to seek shelter in San Juan; he would have to be a mad man to do so. The fortress was heavily guarded, but an old saying came to mind, "any port in a storm."

Calling out to Brendon, the cabin boy, Redbone ordered him to bring Mr. Schmidt and Mr. Toner to his cabin. When the men arrived, Redbone described the intricate details of his bold plan.

"Listen to good, ye blood brothers; we all be in a fix; that much ye guessed already. There be a gale coming down upon our heads, from which there be no escaping. We must seek shelter or perish. Me plan ye may think foolish and outlandish, but believe me, there be no other choice."

"Continue, Captain, we supported ye all this time; tell us what we must do," said Mr. Toner.

"A few leagues ahead be thee opening inlet to San Juan. Although guarded by Castillo San Felipe del Morro, I believe seeing a distressed ship will quiet their guns and allow us safe passage into thee harbor. But hear ye men, if I be wrong, then I do not need to tell ye what will happen. We'll be blown out of thee water. That is why we must make this ruse as believable as possible. Above all else, keep yer cannon hatches closed, bare no flag except the flag of truce. Take oil and fill thee pots to overflowing on thee main deck. They must remain to burn, no matter how much rain this storm produces. We have to give the illusion that our ship is burning out of control. Do ye hear men?"

"What then, Captain, after the storm passes?" Schmidt asked.

"Oh, that I knew such an answer, but sadly, no, I cannot say. Men, it's been a pleasure knowing ye, but for now, there is no time to remember thee past. Look ahead, boys; soon, thee fortress will come into view. Act quickly, or else all will be lost. You have yer orders; get to it, boys."

In haste, both men scrambled out of the small captain's cabin. The gun hatches closed tightly, and a white flag draped off the stern. Dozens of pots were burned, sending black plumes into the rain-filled clouds. Thick smoke trailed behind, giving the illusion of a crippled ship. Those at the fort would assume the wreck would soon succumb to the damage and sink. As a result, no one paid them any mind, and they slowly slipped past the fortification and followed the mouth of the inlet as it turned inland.

Redbone had every anchor possible let loose in the shallow inlet. All sails were stored tightly in place. There was nothing to do except wait for the pending doom that announced its fury by the howling wind and sheets of pouring rain. Still, the pots remained lit, causing no damage to their ship. For now, the illusion was meant to keep the Spanish from firing on them and destroying them where they anchored, although anyone caught in this hellish storm would be preoccupied with staying alive.

Watching from the quarterdeck, Redbone was blown to the deck a time or two as he gripped the railing, staring up at the fortress, expecting to see the hellish booms of cannon fire. Still, he often returned to the quarterdeck and carefully eyed their predicament. Seeing no way past the fort, he wondered how in the hell he would get out of this mess. Sometime in the early morning hours, the typhoon turned north, and the howling winds abated. Seeing a break in the weather, Redbone did not hesitate to go into action. He ordered his men to let loose the chains that held them firm and shouted orders to get underway. The burning oil pots no longer gave the illusion of a ship on fire. Instead, men scrambled to get underway.

Alone on his watch, a single soldier named Pedro ran about the curtain wall, shouting that the ship was leaving. Still exhausted from fighting the storm, most soldiers were at home with their families; no one paid him any mind. Pedro could only watch the *Hell's Fury* sail out the channel unscathed into the Caribbean waters.

Redbone was relieved that his plan had worked brilliantly. The remainder of the passage was smooth sailing, and when they reached Barbados weeks later, they had to tie up to the docks, having discarded their anchor chains back in San Juan.

IN BARBADOS, THE BUSINESS of trade was in full gear. Ahead of the pirate's ship was another ship unloading its cargo. Redbone and his crew sought refreshment as soon as they disembarked. It had been a tiresome voyage, and with the memory of Tortuga still fresh in their minds, they hoped Barbados would be more welcoming. Still armed to their teeth with muskets and swords, the crew was ready for a fight if one should occur.

Stopping cautiously at a tavern named Peg Legs, they walked inside. There was music playing and girls scouting for clients, but little else; apart from a few stares, no one paid them any mind. Most of the crew remained on board the *Fury* in case of a repeat of what happened in Tortuga. Redbone brought his first mate, Mr. Toner, and Hunter.

Finding a table at the back, Redbone glanced about the small tavern for any sign of trouble, but after some time, the small band of pirates began to relax. Those seeking the company of the female persuasion were soon rewarded. A couple of hours had elapsed when a large black man walked into the public house. Sitting down near the door, he surveyed the room and, seeing Redbone and his pirate companions drinking, called over to the innkeeper and whispered something into his ear.

The innkeeper turned and stared at Redbone, nodded, and hurriedly disappeared from view. The man received his ale a moment later and drank it in one large gulp. Wiping his mouth on his sleeve, he glanced again toward Redbone and called out to a pirate sitting at the opposite table. The swashbuckler looked at Redbone, who was gripping his sword by this time, expecting a fight to break out. Redbone explained the situation to Schmidt. He, in turn, informed Hunter, who was now watching the mysterious brigand sitting at the table.

Before another ale could be delivered, the black man stood to his feet and motioned to the others. The room became quiet, and the music stopped. The prostitutes scampered away. All that was left was the group of pirates looking for a brawl.

Redbone stood to his feet and addressed the other pirates, saying, "Arrrr ye listen, man, before ye come one step closer, allow me to say ye do so in great peril to life and limb. State yer business before it's too late for all, and ye finds yerselves on thee dirty end of ye stick."

The buccaneer leader stopped, looked back at his companions, then looked Redbone square in the eye. "Tell me, man, is it true that you are the famous pirate captain, Redbone?"

"Aye, that be true, well enough. Tell me, man, who

be asking?"

"My name is Rupert Dupont, Captain. We are a small group of Corsairs stranded on the island of Barbados. We've heard reports about the Iron Born throughout the Caribbean. Captain Redbone, you have already become the most hated and beloved pirate captain sailing these waters. Dead or alive, there is a sizable price on your head."

"Avast ye! so tell me now, do ye expect to cash in on this reward booty?"

"Unquestionably no, Captain. We, the surveying men aboard the *Tempest,* wish to join your crew. Look now, Redbone, and see for yourself; we are a strong and stout group of sailors, a worthy addition to your crew if ever there be a buccaneer!"

"Tell me, man, do you believe in fate?"

"Aye, Captain, as all my companions, we are firm believers in the eternal God above."

"Very well, the type of believer I speak of believes that fate plays a hand in whether or not they survive the dance with thee Bloody Hag. Ye will have an opportunity to share in this dance if ye hope to become a member of thee Iron Born brotherhood."

"So, the rumors are true. A mark upon the wrist you all share?"

"Thee men you see seated at my table have all shared in thee ritual. Ye will be no different if yer souls seek adventure and treasure. If ye can survive the test, we have a place for thee at our table. But know if there be a weakness in yer being, thee sharks will dine on what's left of thee. What says ye man, are ye willing to abandon the life ye once lived and take that chance? If fate plays ye the fool, ye surely die, but if not, ye be a unique privateer that none could have ever imagined."

"Aye, aye, captain, Redbone, sign me up."

Turning around to address his companions, Rupert shouted, "What say the rest of you? Ye be willing to join me in this dance? Don't tell me there be any afraid to dance with the Hag?"

Cheering and shouting was the only response. Afterward, sometimes into the late hour, the men carried torches to light the pathway back to *Hell's Fury*. Shortly before midnight, the ship's deck was a beehive of activity. When the morning dawn appeared, the men littered the main deck, having completed the ritual. Twenty-three souls in all survived the test, and only one perished. At sea, the man's body would have been tossed overboard, but at the request of the scallywags, the dead man was taken to the cemetery and buried.

Over the following weeks, ship repairs were foremost on Redbone's mind. He had not forgotten that the wreck of the *Tempest* lay in shallow waters not too far from shore. Besides salvageable cargo, what Redbone wanted most were the brass cannons. He eagerly paid for a crew to retrieve them from the clear blue waters. Standing on the salvaged vessel's deck, Redbone watched the men struggling to haul the precious items aboard. He recovered six guns from the deep waters, with another four promised the following day. Each cannon weighed near twelve hundred pounds.

Enslaved people outnumbered the free inhabitants of Barbados; they were the central workforce when it came to repairs needed upon the *Hell's Fury*. Redbone never could stomach the thought of one man belonging to another and hated the practice of slavery and the cries of an enslaved person being beaten by his master. Redbone ordered the whip masters off his ship. Once they were gone, the cook would bring the worker's food and wine. Young Henry, *Hell's Fury*'s only shipwright, watched it all.

When the repairs to his ship were almost complete,

Redbone plotted a new course out to the ship lanes of the Caribbean. It had been too long since he felt the jingle of a coin in his pocket, and now, more than ever, he had a formidable fighting force to do his bidding. Although Henry could not understand the sympathetic attitude of his ruthless captain toward the enslaved people, he walked away thinking that perhaps Redbone had a heart after all.

WHILE WATCHING THE gunwales being painted, Redbone had a couple of visitors. A man and woman finely dressed in colorful clothing met him at the docks, bowing to him.

"Captain Redbone, my name is Humphries Jasper Walton; I'm the Earl of Manchester. Here in lovely Barbados, I oversee the shipments of tobacco to England. My lovely wife, the Duchess of Canterbury, Marie Abigale Hertford." Bowing slightly, the lady approached, offering her hand, which was proper in those days. Redbone, planting a small kiss on the lace fabric, quickly asked, "What business brings ye to me ship, sir?"

"Captain, we have received reports of what you have done to Tortuga and its thieving governor. The crown has no arguments with you or your men; instead, we hope you will join us for dinner this evening."

"Aye, dinner, ye say?"

"Yes, Captain, we don't often meet such a famous buccaneer as yourself. Won't you please come? I have told my children stories of your heroic struggles to leave that dreadful place, Tortuga. They play swashbucklers in their spare time, fighting the Spanish. To have you as our guest would bring them such happiness, Captain," the Duchess explained.

"Although I appreciates yer hospitality, sir, I

cannot promise ye to make it for dinner. With so many preparations still to complete, I be unsure I can tear meself away. Ye see, I plan to set sail soon."

Marie grabbed Redbone's hand and cried, "Oh, Captain, please come! My children are looking forward to your visit!" Something about the smile the lady gave or how she held onto his hand made Redbone suspect this lady had her reasons for inviting him for dinner. Redbone stared back into Marie's blue eyes, saying, "Arrrr, why ye could not forgive meself to see the disappointment on ye little tykes' faces?"

"Splendid, Captain. See you at seven?"

"Aye, yes, of course, but ye should know I always bring the first mate along. Look yonder, can ye see thee giant ordering ye placements of ye cannons? That be Mr. Schmidt."

"Oh, I see, Captain; no matter, please bring Mr. Schmidt along for supper."

"Very well, if ye will excuse me, there is much work to finish."

Bowing, the Earl and Duchess discharged themselves and walked away. Afterward, Redbone called out to Schmidt, saying, "When ye be done, wash yerself clean; it appears we are guests of the Earl and Duchess this evening for dinner."

With a simple nod of agreement, Schmidt returned to work, setting the cannons in place on their gun carriage on the four-wheeled wooden cart.

By the evening hour, the pair of pirates appeared at the Earl's house and knocked on the door. Soon, an elderly negro opened the decorative door and motioned for them to enter. Standing in the foyer, the two brigands looked about the embellished surroundings. From a distant room, two children, a boy around ten and a girl eight came running toward the front door, followed by the Duchess, who advanced as if she was skating across the floor on ice, her silky dress flowing behind her. "I'm so glad you could make it for dinner."

"Please allow me to introduce me first mate, Mr. Howard Schmidt."

Sticking out her hand, the Duchess presented it to the large man and waited. Mr. Schmidt reached out for the delicate appendage and kissed it gracefully.

The boy turned to the Duchess and asked, "Mother, are these real pirates? Look at how they are dressed; surely, they are nothing more than circus performers you hired to impress Abigail."

"Abraham, don't be rude; I swear, child, you're growing up to be so much like your father." Turning to Redbone, Marie quickly apologized. "Please forgive my son's rudeness. I have tried my best to raise him with proper manners but being so far from our home in England. It's difficult; you must understand."

"Aye, give me a minute and allow me a word with this young whelp."

Redbone drew his rapier from its sheath; the sharp metal reverberated as it was pulled free. Holding the weapon of death before the child, Redbone said, "See ye here, young pup; look close at the remnants of human blood still coating me steel blade. Tell me, true boy, still believe us to be circus clowns?"

The look on the lad's face was priceless. His knees began knocking, and he turned white as if the blood had run from his body.

The girl looked up at Mr. Schmidt, to whom she'd taken a liking, and said, "Could I sit next to you at dinner?"

"What——what was that child?" Schmidt questioned.

"Now, Abigail, please play in your room; dinner

will be served shortly. Quit pestering our guest."

"Yes, Mother, as you wish." As she stopped to curtsy before the swashbucklers, Abigail looked up, smiled, and then hopped happily away.

"Gentlemen, can I offer you some refreshments?"

Redbone, returning his saber to its sheath, responded, "Arrrr be partial to cognac if ye have a bottle close by."

"Yes, certainly, Captain; how about you, Mr. Schmidt?"

"Tell me, M'lady; you wouldn't happen to have a bottle of Massandra Sherry de la Frontera?"

The Duchess laughed. "I'll have to ask my husband, Humphries. Please come inside and make yourselves comfortable while I attend to dinner."

The two buccaneers were offered seats in a drawing-room. A few minutes later, both were handed crystal glasses filled with their requested liquors. Sometime later, they were joined by the Earl, eager to discuss the latest government policies on piracy. When a servant arrived to tell everyone that dinner was served, Redbone lingered behind, gripping his sword, half expecting a trap of some sort. Always cautious, he trusted no one.

When Redbone arrived at the dining room, the Duchess eagerly asked him to sit at a place of honor opposite her at the table. The Earl, already enjoying his soup, paid Redbone no mind as he slurped away. Mr. Schmidt, customarily waiting for his captain, sat down after Redbone. Next to him, little Abigail could only smile. Abraham was absent from the table. The Duchess announced he would not be joining them; he felt a sickness coming and decided to stay in his room for the evening.

The meal tasted divine but became increasingly uncomfortable as the Duchess seemed fixated on getting her husband drunk. No matter how often he drank, his wine glass was quickly overflowing. The Earl made cruel jokes and sang about his beloved England, telling everyone how much he missed his dear mother. When the subject matter changed to hanging pirates, the cheerfulness ended.

After calling for a servant, the Duchess ordered the servant to help the Earl to bed, saying he'd had too much to drink. Turning to Abigail, Marie told her to play in her room.

"Mother, I want to play a new song I learned on the piano for our guests."

"No, not this evening; you can play for them another time, perhaps before they set sail."

Seeing the child's disappointment, Schmidt gripped her tiny hand and looked her in the eye. "Using my imagination, I shall dream of you playing a concerto in the finest European theaters. For now, we will make that another time; go, child, do as you're told."

The child got out of her chair and hugged the big man tenderly. Not sure what to do, Mr. Schmidt looked over at his captain. Redbone grinned, seeing his first mate confronted by the innocence of a child. Afterward, the girl ran off, leaving the adults alone.

"Gentleman, please let's retire to the library."

Once there, Marie's demeanor changed. She gripped Redbone's arm. "Captain, you must help me, please."

"Ma'am, tell ye, what matter has ye so distressed?"

"It's my childhood servant Poppy; I'm afraid he's to be hanged this Friday at dawn."

"Blimey, what does this matter have to do with us? We are pirates and nothing more; why should this concern us, brigands?"

"You are my last hope to save Poppy! You see, he was only saving his daughter Evette from being raped. You must help me; I will give anything to save him."

"Aye, choose ye next words wisely, as if ye be making a deal with thee devil himself, Ma'am. Be warned; we are cutthroat pirates, not slave liberators," Redbone hissed.

"No, you're mistaken, Captain; I believe there is another side to you that few can see. I have heard rumors about how you have cast off the whip masters from your ship and your acts of kindness toward those half-starving slaves working on repairs. A price, there must be a price. Name it, and it will be yours. Gold and riches, I have enough to entice you. If it's the sensual persuasion, I'm an experienced woman and have had many lovers. I have spent time at the French Court, The Palace of Versailles. I'm only a lady by title; believe me, Captain Redbone. My husband would never imagine the life I lived before we married."

"Aye, ye seem desperate enough, Ma'am, but tell me, what of Humphries, yer husband? What will be his response when he discovers that this Poppy has escaped? Will he not suspect ye are behind it all?"

"Believe me, he will know."

"What then?" Redbone argued.

"No doubt, I will be beaten with a rod below my head and shoulders so as not to leave any bruising, but I do not care. I love Poppy as though he were my father. At times I wished he was. But enough, tell me, Captain, will you help me?"

"Arrrr, it's as if I be the one speaking to the devil, and he has appeared in ye form of a woman. Yer offer both excites and thrills the imagination, but I cannot put me men in harm's way to satisfy me lustful desires. Me price, you must know, is no less than a thousand pieces of eight."

"That much coin...I'm afraid I don't have it with me,

but my precious jewels are far more valuable. Now, Captain, will you help me, or am I to look elsewhere?"

Spitting into his hand, Redbone announced, "Aye, ye bargain be struck, now ye shake on it, Ma'am. Me word as a gentleman is me bond."

Spitting into her hand, the Duchess grabbed hold of Redbone's, gripping it firmly. "The bargain is struck; just give me time to go to my boudoir to retrieve your wages."

"Aye, be quick. I have little patience when it comes to waiting; ask me, men."

Leaving her guest, the Duchess hurried upstairs to her room. Quickly rummaging through her armoire, she opened a secret door and removed an ornately decorative necklace Humphries had bought her for Christmas. It was made from gold, and the center stone was a large diamond set in the middle of a row of rubies; Marie would give it away and more to save Poppy. Its value was worth more than a thousand pieces of eight. She also took a pair of diamond earrings to ensure the pirate was happy with his arrangement.

Downstairs, the Duchess felt relieved to see her pirate guests hadn't left. Walking up to Redbone, she handed him her gold necklace. "Here, Captain, this should be enough payment, easily worth more than a thousand pieces of eight."

Redbone held the valuable item, lifting it near the chandelier's light. The diamond sparkled in its brilliant colors. Its weight felt heavy in Redbone's hand. Staring back at Marie, he said, "Blimey, it seems valuable enough."

"Here, Captain, in case you find displeasure of any sort, take these as well; the two large diamond earrings are easily worth five hundred pieces of eight by themselves. You have all you need; you will find Poppy in the jailhouse. I doubt he will be under guard, as he is old and harmless."

"Aye, well enough, M'lady. But before I go save yer manservant, I must depart with a kiss, for leaving is such sorrow, and I fear that we shall never meet again."

The Duchess, an attractive woman in her forties, seemed surprised by his statement, but regardless, she stepped forward, offering herself without hesitation. Redbone smiled, grabbed her delicate form around the waist, leaned in, and slowly kissed her.

At first, she was unsure how to respond; it felt awkward but pleasant, arousing a moment later. The captain, experienced in swordplay and wooing the womanly desires, took his time. The Duchess felt her gold jeweled tiara pulled from her hair. She stopped the passionate kiss and stared at Redbone with a look of surprise.

"Ma'am, I be taking this trinket as well. It will be me price for saving Poppy's daughter. No doubt, once ye constabularies learn of Poppy's escape, they be coming after his family next.

"But I've already paid you, Captain."

"Ma'am, I, be a pirate not by name alone. I will decide when I be paid in full. Now, if you will excuse me, I will be off to save Poppy before his appointment with the gallows."

"Please tell me, Captain, how do I know I can trust you to deliver Poppy safely? How can I trust a pirate to keep his word?"

"I have seen for meself yer Barbados island's defenses. Thee slaves upon this island outnumber white settlers three to one. What military forces are here on this island will be no match for ye Iron Born. Here, I am King and will take whatever I desire, including the virtue of a high-bred lady such as yerself! Now step aside before I forget me manners!"

The Duchess knew she dared not press the issue further if she hoped to escape unharmed. As they left, Marie shouted, "God's speed, Captain! Save Poppy and Evette, his daughter, as well; please hurry."

"Aye, it will be done soon enough; ye have me word. Goodbye Duchess. I doubt we be seeing thee again. Now tell me what this Poppy fellow looks like?"

"You have seen our house servant, Jasper? They are brothers; they could be twins well enough."

Redbone threw the valuables to Mr. Schmidt, and he grabbed the bottle of cognac on his way out. Redbone, for his part, considered setting sail on the morning tide, forgetting his promise to the Duchess and putting Barbados behind them, never to return. However, he couldn't discount the fact that burning too many bridges would be a mistake, especially when they needed a safe harbor for anchorage.

Preparing to save an enslaved person from death was something that Redbone never expected. He was a pirate, not a liberator. He called in his quartermaster, Mr. Toner, who told him the stores had been filled, and they could sail anytime he chose.

EARLIER THAT MORNING, Redbone had notified Mr. Schmidt that he wanted to get underway; there were signs of laziness aboard the *Hell's Fury*. Besides his original crew, the scallywags seemed lackadaisical and went about their days joking and making merriment. No, being a pirate, let alone an Iron Born pirate, was a life filled with danger and peril. These new men would soon experience that fact for themselves.

But for now, Redbone stood silently upon the quarterdeck, looking at Bridgetown, the capital of

Barbados. He realized that Hunter would be perfect for the job of rescuing the slave, and from what Redbone saw of the jailhouse, it would not be too difficult. It was a delicate matter, and one fact was obvious: there could not be any loss of life if they had ever planned on returning to Barbados.

Having one last look about the deck, he saw two men on guard. Feeling that all was safe and secure, he retired to bed, although once he crawled beneath the sheets, his soul was troubled; something felt amiss, as if an unseen danger approached.

His discomfort could be easily dismissed as nervousness about the slave's rescue, but it felt like something more. Perhaps in the morning, his reasons for apprehension would present themselves, but for now, he pushed it aside, turned over, and fell fast asleep.

Chapter 11

AFTER ENJOYING HIS MORNING tea and crumpets in his cabin, Redbone considered that perhaps they should have rescued the enslaved Poppy the night before instead of putting it off. Nonetheless, with preparations now set in place, Hunter was to break Poppy out of jail that night. Instead of swords or muskets, they were given bailing pins and clubs.

But all that changed when Redbone heard a rapid knock on his door.

"Aye, come in."

Mr. Schmidt walked in, a look of terror on his face. "Captain, sir, have you seen what sailed into port this morning?"

"I have; nothing to do now; we be sitting ducks for sure." Standing to his feet, looking out his cabin windows, Redbone thought, Few *things in life could cause a pirate captain's knees to knock. Not a sea battle with a formidable enemy upon the open sea or the fear of shipwreck upon a rocky shoreline in a severe storm. But a British man-of-war coming into port, with her gunport available, ready to blast the* Hell's Fury *out of the water? This sight was something most frightening.*

"What are we to do, Captain? What orders should I give the men?"

"None, do you hear me, man? There be no orders

or commands. Ye know for yerself, if this warship wanted to end our days, nothing could be done to stop it. Please pass the word, and keep our weapons locked away— nothing to do but wait. Come ye, sit down and have some tea, man, relax yerself. All we can do is wait; besides, we are guests of the Earl's, don't ye forget!"

"Never in all my days have I feared to stare death in the face. No time like now, Captain."

"Aye, hear ya. Come sit; let's enjoy the morning as if nothing is wrong; if this day is the day to die, then so be it. We'll know soon enough whether they mean us harm."

Looking at Redbone with surprise, Mr. Schmidt responded, "I suppose that's why you're the captain; anyone else would send our mournful reply broadsides into that ship. Instead, you invite me to enjoy some tea and crumpets. Redbone, sir, you are a bit of a mystery to us all."

"Yes, I suppose it be true, man; inform thee crew of me orders and return here to me cabin. We'll spend thee rest of ye day relaxing. It won't take too long before we understand their intentions. Many British sailors will never see their beloved England again if they are hostile. For that, you have me word."

"Aye, Captain, as you wish."

As expected, toward midday, a young Negro appeared upon the docks carrying a letter from the Governor, requesting Redbone's presence that evening for dinner. It seemed that his estimation of the situation was correct. Not too hasty to shed blood, Redbone grinned when he read the note. Turning to his first mate, the pirate captain handed Schmidt the invitation to read for himself.

"It seems that you were correct in your approximation, Captain. Much to the relief of myself and the crew."

134 Timothy Patrick Means

"Aye, one day when yer captain Mr. Schmidt, ye'll discover that force isn't always thee answer; sometimes a matter requires finesse. For now, come, we must prepare ourselves for dinner. We mustn't keep thee Earl or thou British captain waiting."

"That be true enough, Captain; let us prepare for the gallows with our brave faces displayed. After all, what do we have to lose except our lives?"

"Ye have it all wrong, Mr. Schmidt. No, they should be afraid. We are Iron Born pirates. We do not fear death but embrace thou afterlife, knowing that we lived life to ye fullest without regret. We buccaneer who stand in their presence are not mortal men who seek treasure and fortune but gods of the sea who give life or take it, depending on our good pleasure."

"Good thing I sharpened my ax; I have a feeling I'll be needing it soon."

"Think positive thoughts, man, and good things will come to ye in time. Life is not always sour melons."

A few minutes later, a knock was heard on the captain's door. "Arrrr, come in now and be quick," Redbone shouted. Instantly the door squeaked open, and there stood Brendon, the cabin boy, with the governor's servant.

"Captain Redbone, sir, this lad has a letter for you."

"Aye, he does? Be quick; hand it over then."

The servant approached apprehensively and handed over the letter with a shaking hand. "Ye have nothing to fear, lad, be quick and give me thou letter."

Taking the note and dismissing the servant, Redbone walked closer to the cabin windows and tore open the envelope. As he began to read the letter, he experienced a pleasant aroma, no doubt the expensive cologne of the Duchess. The Duchess pleaded with him to hurry and save Poppy before it was too late. The note finished, "Please hurry, Captain, before Poppy hangs," and was signed, "Your desperate aficionado, the Duchess of Canterbury, Marie." the arrival of the British warship in the harbor meant that there was little anyone could do. Still praying for a miracle, she explained that her husband planned to invite the British captain to Poppy's hanging the following day. He would be there for dinner with his officers. To refuse the dinner offer would be a mistake, an insult dangerous to everyone involved.

Handing the letter to his first mate, Redbone announced, "It seems we are in a bit of a pickle, Mr. Schmidt. Cool heads and a calm demeanor be the order of the day."

A moment later, handing back the letter, Schmidt announced, "What's best for us is to get the hell out of Barbados as soon as possible. There be no winning this fight, Captain. It's sad, but I believe you have met your match. Look over yonder. Ye see the British man-of-war breathing down our necks? Captain, let us flee, not as cowards but as men with little choice in the matter."

"We have sailed together for some time, Mr. Schmidt, have we not?"

"Yes, that be true enough, sir."

"Tell me, man, have I ever led us off course?"

"No, Captain."

"Every morning ye wake, it be a new day; thee past is simply thee past. Today be no different. Chart a new course to see where it leads. As I told you before, it would surely be over if this battleship was meant to harm us. Man, have assurance in that, if nothing else."

"Again, that's why you're the captain of this ship. The truth, sir, I hope you are right about all of this. I will leave you, sir; I have duties that I must attend to. For my part, I see no way out."

"Aye, that's understandable. Something I have learned over thee years is that in all circumstances, there is a natural order to things; ye must take each difficult situation as it comes. To save a Negro servant and avoid being blown out of thee water by ye British, all of this in one day could boggle yer mind. First, have dinner with thee, Earl, save ye servant, then escape with our very lives without terminating our welcome." Redbone laughed as Mr. Schmidt shook his head and walked out to attend to the ship's affairs. He had just appeared on deck when he ran into Harv-Dog, the navigator, who approached cautiously.

"Tell me, Mr. Schmidt, what is the captain planning? Whatever it be, I hear his amusement coming from his cabin. In times past, when I've heard that booming jubilation, it has meant we are in a pickle that he must work out. Tell me, are we in a fix, Mr. Schmidt?"

"Harv-Dog, can you not see the man-of-war blocking the harbor?"

"Aye, it is the topic of discussion throughout the ship today; frankly, the men are scared."

"Everyone sees this predicament much the same, except Redbone, who sees things differently. To him, the fact that the British haven't fired a broadside into our hull means that they are no threat to us. No, strange as it sounds, our captain and I are invited to dinner with the Earl and the British captain. I will have my ax at the ready, but while both Redbone and I are away, I will have our gun crew prepared to fire a broadside at that man-of-war. Although none will guess with our gun ports closed, each gun station will be on high alert throughout the night.

"I've sailed with both you and Redbone for some time now. I had a choice and cast my lot with you two and the promise of creating a new band of pirates. I bear the mark upon my wrists. I entered a contract and forsook the one I had with Captain De Vries and crew aboard the *Triumphant*. Some could consider me a traitor, but I believe in the Iron Born. Now, hearing the hilarity coming from beyond that cabin door, I'm certain all will be well. Please excuse me, Mr. Schmidt, for we all have our parts to play. For my part, I will steer us clear of this harbor when called upon to perform my duty. I wish we're not dodging cannonballs while I steer to avoid the rocky inlet."

"A fine sailor and navigator you are. I do not doubt that you'll perform your job flawlessly. But if that were the least of my troubles, I'd consider it a relief, for apart from this British ship business, we're to rescue a Negro slave from hanging by morning."

"What, man? Tell me now, Mr. Schmidt."

"The details are not your concern. Do your part, and we'll sail free of danger. I bid you farewell. Keep watch, stay on alert, and above all else, stay at your post and be ready."

"Aye, for that, you have my word."

He stood silently, watching the ship's only navigator hobble away. Mr. Schmidt thought, *I, for that, I'm assured.*

APPEARING AT THE MANSION for dinner, Redbone and Schmidt were led to the study where the British captain and the Earl discussed the production of tobacco shipped to England.

"Oh, I see our guest of honor has arrived," the British captain said. "Please allow me to introduce myself. I'm Vice Admiral Montgomery of his Majesty's Royal Navy; Captain Edmonton and Lieutenant Cornwall are with me."

"Arrrr, how do you do, gentlemen? My name is..."

"Oh, no need for introduction, Captain Redbone. Already your reputation precedes you. I must commend you on the work you've done in Tortuga. That dreaded place was nothing but a nest for bandit rats. I only regret that you didn't sink all the ships that call that place home. No, sir, you've done a service for the British crown, and I would like to shake your hand, sir."

Redbone shook the man's hand, although he suspected that one day that hand would be at the end of a sword trying to cut him asunder; for now, he ignored his concerns and smiled.

"Come in, gentlemen, let us share in a drink and toast the future success of our British military men who are on a mission to eradicate the Caribbean waters of all pirates—except you and your men, of course, Captain Redbone," the Earl proclaimed.

Taking a glass of cognac from the Earl and lifting it, Redbone announced, "Aye, to ye ship's success. Tell me, Captain, the name of yer ship, sir?"

"She is called *HMS Victory*, the first-rate ship in his Majesty's service with an armament of over 100 guns."

"Arrrr toast to *Victory*, may her hull never be covered in barnacles, and may her sails always find a favorable wind," Redbone announced and emptied his glass.

"A toast to your ship, Captain Redbone; I believe she is called *Hell's Fury?*"

"Aye, that be true enough, Admiral Montgomery."

"Lift your glasses high, gentlemen. A toast to *Hell's Fury,* may she always find a booty of Spanish treasure, wins the day in her fight with other pirates raiding the British Commonwealth, and sink all those other pirate dogs!" Cheers broke out, especially from the Earl.

Montgomery seemed unaware of Redbone's true thoughts—that one day they would meet in battle, if not the Vice-Admiral, then definitely one of his captains. Regardless, the rest of the evening was pleasant, especially when the Duchess appeared. She brought a welcoming distraction as she sang for her guests, giving Redbone time to mull over his plan.

His plan was simple that morning before the *HMS Victory* anchored in the harbor. Onboard the *Hell's Fury* was an herbalist, Tobias, who studied plants and their use for medicines. Redbone had called upon Tobias to give Hunter a vile of a special brew of *Atropa belladonna* or sleeping nightshade. It would provide Poppy with the illusion of death. If dead—no need for hanging.

One part yet to plan involved the Duchess herself. Redbone intended for her to ask her husband for the body of Poppy to give him his final wish, burial at sea. Ultimately, the *Hell's Fury* would sail away with Poppy aboard, and no one the wiser.

Now it was becoming more challenging to speak with the Duchess. Vice Admiral Montgomery seemed smitten with the lady and wouldn't leave her side. Despite this, soon came the news that Poppy had died in prison. Immediately, the Duchess broke down in tears while her husband unfeelingly announced, "It's a good thing that lawbreaker died. Negro servants should never go around killing their masters; it's not good for business, you understand."

"Poppy was a good man; he was only defending his daughter from being raped," the Duchess responded sharply.

Seeing his chance to intervene, Redbone stepped

forward, saying, "Me lady, please forgive me rudeness at such a time as this, but will ye still want to give thee man a proper burial at sea, as we discussed earlier?"

"A burial at sea, Captain?" the Duchess replied, not catching on.

"Blimey, you remember, Duchess. Why it was here in this very room while we were departing just last night that you confided in me about your dear Poppy wanting to be buried at sea? If ye remember correctly, ye said thee man always dreamed of becoming a mariner and sailing the warm waters of the Caribbean."

A wink, was it a wink in Redbone's eye she saw? Redbone was up to something, and without hesitation, the Duchess answered, "Yes, yes, of course, you must forgive me; I'm not thinking lucidly. You are right, Captain Redbone; thank you. Dear Poppy must be buried at sea. The man had always visited the harbor hoping one day he'd fulfill his childhood dream of sailing aboard a merchant ship destined for unknown ports of call."

Stepping in front of Redbone, Admiral Montgomery put in, "Please, Ma'am, if this Poppy meant so much to you, then, by all means, allow the British Royal Navy to assist you in giving this man his burial at sea. Please give the word, and my men will gather his remains and send him off with honors suitable for an officer aboard my ship; none could be finer a sendoff."

Humphries, the Earl, unexpectedly shouted, "I must protest, Admiral; this Poppy was nothing but a common criminal. You will not give this man a good send-off as promised to the Duchess. Your actions, sir, will be in my report to the Admiralty. Now, listen to me, all of you; Poppy was a murderer and nothing more. He does not deserve a hero's burial at sea. And I will not hear of it. The better choice is to let the pirates have him; if he is to be buried at sea, then they are the ones to do it, sir!"

The tension between the two aristocrats changed the mood. Vice Admiral Montgomery announced to his host, "Oh, it is getting late; you must excuse my men and me; we must return to our ship, military business, you understand."

"Yes, of course," the Earl responded and began to lead the British officers to the door. Still, Montgomery approached the Duchess, grabbed her hand, and kissed it softly. Looking up at the lady, he apologized and said, "I'm sorry to hear of your loss; this Poppy must have meant a great deal to you."

"Yes, Admiral, he helped raise me as a child; I will miss him greatly," the Duchess explained as she began to weep again.

"Come, gentlemen, we must leave. Captain Redbone, may I have a word?"

"Yes, certainly, Admiral."

Walking together toward the door, Montgomery asked, "Tell me, Redbone, what are your plans? What will you do once your ship has finished her repairs?"

"Arrrr me ship and crew plan to sail west toward Aruba. On the way, I hopes to encounter a fatted Spanish galleon, loaded with precious jewels and gold departing Hispaniola."

"What you did in Tortuga was remarkable, and I'm here to say that you will always find safe passage in any British-controlled harbor. But hear this warning, if your loyalty wanes and you raid English interests, you will become my enemy, and I will hunt you down and sink you without mercy."

Ignoring the Admiral's words, Redbone changed the subject. "It's a shame about thee Duchess's manservant.

Why, just yesterday, over dinner, she confided in me that Poppy wanted to be a mariner. For me part, I will oblige thee lady and take his body out to sea."

"A notable gesture, Captain, from a pirate such as yourself. I feel that if circumstances were different, we could be friends. My only wish is that you heed my warning. I realize you're a cad and cutthroat. No honor exists in men of your type. Still, it was a pleasure meeting you, sir."

"No, I'm sorry to say, Admiral, that yer wrong. There is honor among me pirate brothers. Especially brothers born of Iron and Blood."

"Yes, Iron and Blood, as you say! Take care, Captain, until we meet again."

"Until that day, Admiral." Watching the military officers depart, Redbone laughed, thinking what pompous asses they were. Turning back to the Earl and the distraught Duchess, he asked, "Lord Humphries, may I obtain a letter from you asking for the body of Poppy."

Turning to his wife, the Earl asked, "Why haven't you told me that Poppy wanted to be buried at sea? This news seems preposterous."

Wiping her tears, Marie approached her husband. "Yes, it's true, ever since I read him the story about Jonah and the whale from the Bible. Please, Humphries, you must agree to give Poppy a burial at sea. I will never forgive myself if he is not."

"I suppose. Tell me, Captain, what would it cost me to bury the slave at sea?"

"Oh, I could not take any coin; look how ye treated us, Iron Born, here in Barbados, why it's as if ye be family! Please, write me thee necessary documents to retrieve ye man's body, and in ye morning, we shall set sail and be on our way. Now, listen to me; please never forget this day and how thee Iron Born came to yer service."

"Believe me, you buccaneers shall always find safe harbor here in Barbados; you have my word."

"Arrrr. Be quick; soon, thee man's body will give off a stench that none aboard the *Hell's Fury* will find pleasant."

"Please, give me a moment. I shall return shortly."

Now alone, the Duchess quickly grabbed hold of Redbone's arm, saying, "Tell me, sir, is Poppy dead, as you say?"

"Ma'am, what pray tell is me word worth if I change it back again? No, yer dear Poppy has been given a special assortment of drugs. Yer man is simply sleeping. Soon he will awake, and we must get him before that happens, or thee plan will unravel. I haven't much time."

Gratefully, the Earl appeared at that moment with a letter in hand. Redbone ripped the letter from his hand and walked out. Behind him, Mr. Schmidt said nothing but grinned as they walked away.

Chapter 12

On the *Hell's Fury* deck, Redbone was anxious to talk to Hunter, his assassin. He trusted the man most in dealing with delicate situations requiring a certain finesse. Unfortunately, he was nowhere to be found. The evening was growing late, and Redbone's plans required perfect timing if this was going to work and they were to escape Barbados alive. All ye plans of mice and men are subject to failure. Still, he must try.

Standing alone on the quarterdeck, he looked into the darkness of the sleeping harbor, searching out any sign of Hunter and his men. *The plan was simple: locate Poppy's cell, his appearance was already recognizable by his clothing, and sneak to the back of the prison. Then call Poppy from the small iron-barred window through the back wall, give Poppy the elixir, and let Poppy play dead. What could be simpler than that?*

Again, he thought of Tortuga and how simple it had seemed to take refuge in that pirate haven. But Redbone had learned that his options for a protected sanctuary were dwindling. He remembered the Admiral's warning.

Redbone was a buccaneer, first and foremost. He would not align the Iron Born brotherhood with the British interest and ambitions to rule the Caribbean.

Despite his invitation, the Admiral seemed to take his liberties wherever he pleased. *Why his interest in the Duchess? She never showed interest in his advances. Her only wish was to rescue her manservant Poppy, not a roll in the hay. The admiral did not see that.*

Soon, a small regiment of pirates appeared from the darkness and approached the ship. In the dim light, Redbone immediately recognized Hunter. *At last*, he thought. *Things are beginning to move in the right direction.* He still held the signed letter in his hand. Next, he would hand over the letter to the jailer and retrieve the body of Poppy before the nightshade wore off, and then he would conceal Poppy below decks and sail off.

Hunter reached the quarterdeck where Redbone was waiting. "Captain Redbone, sir, I'm sorry to report that we ran into a bit of a snag."

"A snag? Tell me, man, and be quick about it."

"This Poppy wasn't alone in his cell. The scoundrel listened in on our plans to break him out. When I finished telling him to drink the nightshade and what would happen, this other prisoner demanded that we include him in our plans."

"That rogue shall die. We have no time for this upheaval. Soon ye morning will break."

"I understand your disappointment, captain,"

"Well, tell me, man, where be this Poppy now?"

"He's dead!"

"Dead truly dead, or make-believe dead" Damn ye!"

"No, I'm sure he's dead. His cellmate, the man that was to be hanged alongside him, was furious when I told the man he was not to be rescued; he picked up a stool and bashed Poppy on the head. He beat the man's brains out."

"So Poppy is truly dead. All this ruse to fool everyone so thee man could be saved, and now he's been murdered. Aye, it makes me blood boil."

"Yes, Captain, a sad day indeed."

"No, Hunter, we must cover up our intentions, or else our hoax will be discovered, and we are thee ones holding ye dirty end of the stick. Blimey, now listen, Hunter, this murderer back at yonder prison, how desperate was he to escape the noose?"

"The man seemed desperate to me."

"Wait, tell me, what of thee elixir?"

"Never had a chance to give it to poor Poppy before his cellmate crushed his skull; I have the vial in my pocket."

"Splendid, give it to me. Let's visit this prisoner who murdered Poppy."

"Of course, Captain, follow me; it's only a short distance inland."

Leaving Mr. Schmidt in charge of the *Hell's Fury*, the small party headed to the prison atop the hill overlooking the harbor, climbing uphill along a rocky path.

Redbone's plan for a leisurely departure had escaped him as if sand were running through his fingers. Nonetheless, he was determined to put things right. Yes, the Duchess would be disappointed to learn the truth, but he couldn't change course. Poppy was dead. To the prison guards, retrieving his body would be a welcomed relief, a job they wouldn't have to do themselves.

Arriving at the back wall, Redbone followed Hunter to a particular cell window. Whispering into the darkness, Hunter called to the man inside. A commotion was heard. And at the barred window, a dirty face appeared. "Yes, I'm here," the man called out.

Hunter leaned closer. "Listen to me, man. I've brought my captain; he has a plan for your escape. You must listen to him if you want to save your life!"

"Yes, of course; hurry before the guards find you."

Redbone walked up to the window. "Aye, listen to what I be saying, man, listen well. If ye hope to escape, ye have best follow me instructions to thee letter."

"I will, sir but tell me, first, why would you be helping me escape? What possible reasons would you have for saving a humble slave?"

"I have no time for yer questions. Here take this; it's the elixir that my man Hunter was to give Poppy, ye man thou bludgeoned to death. To me, fellow Iron Born and meself, you seem ruthless and desperate enough to want to survive. A significant asset to me pirate band. Ye will fit perfectly with me crew. Quickly, no time to waste. Join now, or stay where ye lay; it makes no difference to me."

"Please, Captain. I know I can be an asset to your crew. Quickly man, give me the potion! All I need to do is act dead, correct?"

"Aye, it be true enough; here it is, your ticket to freedom. Down it before the guards see us."

Grabbing the small glass vial, the man winked his eye. "Now, there be no shenanigans or mischief in your offer, is there, Captain?"

Redbone shoved his hand through the bars. "Man, hear me now; I have no time for yer hesitations or regrets. Take the offer or not, damn ye; thou be testing me patience for sure. In my hand, I has a letter from the Earl. I'm to take Poppy's body to sea for a proper burial. Soon, ye shall see me and my men appearing in yer cell. Play dead, and I shall ask the guards for yer body and Poppy's. Drink up; it be yer last chance!"

After a moment of hesitation, then grabbing the potion from Redbone's hand, the man quickly drank down the contents and stood back against the wall. "What is this? It tastes like goat piss?"

"Aye, give it a few minutes to work, man."

"Now, tell me, Captain, this is supposed to give the

guards the illusion of my death, is it not?"

"It be true. Tell me, how do ye feel?"

"Strange, I feel, strange. My stomach is beginning to ache me so."

Redbone turned to his men. "Arrrr, come, boys, we must retrieve Poppy's body and sail before the morning tide."

Inside the prison cell, the man appeared at the window, gripping the iron bars, looking desperate, "Captain, don't forget your friend, Antony Black. I will be waiting for you inside." He began to cough up blood. Wiping his chin and tasting the blood on his tongue, the man screamed, "What trickery have you played on me, ye bastard? What have you done!"

"Aye, first and foremost ye fool, Poppy was the man to be rescued, not a scalawag, such as yerself. The Iron Born will never be held hostage. Not by ye or any other bamboozler thinking, we be simple. As for you…"

Before Redbone could utter another word, the man fell to the ground. Turning to Hunter, Redbone announced, "Blimey, time to recover Poppy's body; let us be quick before dawn appears."

"Captain, what of the man who killed Poppy?"

A smirk appeared on Redbone's face, and he responded, "Leave him where he is; the man be in for a rude awakening, he will."

Hunter looked surprised by Redbone's statement. "What do you mean, Captain?"

"I have no time to explain. Let's be off and recover Poppy's body. Ye explains me meaning on the morrow when we are free of Barbados."

"Aye, Captain, you lead the way."

At the prison entrance, Redbone banged on the metal doors, shouting, "Come ye men, answer the door. I have news from your Earl."

Through the small iron bars window, a lantern appeared. A curious man's face appeared. Looking over, Redbone, the man asked, "Yes, what business do you have this early in the morning, sir?"

"I have with me orders from yer Earl telling you to release the body of a man named Poppy to me care."

"Poppy, you say?"

"It be true enough, man! Open these cursed doors at once. I, be on a timeline and must leave Barbados before the morning tide; be quick about it."

"Orders from the Earl, you say?"

"Aye, here in my hand, damn ye. Now open these doors, or else I break them open."

"Hold on, man. I must wake the captain of the guards."

"That is no concern to me. Here, take thou orders and stick them under your captain's nose. I be sure once he sees ye royal seal, he'll be happy to help us."

"Hand over the paper, and I'll show it to my captain, you pirate."

"Arrrr, a pirate indeed. Be quick, man, or else I take yer words as an insult!"

"Yes, yes, wait here." The lantern followed the long hallway and disappeared. Redbone turned to Hunter and his companions. "Lads, be quick about gathering Poppy's body; we haven't much time before dawn. Speak few words to these fools, and let us be on our way fast."

Hunter and the men nodded in agreement. Redbone had a plan; it was best to follow his orders.

A few minutes later, a commotion came down the dark hallway. As Redbone looked within, he saw two men approaching the entrance—the guard he had first engaged and the captain of the guards, struggling to button his trousers and fasten his leather belt around his waist.

"Yes, what do you want at this dark hour?" the guards' captain yelled.

"Tell me, have ye read the Earl's letter?"

"Yes, I have it in my hands." Lifting it closer to the lantern, he continued: "It says something about handing over the body of a prisoner named Poppy to your care?"

"That be true enough. We're here to take poor Poppy's body for a burial at sea."

"A burial at sea, why that sounds absurd to me, man. Tell me, Captain, why such a need to take his body at this early hour?"

"Ye simple truth, sir, it all has to do with catching thee morning tide, of which there are few hours left. Soon, yonder dawn will break, and our chances of getting underway will disappear quickly. If we hope to leave yer fair city, it is now or not until thee next tide."

"Yes, yes, of course. As a youth, I spent some time at sea and studied the trade routes and sea currents myself. It does not matter to me what you do with the body of this murderer."

"Arrrr, be only carrying out the Duchess's request. This Poppy was a servant of hers as a child. I would not want to disappoint the Duchess of Canterbury."

"Nor, sir, would I." Turning to the guard, the captain said, "Give the man whatever he wants."

"Whatever he wants, Captain?"

"Yes, you heard me, Mr. Porter, be quick about it, too; these men have a tide to catch!"

"As you wish," Mr. Porter responded, unlocking the heavy door. He ushered everyone inside. Locking the door behind them, he said, "Follow me; I'll take you to Poppy's body."

Soon, the small band was led to a group of cells where men slept, snoring loudly.

The guard, Mr. Porter, turned the corner and

walked down a set of stairs. He stopped at a locked door and announced, "Here we be, the place where we're storing Poppy's body. It's too bad what happened to him; you would not find a more pleasant fellow, a gentler soul that did not deserve to die as he did!"

He looked inside and saw Poppy's corpse lying in a crude wooden coffin. Redbone turned to Mr. Porter. "Arrrr, about that man who killed our dear friend Poppy, tell me where he be. I have a mind to meet this killer."

"Oh, you want to meet Mr. Black, do you?"

"Aye, yes, it would do me heart good to meet this killer, so I can spit in his face and curse him to hell."

"Well, I have orders to aid you in your endeavors, so follow me then."

Walking back upstairs, the small party stopped at one particular cell. There was no movement or sound from inside. Mr. Porter unlocked the cell door, shouting, "Mr. Black, you have visitors. These men want to meet the man who killed their friend Poppy! Wake up, you piece of cow dung." Still no response. Mr. Porter kicked the man's feet and got no reply. He brought his lantern up against the man's face. The guard could see Mr. Black's eyes open, staring back at him, obviously dead.

"Curse you to hell, Mr. Black, for dying on my watch."

"Tell me, what do ye plan to do with this Mr. Black's remains?"

"Not sure; in most cases as this, he'll be buried over at the church. Why are you asking, Captain?"

"Arrrr, shiver me, timbers says me. Truly, I can't be sure, but from how the man is dressed, he looks to me like a merchantman or sailor. Perhaps it would be proper to give thee rogue a burial at sea, along with this man Poppy."

"It's up to you, Captain. I would be forever in your debt. It would mean less work for me. I'm the one that's usually digging the graves for these scoundrels. Would you please take him with you? I beg you."

"Aye, first and foremost, I want to ask if ye would gift wrap thee man in a box for easy transport to me ship?"

No worries, Captain. We have a horse-driven cart for such matters. We'll have these two loaded up and transported to the harbor in no time at all. You can have your men carry them onto your ship. From this time onward, I wash my hands of Poppy and Mr. Black."

"Done it be, man; let us hurry." Turning to his crew, Redbone shouted, "Ye heard thee, fellow, pick up his worthless carcass and bring it along, lads!"

A short time later, Redbone was standing on the quarterdeck of the *Hell's Fury* about to set off when a coach appeared, racing toward the docks. Redbone could see the Duchess, wearing a bright blue dress, sitting at the back of the open carriage, holding onto her hat.

Redbone had hoped to avoid the Duchess and sail away, leaving her none the wiser about what happened to Poppy. But for now, all he could do was wait as the coach abruptly stopped. The Duchess paused for the two servants to place a small stool at her feet. Grabbing her long colorful dress, she held a servant's hand and alighted from the carriage.

There to meet her was Redbone, the crew standing by, waiting for orders to shove off.

"Captain Redbone, sir, I wanted to wish you a safe journey," The Duchess announced loudly.

"Thank ye, Ma'am," Redbone responded tactfully.

"Please tell me, Captain, where are the remains of Poppy? I must see him!"

"Um, thee man Poppy is down below in ye hull,

away from the sunlight. It be best to avoid having his remains rot in thee sunlight."

"Rotting in the heat! Excellent, Captain!" A wink from the Duchess, showing appreciation that the ploy was being played out as planned. Redbone had the decision to make; should he tell the Duchess about Poppy's murder? Or should he tell her a lie?

As he considered his choice, strange noises began to be heard from below. Mr. Black was waking to the horrible realization that he was trapped inside a coffin with no chance of escape.

Hearing the peculiar cries for help, the Duchess thought it was Poppy but quickly realized it was not his voice. Distracted by a pirate escorting a young black girl up the gangway, the Duchess recognized the girl as Poppy's daughter Evette. The Duchess felt confused.

The buccaneer accompanying Evette walked up to Redbone and announced, "Captain, sir, here be the miss ye asked me to fetch. She was apprehensive about coming, but I convinced her to join me by promising her a better life away from Barbados."

"Thank ye, Hunter, that will be all; please take yer place and prepare thee ship for departure, sir."

"Aye, Captain," Turning to the young girl, Hunter announced, "You won't regret your decision, I promise you."

"I have little or no choice, sir. Already I've received threats from the whip master's household promising to take revenge on me for what my father did. I have little hope of survival."

"Evette, I'm so sorry for how this all played out. Please believe me. Still, I see a brighter future for you, far away from the danger of dying," the Duchess said.

"I wish my mother was here to aid me. I feel so alone in the world. Especially since the death of my father. I cannot say what will happen to me now."

Looking over at Redbone, the Duchess sought to assure Evette that everything would be well. She leaned close to the young girl and whispered, "Evette, your father is not dead but is merely sleeping, pretending to be deceased."

"No, I'm sorry, ma'am. I'm not sure what others have told you, but my father was murdered by another prisoner last night. My poor father Poppy had his head bashed in, according to a prison guard who visited my home last night."

"No, wait a minute, that's not right." Turning to Redbone, the Duchess asked, "Captain Redbone, sir, tell me, what is Evette saying? Poppy is alive down in the hull of this ship, correct?"

"Alas, poor Poppy met his end by a wooden stool. That much be true; it is. Excuse me, Ma'am; there be no easy way to tell ye. Still, as part of our bargain, I rescued his only daughter, Evette."

"Poppy's dead!"

"I'm afraid it be thee truth."

Hearing the disturbing news, the Duchess broke down crying. A few minutes later, she angrily turned to Redbone and slapped him across his face. "Curse you, sir, curse you for double-crossing my good nature. I arranged for the rescue of dear Poppy and what I got was a dead man and nothing more."

"Aye, it be a sad outcome surely, but now listen to me, all of ye. What happened to Poppy was nothing more than fate. It couldn't be helped. He was killed before we could get him out of prison. But do not be discouraged. For we have not only rescued Poppy's daughter, but we also have thee man who murdered him down below in the ship's hold."

"You have my father's murderer?" Evette shouted.

"Arrrr, it be true enough. Now, hear me, ladies.

Have any of ye taken the time to notice thee deck upon which you're standing? Upon this quarterdeck, I be both captain and commander; only God himself commands more respect here. Thee man did not realize his mistake when crossing paths with ye Iron Born. This murderer will pay for his crimes in ye ghastliest way imaginable. Arrrr, both can rest assured he will soon die for his corruption."

"Captain Redbone, the deal we made was for the rescue of Poppy, not the execution of some bandit."

"Aye, but this man will pay for his mistake. For that, ye have me word!"

"Your word, Mr. Redbone? I'm beginning not to trust you, sir."

"Aye, ladies, I'm growing tired of these shenanigans and talk! Too much talking wears on a man. Usually, it's my rapier that does all thee talking. So, excuse me for rudeness, but we're about to set sail and dismember Poppy's murderer."

"You'd perform such an act on a man? I've heard stories of human mutilation. I always considered such acts cowardly," the Duchess argued.

"It's no more than thee scalawag deserves. My father was an honorable man. The man below in the cargo hold killed him for no reason." Turning to Redbone, Evette announced, "I wish to see this man brought to justice."

"Aye, ye do, do ye?"

Stepping forward, the Duchess announced, "Me as well, Captain. I want to see justice carried out, a pirate's justice."

Rubbing his eyes in frustration, Redbone took a moment before answering. Then he began to curse aloud. Ladies hardly hear such words. "Blimey, ye want to see the man's blood spilled? Once your eyes are privy to such things, they can never be blotted out. Ye will forever remember hearing the man's screams and seeing the red blood dripping from his body. His eyes plucked out of their sockets. The man's entrails are soon exposed, pouring out onto the deck. Finally, he'll be drawn and quartered, parts of him thrown out into thee sea for shark food. So, tell me, ladies, still wish to be part of the ritual, do ye?"

A cold expression glazed over Evette. She considered what Redbone was saying. Still, there had been such executions played out in Barbados before. It was no less dreadful when an accused had paid for their crimes against the state. She would be a part of the man's murder whether or not she looked on. There was no place for her to run to escape the man's cries of pain. Looking back at Redbone, Evette said, "Captain, as you explained earlier, you're both lord and commander aboard this ship. You have the authority to grant wishes, do you not?"

"Aye, tell me, lass, what do ye want?"

"Spare the man the misery of torture and merely behead him! Make his death quick and painless. Pardon him for his cowardly act and show compassion."

Hearing Evette's plea for the accused, the Duchess approached, saying, "Captain, you owe me a debt. I would consider it paid in full if you would allow such an act of compassion. Thinking of the man's torturous ending, I couldn't live with myself in all good conscience."

"Hear me, ye wenches. And do not take advantage of me good nature. Ave has always intended to make a man or woman suffer for any dishonorable act against the Iron Born. To show ourselves as sympathetic is a consideration I be not comfortable granting—unless me inclinations have been persuaded. Tell me, Duchess, are you persuading my inclinations?"

Redbone was indeed a pirate, not only in words but in actions. The Duchess hadn't considered herself to play a role in how the accused was to die. Now, she must choose her dignity over a man's torturous death. The whole matter seemed ridiculous to her, and she laughed aloud as she stared at everyone, searching for answers or approval.

Still, a smile appeared on the Duchess's face as she considered all the ramifications. She was here, exposed, with no place to hide. Redbone saw her countenance turn a reddish glow. He did not hesitate but took the lady by the hand and led her to his cabin. As everyone stood by, surprised by what was about to happen, they caught a final glance from the high breed Duchess, an excited smirk upon her face.

Here and now, no one to tell the tale of how the lady's virtue was given freely to save a murderer. Nevertheless, three hours later, she and the captain reappeared, her smile and ruffled hair showing their heated negotiations. As the Duchess turned to leave, she removed a ribbon from her dress and placed it around the arm of Captain Redbone. "Thank you, Captain, for your kindness. Safe journeys, and when you pass this way again, please revisit us, won't you?"

Bowing properly, Redbone addressed the lady. "Aye, thank ye, Duchess, for such a pleasant morning. Until we meet again, ma'am."

"Until that day, sir."

Once the lady was back at her carriage, Redbone began shouting orders to his crew to depart. The navigator, Harv-Dog, made the arduous task look easy. There was little time left before the tide changed. Soon the sail unfurled, and they shot through the narrow passage out into open water, skirting past the British man-of-war.

Redbone had made a promise not to disembowel this

murderer. However, now at sea, the man's life hung in the balance of Redbone's resolve. This pirate Captain was free to deliver justice in any way he pleased.

As they sailed away from Barbados, the Hell's Fury set anchor on a nameless island sometime near midnight. With torches lit, all the crew members appeared on the main deck. They buried Poppy's body at sea, and everyone drank to Poppy's journey into the afterlife.

Mr. Black was another matter altogether. He was brought up top onto the main deck. There his wooden coffin was wrapped in heavy chains. A thick lock through the steel loops was left open. Evette was called topside and was brought to see Redbone so she could decide a man's fate. Seeing the wooden coffin and hearing the man begging for his life inside, Redbone turned to her, saying, "Aye, hear me, lass, there inside the wooden crate is thee man that murdered yer father. True to ye Duchess's request, he has not been hurt or suffered the loss of his attachments. Thee lock is left open. Few have ye chance as thee to confront thou murderer of their beloved parent. Still, ye have an opportunity to deliver justice as ye see fit, and I will honor yer request whatever thou choose. Now, tell me, girl, set him free? Or close thee lock and deliver his remains to Davy Jones?"

Evette stood by, eyeing the coffin. She thought of her loving father, who killed the man trying to rape her. Her father paid the ultimate price for intervening, and now to avenge him seemed the logical choice—but what a choice for a sixteen-year-old girl. Evette, looking at the many pirate faces around her, saw compassion and pity on the faces of these bloodthirsty cutthroats; a choice, her choice, was now on the table. She considered her options. Time was slipping through her fingers. Captain Redbone was not someone whose time she should waste. "Captain, I've made my choice!"

"Aye, out with it, lass,"

"I choose…"

THE FOLLOWING DAY, the sun burst over the horizon as a new course was plotted for St. Mary's Island. There the Iron Born allies were more friendly. There was no chance of a British Vice-Admiral changing his mind and blowing their ship out of the water.

Redbone received news of a possible cache of treasure being recovered by the Spanish. A close friend and fellow pirate named Robbie had come across the news that a fatted ship, the *San José*, was a 64-gun, three-masted Spanish galleon that had sunk in a sea battle off Cartagena, Colombia while laden with gold, silver, and emeralds. Redbone's interest was piqued; he wasted no time in setting sail.

Evette stood on the bow as the waves crashed into the hull. They were making their way to New Providence Island, Bahamas. The journey would take weeks, and she would be alone with her thoughts.

Hunter, the pirate she met back in Barbados, appeared.

"Do you care if I join you, ma'am?"

"I will enjoy the company if the truth is told. I feel so alone in this world."

"I understand what you're going through; believe me, I do. I also lost my father at an early age. He died at sea, shipwrecked on a rocky shore; none could save him, I'm afraid."

"Yes, but please tell me, do you feel I made the right choice? I'm having second thoughts about the matter."

"It was your decision and yours alone. I do not

always agree with what my captain does, but he is my leader, and the crew and I trust him to make those difficult decisions."

"Perhaps you're right."

"Trust me, in time; you'll see that you made the correct choice."

"I hope so; thank you."

At that moment, Hunter's name was called, and he excused himself, promising they would talk again. As he left Evette alone, she stared into the murky dark water and thought, "I hope I made the right choice, but time will tell."

Chapter 13

WHILE SKIRTING AROUND JAMAICA and Cuba, avoiding Tortuga, they arrived at New Providence Island, Bahamas. The actual township wasn't that large, and it didn't take any time before they'd found the pirate Robbie in a smoky tavern, drunk from rum, singing, with a prostitute wrapped around his neck. A few pirate ships lay in the harbor, unmolested, left in peace. They were still keeping a worthy eye out for pirate enemies.

Sitting at the table, Redbone looked at his old friend and smirked. "Aye, Robbie, ye old sea dog, I, Redbone, come to see ya."

The man tilted his head toward the voice and narrowed his eyes. A broad smile appeared on his face. "Captain Redbone, my old friend, is that you come to see me?"

"Aye, it be true enough, man. I has traveled a long way to see ye! Arrrr, not speak of it now, but perhaps we'll have words on thee morrow, ye and me?"

Turning to the whore in his lap, Robbie announced, "Forgive me, where are my manners. What did you say your name was again? Oh, wait, I never asked!" The man broke out in laughter.

"Aye, indeed," Redbone replied. "Tell me, Robbie, where a man tee gets a drink around here?"

Robbie turned toward the bar and yelled, "Hannah, come here, girl; I want you to meet an old friend of mine."

Redbone turned to eye his first mate for his reaction. Mr. Schmidt smirked. In no time, a girl appeared carrying goblets of rum. A lit cigarette hung from her bottom lip; she wore an apron around her body. She placed the glasses and asked if they cared to have something to eat.

Redbone looked up, reached around, and smacked her bottom. A smile appeared on his face. "Aye, wench, what do ye have available?"

"Sir, truly, if ye smack my arse again, I say it'll be your hand on a plate."

Hearing the server's comments, Redbone laughed and reached for his goblet. When he did, his coat sleeve pulled up, exposing his wrist, baring the sign of the cup with the two crossed swords. The lady recognized the scar, signifying Redbone as an Iron Born pirate. She drew back in fear. Rumors of the band of pirates had already run throughout the Caribbean. Now, in front of her was not only an Iron Born pirate but the captain of the cutthroat crew, obviously, the meanest rogue of the bunch.

"Excuse my manners, Redbone; I didn't mean anything by it, sir, just the ramblings of a foolish woman."

Redbone understood the reason for her sudden change of temperament. He lifted his glass, took a long swig, smiled, and responded, "Tell me, what be that boiling in thee pot?"

"Tonight's special, a delicious stew of turnip greens, carrots, and corn, including boiled game hen. All combined with my special seasoning. It's most favored among my customers, sir."

"Aye, it smells quite good. What do ye say, Mr. Schmidt?"

Finishing his rum, the Iron Born first mate replied, "It does, Captain; I shall have two bowls myself, with a bread loaf."

"Ye hear me first, mate Mr. Schmidt; we'll both be

having your special." The girl stood shaking. Again, Redbone smacked her arse and shouted, "Hurry, Ma'am, Mr. Schmidt is a bear when he's hungry."

"Right away, sir," In a flash, the woman disappeared into the kitchen. Robbie watched Hannah's reaction and laughed. Turning to his friend, he said, "Redbone, you shouldn't frighten the locals. Hannah, be harmless enough."

"No need to bother yerself with such concern Robbie; you already have your hands full; I can see this for meself."

"No worries, my old friend." Lifting the intoxicated girl from his lap, Robbie shouted, "Now lass, take me bottle up to ye room and meet me there. Warm the sheets for me, and I shall join you shortly." The girl grabbed ahold of the bottle of rum and staggered up to the stairs. A short time later, a door was heard slamming closed.

Hannah appeared, her arms full; she quickly set down three bowls of steaming stew, two for Mr. Schmidt and the third for Redbone himself. Looking up at the hostess, Redbone asked, "Tell me, ma'am, do ye have accommodations for the two of us for the night?"

"Sorry, sir, we only have one room available."

"Oh, that won't do. I refuse to sleep in the same bed as me first mate, and if ye look at the man, you can see he's as big a horse. Besides, Mr. Schmidt won't be too fond of sleeping on the cold floor. No, I be sorry, but one of yer guests will have to find other lodgings for thee night!"

Margret Collings would be the local choice; she was a high-bred woman with a fear of pirates and could be convinced to leave her room. Hannah knew resisting the captain's request could be costly, especially for her or the guest who had just lost a room. She nodded her head in agreement.

It had begun to rain, making walking through the

muddy streets miserable. As the evening wore on, drunk patrons staggered out of the tavern into the cold weather. Sometime in the wee hours, Robbie staggered up to his room, leaving Redbone and Schmidt to talk.

"Captain, are you sure about this man Robbie? Do you think he can be trusted?"

"Mr. Schmidt, don't ye be judging thee man on his appearance. I've known Robbie for many a year. He's always been honest in our dealings."

At that moment, Hannah reappeared, carrying two more goblets of rum, saying, "Gentlemen, the pub will be closing for the night; it is getting late, and already the cook has left. Please take your time and drink your rum; leave the cups on the counter when you are finished! Good night, sirs!"

"Aye, good night indeed, lass. Tell me, do ye hear thee rain outside and ye blowing wind? It's bound to be a cold night. Why would ye risk catching a cold or worst? Wouldn't it be better to stay thee night with meself and warm me sheets? Why I promise ye a good time! Besides, I won't snore—not to my knowledge, anyway!"

Hannah was, after all, alone. Staring at her was a man whom she was sure was not accustomed to hearing the word no. A known killer, a pirate captain, an Iron Born. Redbone was sure he knew her response, but Hannah surprised him.

"Excuse me, but no. Although I'm flattered by your offer, Captain, sadly, I must decline. I have a baby to get home to."

"A baby, ma'am. Blimey, that does indeed complicate things a bit. So, tell me, who be watching ye child presently?"

"That answer is simple enough, sir; it is my dear mother!"

"Aye, I see; that will be all then, I suppose. Tell me, how soon will our rooms be ready?"

"I haven't informed Margret Collings that she will be staying elsewhere. I still need time to change the sheets in that room before it is ready."

Mr. Schmidt stood to his feet. "There be no need to change the sheets. Compared to where I'm used to lay my head, a soft pillow and mattress will be a welcome change."

Seeing how large the man was, now that he was standing, Hannah said nothing else and quickly ran upstairs. Schmidt heard a pounding on a door a moment later, then two women whispering, then a cry. "What did you say, pirates?" A second later, steps were heard coming down the stairs. They were given the evil eye as a gray-haired woman, carrying a bag and wearing her nightclothes, rushed out the door. Hannah followed her, dropped off two sets of keys, and bid the men goodnight.

After finishing their rum, Redbone and Schmidt walked up to the top of the stairs. The keys had numbers carved in wooden markers. A squeaky bed was heard echoing out in the hallway. No doubt Robbie was warming the sheets. Redbone and Schmidt were grateful that the passionate sounds stopped with a man's grunting. Opening the door, Redbone turned to his first mate, saying, "See ye in the morning, Mr. Schmidt."

"Yes, Captain, in the morning, sir. Good night."

THE FOLLOWING MORNING, Redbone was up at dawn, requesting breakfast. Both Robbie and Mr. Schmidt met him in the dining hall sometime later.

After enjoying a hearty breakfast, Robbie suggested that the three take a stroll down by the docks. Along the way, they talked of Redbone's plan to raid a Spanish settlement in Cartagena, Colombia. Robbie had it on good authority that the Spanish were recovering a wreck with divers, but it was a slow process and would take some time to bring up the treasure hold of precious gems. In the meantime, the valuables were housed in a temporary shelter on the beach. All the gold and jewels were there for the taking.

Robbie's plan made sense, although Redbone asked himself why the Spanish wouldn't guard the treasure with warships. Was it that simple?

Something unknown to the other two men was that Redbone had a king's ransom worth of gold and jewels already back at the Turks and Caicos Islands. He still believed it intact, despite the trick played out by that cursed witch, where he saw Montoya alive in the vision. The man couldn't still live; he'd shot him in the head!

Soon, however, Redbone would have to return to the islands to claim his treasure, but how? His pirate crew constantly surrounded him. No, he'd have to wait for some time to be alone in the distant future. Perhaps a time in his life would come when he needed the booty to quit his pirating days. Still, he had a nagging feeling that his treasure had been compromised.

Not even Mr. Schmidt knew about the treasure. The only plausible solution would be to hire a merchant ship and travel to the Turks and Caicos Islands. But life aboard a pirate ship is not that simple; if he deserted his ship and crew, no doubt upon his return, he'd discover a new captain in charge. No, he'd worked too hard to see his dreams of a pirate brotherhood become a reality; to abandon his hopes now would bring about inevitable disaster, and he would have to fight this new captain challenger to the death.

Still, hearing Robbie's plans to capture a Spanish hoard of treasure was the news he needed to hear. Already he's overheard complaints about empty pockets amongst his crew. Redbone, the exceptional visionary of a mighty fighting force, knew his men needed a new treasure to hunt. To pack the crew's pockets with gold was a need that couldn't be ignored.

"Arrrr, I've heard enough; we leave on the morning tide," he declared.

A man of few words, Mr. Schmidt nodded his head in agreement. "I'll check with Mr. Toner to see if he's finished gathering supplies for the journey."

"Arrrr, it will be a sad day," said Robbie. "I'll inform, my lady of the night, that I have a journey ahead. It's sad to think I'll be sleeping inside a dark musky hull with men snoring about, but such is a pirate's life; we cannot always have comfort for our old bones, can we?"

"Alas, Robbie, ye haven't changed a bit, always thinking of your man pole."

"Yes, it be true enough, Redbone. I imagine my pole will be getting a workout tonight; it will."

"One last night in New Providence. I'll inform the crew," Schmidt announced.

"Mr. Schmidt, add a stern warning. I will not take kindly to any man being imprisoned for unruly behavior. Warn each who is departing the gangway that they are to sleep in their bunks tonight, not in the arms of a passionate lady. Upon our return, their pockets full of booty, they can sleep as long as they wish and with whom they wish, but for now, see that each of them heeds me warning."

"Aye, Captain."

"One more thing, before you go, Mr. Schmidt, have the cabin boy Abisai bring the sailing charts I keep under me bunk in the leather pouch to my room at the inn."

"Right away, Captain."

Afterward, alone with Robbie, Redbone proclaimed, "Hear me now, me old friend, this warning is for ye ears as well. Say goodbye to ye lady, but do not spend the night. On the morning tide, we sail, with or without ye, man."

"Enough said, Redbone, ye be coming across clearly enough."

Robbie departed, and Redbone stood alone, staring at his ship in the harbor. It was a beehive of activity as men gathered supplies and prepared to leave. Each man had a job, and he did not doubt that his ship would be ready to sail by morning. Experiencing a headache, Redbone rubbed his eyes; the pressures of being a ruthless pirate captain took their toll on his earthly body. He wanted to be alone with his thoughts. He decided to enjoy a night of quiet solitude at the inn before returning to the floating fortress in search of treasure.

When he arrived at the inn, the evening was still young, with few patrons. He took a table near the window where he could be alone, and Hannah appeared.

"Tell me, Captain, will you stay for dinner this evening?"

"Ye be correct in your estimation, lass. I will be staying the night. One last time here in your establishment."

"Then, can I bring you something to drink?"

"Aye, that would be nice of ye. Have you something in the way of cognac, lass?"

"Yes, indeed, Captain, we have a wide assortment of spirits on hand."

"That will do nicely."

"Very well."

Redbone took the sailing charts and spread them across the table as he began to study the dangerous route to Cartagena. The Spanish Main consisted of many islands occupied and controlled by the Spanish. Although Tortuga was off-limits, there were other pirate harbors in which to take refuge if need be.

The golden prize was irresistible for most pirates, which was undeniably why Robbie had information about the sunken treasure ship in the first place. The route Redbone had in mind would skirt around Havana through the Yucatan channel heading directly south, avoiding the

Mosquito Coast. Spanish ships often took this route when returning for more treasure.

Hearing his name, Redbone looked up and saw Evette standing next to him.

"Good day Captain Redbone. May I have a word with you, sir?"

"Aye, indeed ye may, lass. Please seat yerself and tell me the tale of a new life here in beautiful New Providence!"

"Captain Redbone, I must thank you for your kindness and consideration. Here, there are no preconceived notions that I'm a slave. Yes, slavery is still freely practiced, but with your help, I've had liberties as if I'd been born a free woman, no one's property."

"Lass, you've had a bit of a rough patch, losing your father as you did. Why would I complicate your life any further with this slavery nonsense?"

"Yes, very true, Captain, but you didn't have to arrange for me to obtain employment as a seamstress. The lady I work for has shown me great kindness. Although I have just started, I can tell she will treat me not as property but as a person. I truly wish I had more time with you, sir, but I do not. I was on my way to the butcher's house to take measurements for curtains. If I do not see you again, you have my thanks for all you've done, Captain Redbone, knight of the Iron Born!"

"Arrrr, lass, it is the least I could do."

"Captain, before I go, what of Mr. Black? How is he surviving as a pirate?"

"Aye, Mr. Black. The man has surprised us all, lass. Truth be said, I was hoping for his death when thee man went through the Bloody Hag trial, but I was astonished to discover he is resourceful. I imagine the morning he woke; he felt grateful to be alive.

"Take care, Captain. I shall pray for you and your crew every night that you have a safe passage, no matter where the winds take you."

"Aye, that be nice. Until we meet again, Miss." Returning to his charts, Redbone completely missed Evette's sorrowful tears as she walked away.

The conversation had played out under the watchful eye of Hannah, who, for her part, began to see a different side to the frightful, cutthroat captain. Hannah brought Redbone his drink. She stood back and waited before saying, "Tell me, Captain, how did you sleep? Was the room comfortable and to your liking?"

Redbone laughed. "Even now, I feel the boat moving, side to side. Compared to the ship rocking, yes, the room was pleasant enough. Still, the sheets were a bit icy. A warm body would have made all the difference."

Taking a hand-rolled cigarette from her apron, Hannah lit the tobacco, breathed it into her lungs, and responded, "That may be true, Captain, but believe me, your night alone was more sleep than I experienced. The truth be, I had to share a bed with Margret Collings. There was simply no other place for the woman to lodge for the night. So, I offered to share my bed with her. Regrettably, the woman snored like a bear; she did."

"Most regretful, indeed. The good bit of news is we will soon be gone on a new adventure. My first mate is preparing our ship for departure on the morning tide. Please have Miss Collings return to her room if she wishes."

Hannah inhaled a drag, expelling her tobacco above Redbone's head. "The truth is, I will be closing the tavern late, as usual. I do not wish to wake the woman in the middle of the night. I've considered staying in her room this evening. Still not sure how the day will play out. We're always receiving new guests, you understand."

"Yes, after tomorrow, things should return to normal. You'll be able to return to your boring life as a handmaiden. For me part, I will be plotting courses toward a new adventure. It's doubtful our paths will cross again. Blimey, wench, you've shown me and my first mate kindness. I want to settle up now if it's all the same to ye; tell me what I owe?"

"Let me see, a room for the night usually costs four pieces of eight for one guest. You had two rooms, both you and your first mate, plus the cost of dining. I'd say to be square, pay me fourteen pieces of eight. I'm giving you another night for free."

"Aye, again, Lass, ye have shown me kindness unexpected for a man of me nature and upbringing." Reaching into his pocket, Redbone dropped two gold doubloons on the table. The metallic items rang out, twirling around in separate circles before they came to rest, showing the royal seal on the face of each coin.

Hannah never expected to receive such an exuberant amount. "Captain Redbone, you expect change, correct?"

"Nay, it be all yer to keep. Let's say it be a little help for ye raising that child of yores. What bit of information I expected to hear but did not was the telling of the lad's father. Where he be, lass? I see a ring you be wearing around ye neck. But ye fail to mention the man?"

"Why are you so interested in knowing about Paul?"

"Arrrr, shiver me bones, lass. Ye see before thou a man who's traveled thee seven seas. On all me explorations, one truth rings true, it does. The loss of a beloved is something ye heart never recovers from. It be obvious to me, thou man is dead or lost at sea, or else ye be wearing that ring around yer finger, instead of yore neck. You are tied to the man through a promise, are ye not?"

Hannah began crying at the memory of her beloved and turned to leave.

"Wait," Redbone shouted. "Lass, I did not mean to offend ye. Please believe me. Here, takes yer payment. Go out and buy a new dress, buy yer child a pony or whatever else yer heart desires."

"Thank you, Captain." Taking the money and slipping it into her pocket, she wiped her eyes with her apron, smiled back at Redbone, and announced, "Where are my manners? I'll soon return with your drink. Thank you, Captain. I do not believe the stories I've heard about you, for what it's worth. All I've been shown is nothing but kindness. Those rumors cannot be true; just a hoax thought up by jealous men lacking good morals."

"Lass, I'm not privy to what stories you've heard but know this, it's not wise to cross paths with the Iron Born; it's simply not healthy."

"Regardless, Captain. I have my own opinion and will keep that to myself. Your drink will arrive shortly, sir."

"Aye, indeed, make it quick, me throat is parched." Receiving yet another spank on her arse, Hannah laughed and hurried away.

Sometime before the dinner hour, the tavern crowd began arriving. Hannah was carrying a handful of drinks to a table of men, but when a patron began singing about crown and country, Redbone decided to set sail to his room and gathered his sailing charts under his arm. As he walked up the stairs, he felt the peculiar sensation of being watched. He turned to look back. Hanna's expression was one of sorrow. None could guess the effects of a kind word on someone hurting.

This cutthroat captain was out of character, but he felt a strange sadness, an emotion usually kept away. The foolishness of exercising such compassion could not be tolerated. Never, no, never. He was a murderer at heart. Damn her, this Hannah. He became angry for feeling human softness, and turning away, he trudged upstairs and closed his door.

Does a murderer sleep peacefully during the night? Do nightmarish remembrances haunt the killer of men until the alcohol fades and he wakes in a panic, realizing what he's done?

Redbone slept soundly in the blackened room, the only light coming from a small window. A light rain coated the glass, dripping down in streaks. Redbone awoke to the sound of his door opening. Immediately he reached for his musket from under his pillow. With his eyes partially closed, Redbone watched the individual reach his bed. He carefully observed the robber to understand what they were after, most likely gold coins or something similar.

As he waited to spring his trap, the visitor began to disrobe. In the dim light, Redbone could see a naked breast. Now completely nude, the intruder crawled under the bedsheets. Hannah had had a change of heart, to his delight. Shoving his pistol back under his pillow, Redbone turned to Hannah and affectionately kissed her.

THE EARLY MORNING SOON appeared, and a few hours later, Redbone knew he must return to his ship and set sail. After getting dressed, he grabbed his belongings and opened the door. He heard Hannah's soft voice say, "Paul was lost at sea three years ago. I've been completely alone all this time. My mother gave me and my baby shelter when no one else would. Captain, you're the first man I've been with since losing my husband, Paul."

Redbone paused and stood contemplating Hannah's words, allowing no reaction or softness to show. Regardless of how he tried to shelter his true feelings, he felt a sting. Should he return to the soft, warm bed or leave? A decision must be made. He walked out with no words to say.

A short time later, he somberly walked up the gangway as the *Hell's Fury* prepared to get underway. Closing his cabin door, he was not seen until the following day.

THE NEXT MORNING, appearing on the quarterdeck, Robbie joined Redbone. "So, tell me, Captain, when do you expect to reach the coast of Colombia? By my calculations, I hope we'll arrive in sixteen days, provided we have favorable winds."

"I've made those same calculations meself."

"Redbone, I have known you for some time; tell me what's gotten ahold of you, sir; you seem a bit off course?"

"Curse ye to hell, man, if ye be wrong about this Spanish treasure, Robbie! Ye will be cut from stem to stern if ye be mistaken!"

"Something's got ahold of your arse, as if a tick be biting your seat, it does!"

"Press the matter further, man. I make ye this promise; ye will not like the outcome."

"By me, dear mother's sake, Redbone, I mean nothing by it. We have sailed together many a year now, don't forget. I will not lead you astray, man. The treasure will be there; I bet my life."

"Aye, you already have."

Redbone left the deck and returned to his cabin, where he kicked over a globe and cursed aloud. "Damn woman, curse ye to bloody hell with all ye sisters, the entire bunch of ye!" He heard a knock on his cabin door. "Redbone, are you all right, man?" the familiar voice spoke.

"Blast ye man, come inside, Mr. Schmidt. Do not stand idle at the door."

The big man walked inside. "Redbone, what has gotten ahold of you? The crew has seen unmistakable changes, including you spending too much time alone in your cabin!"

"Mr. Schmidt, yer observations are duly noted. It

may be true that I might have sailed too close to me emotions of late. Be that as it may, the men can rest assured, I be the bloodthirsty pirate ye have always known me to be. Blimey, I need a drink." He called to Brendon, the cabin boy, for rum. Grabbing his coat from an empty chair at the table, Redbone said, "Me, friend, ye have a seat, man, and get comfortable. Soon we'll have our fill of rum; we will."

A short time later, Brendon knocked on the captain's door and nervously opened it. The boy was relatively new to the pirate crew, having been rescued from the sea when Corsair pirates captured the merchant ship carrying his mother and sister to Port Royal. The burning hulk was all that remained of the sailing vessel. His family members were taken as prizes and sold off as slaves.

Much too young for the ceremony of becoming an Iron Born pirate, Brendon looked forward to the day when he, too, would take his oath.

Brendon's rescue had occurred only a few days after the *Hell's Fury* had left the witch's island. When Redbone found the boy floating on the blackened timbers of the sailing ship, half-dead, he ordered the ship's doctor to do everything he could to save the boy's life. When the boy heard the captain slip and call him "Baggi," he realized he must remind him of someone, perhaps a son he had lost. He didn't dare ask any crew if his suspicions were accurate.

Quickly pouring two glasses to the top, the captain and his first mate seemed enthusiastic to get their drink on. As Brendon turned to leave, Redbone spoke up. "Drop ye anchor, a moment, laddie. Now tell me how old ye are."

"Oh, Captain Redbone, sir, let me see; I turn sixteen next month, sir."

"Aye, close enough, boy. Come over here and pour yerself a glass."

"A glass, sir?" Brendon repeated, not sure of what he'd heard.

"Aye, meself wasn't as old as ye were when I had my first drink. Now, boy, ye listen to me words; this be strong drink, a man's drink. It comes with a bit of a bite; it does."

Unknown to Redbone, anytime the dishes were taken away to be cleaned, any remaining liquor in the glasses was often shared with the other cabin boy Abisai. But those were partial glasses; Brendon was thrilled by the invitation to join his commanders.

"Certainly, Captain, it will be my pleasure, sir." Nervously pouring the expensive liquor into the only available glass, Brendon topped it off and set the plunger back inside the crystal decanter. Holding his glass high, he looked at his two officers and proclaimed, "To your health, gentlemen," and drank down the burning cognac in one swig. After setting the glass down, a smile appeared on his face.

Turning to his first mate, Redbone shouted, "Mr. Schmidt, it seems we have a true connoisseur of spirits amongst us."

"True, Captain, it surely is news to me. But there it is, is it not?"

"That will be all, Brendon; you can take yer leave now, boy. Henceforth, I shall have to keep a worthy eye out on me private stock of spirits." Both men laughed as Brendon walked away and closed the cabin door.

"It be good to share in a laugh, it is," said Redbone. "Believe me, man, I had a bit of catch in me craw, I did; nothing to worry yerself over."

"Glad to see you back to your old self, Redbone. Both of us have put great effort into seeing this pirate band brought together, at great peril and risk, I might add; we've come too far to see it come to nothing."

"Drink up, Mr. Schmidt. On the morrow, it will be behind us, I promise."

"Good to hear, Captain."

That night they drank their fill to forget about their pasts and hoped that the alcohol would wash away the remembrance of living. Redbone, haunted by the soft and pleasant caresses of the woman back in New Providence, drank to escape his emotional state. His resolution was plain enough: he intended to erase all memory of Hannah. But could he escape the dream of an ordinary life he had never experienced, a sting of happiness and love?

Chapter 14

INITIALLY ON COURSE TO CARTAGENA, Colombia, none of the crew understood why their route was diverted, sailing 140 degrees southeast toward the Turks and Caicos Islands. Regardless, Redbone understood his intent very clearly, and when Mr. Schmidt asked for a reason for traveling to that particular destination, none was given. Still, Redbone was the captain, and the crew had to trust him to lead the way to the treasure. Nevertheless, when the *Hell's Fury* set anchor at a deserted island, some swashbucklers questioned why Redbone was so generous about cracking open the rum casks and giving every man drinks overflowing.

The men lowered their captain into the water in a dingy by himself. Grabbing the oars, Redbone set out toward the white sandy beach where it all began and where he hoped the vision of Montoya being alive was a falsehood.

Redbone had left Mr. Schmidt in charge, a man not known for mischief. Redbone knew that the *Hell's Fury* would be shipshape, nothing out of line upon returning.

He paddled hard through the waves to shore, placing his oars in the churning waters to avoid capsizing. When Redbone felt the sand rubbing against the boat's bottom, he jumped out and heaved the boat onto the sandy shoreline before the next wave had time to soak him wet.

Taking a minute to survey the area, Redbone looked

about to get his bearings. Already, months had passed since he left, and the landscape had changed—there was a row of crosses lined up near the trees. Looking toward the sandy hilltop where he had buried his treasure, nothing seemed disturbed. Had Montoya survived? Who else would have buried the men that Redbone had slaughtered? Redbone's anger swelled inside him, and he cursed aloud.

Anxiously he walked up the slight grade to the grassy knoll. When he arrived at the top, he stared down at the sandy mound. Already expecting the worst, he dropped to his knees. Grabbing ahold of his wooden oar, he buried it deep into the sand and pushed it away. It didn't take long before he came across a dead man's remains—the guardians of his treasure were still here.

The tropical heat buffeted him with each movement until he stood and removed his coat, burning from exhaustion. He dug until again he came across another rotting corpse. Then a third. By now, he should have seen a treasure chest of gold and jewels but found nothing. Exhausted, he stood and took a breather. He remembered where Montoya was last seen. He walked over to that place and shuffled his feet deep into the sand. He turned up nothing in the way of skeletal remains.

Montoya was still alive. The vision he had seen was real.

"Curse that scalawag to hell!" Redbone shouted. His words were lost in the passing breeze. Disgusted, he returned empty-handed to the dinghy. After throwing his oar inside the small boat, he was about to shove off when he glanced toward his ship and saw another small boat paddling his way. He recognized Mr. Schmidt by his size and stature. Feeling sour and in no mood to explain his actions, he stood waiting for his first mate to arrive.

As the first mate landed on the beach, he pulled hard to bring the small rowboat ashore. Noticing his captain alone on the beach, Mr. Schmidt approached. "Redbone, we have a bit of a problem. The men are negotiating a mutiny."

"What say ye man, mutiny?" These are the words that no captain wants to hear.

"This Robbie friend of yours must have an alternative motive for wanting us to take him to Cartagena, perhaps to take our ship?"

"Ye could be right, man. Now tell me, who be casting lots with Robbie?"

"It should be no surprise, Redbone, that it is the master gunners from Tortuga, the men you shanghaied into becoming Iron Born pirates. It seems they've been unhappy with their decision to bear the mark."

"Yes, of course, but the fools do not realize they will be found guilty by association alone in any court of law? They took the oath, and even with little choice, they bear the mark; their guilt is no hiding."

"You're an astute man, Captain. Did you not see this coming?"

"It be a daring move on Robbie's part. Indeed it be. But enough of this; we must be off or else find ourselves abandoned here on this beach."

"Yes, quickly then; already, I see movement about the deck." Racing back to the small boats, they pushed off against the pounding surf and jumped inside. They grabbed their oars, shoved them into the salty water, and paddled hard against the waves. The rowboats cut into the first wave, causing a splash that soaked each man through. Looking toward the *Hell's Fury*, Redbone saw Abisai and Brendon, the two cabin boys, standing along the top rail, excitably pointing toward Redbone.

The sound of gunfire erupted as a tropical gust blew toward the shore. Redbone paddled hard against the waves. Panic gripped him. Losing command of his ship meant death, or at best, being left stranded on this hellish tropical island where he had killed so many others.

Besides him were his devoted friend and first mate. Mr. Schmidt pulled just as hard. Aye, a faithful, dedicated companion to the end—his first line of defense. Redbone had no idea what to expect when they arrived at the ship. A minute later, another shot rang out. *Curse and damnation, Robbie, ye have done it now, ye have, man!*

Regardless of his need to get to his ship, Redbone was only human. Soon fatigue set in, yet he knew he had to reserve some strength for fighting. *How did he escape? Fight? How much will it take to regain control of my ship? Curse this vexatious treasure and Montoya. I saw the blood splatter meself.* His anger burned hot with each drag of the oars. Robbie would die for inciting this rebellion.

The closer he got to the ship, the more an eerie inaudible silence grew. Redbone was the first to reach the mooring ladder. He tied off the rowboat and began his climb. Close behind him, Mr. Schmidt carried his shining ax. Redbone crawled over the taffrail and landed on the deck. An assembly of Iron Born pirates stood in a circle, and to his astonishment, in the middle was Robbie, kneeling on the deck, and four other conspirators were already in chains with him. They were guarded by Harv-Dog and ten others holding muskets to the traitors' heads. The group of mutineers waited for their fate to be decided.

A swelling of pride inundated Redbone. To see all the schemers held down by the faithful Iron Born, the true Iron Born whose devotion to the brotherhood was not merely an empty promise but a soul-wrenching dedication to their pirate brothers. What had happened was no surprise to Redbone, who suspected the master gunners from Tortuga would betray them all at the first opportunity. Today, he fulfilled his dream of seeing his men, supportive and devoted to the one cause, bring the Iron Born principles to fruition.

Words, at times, are no more than empty boasting. Redbone knew what the men's crimes were and would not waste time with a trial by their peers. Walking up to the first man, Redbone grabbed him by his collar and lifted him to his feet. Before the man could defend himself or speak, Redbone struck him across the jaw, knocking him down to the oak deck. He quickly removed a small blade hidden under his coat, and as his crew members watched, Redbone, the pirate Captain, reached out and grabbed the man by his hair, shoved the knife under his nose, and brought the blade up one of his nostrils, slicing it in half. The man screamed out in pain and gripped his snout as the blood poured out between his fingers. His moans of pain were ignored. Redbone stood in the center of the circle and looked about. No one spoke.

"Ye men, or should I say, ye worms. Ye have this day betrayed ye brothers in a most heinous way. None today would guess yer hatred of becoming an Iron Born brother. Surely ye must have understood there would be consequences? The foolishness of thinking me own shipmates would betray their captain was yer first mistake. No matter what a mistake, I can easily correct it. Mr. Schmidt, the men before us no longer wish to bear the mark. Please do them a service by removing it for them, will ye?"

"Aye, aye, Captain."

As Schmidt raised his ax to remove the first man's hand, the man shouted, "No, wait! It wasn't our idea but Robbie's! Your friend—it was his idea, not ours; you must believe us."

"Do not fret yerselves with Robbie; I have a special treat for him. Mr. Schmidt, carry on."

One by one, each man was brought to the deck. Their arms were stretched out, held apart by ropes. Mr. Schmidt's ax severed their hands in one fell swoop.

Afterward, the rebels were discarded on the beach,

their wrists seared with hot irons to prevent blood loss as a sign of mercy. Without bearing the proud mark of the Iron Born, those who survived to tell the tale would be useless to anyone.

Robbie bore no mark upon his wrist; his disloyalty was toward Redbone, not the Iron Born. But still, they needed him to find the encampment where the treasure was located. He was thrown into an animal cage and kept on deck, a spectacle for all to see. Robbie's life was spared—for now.

Incarcerated in the small cage, Robbie had little choice but to give Redbone the heading toward Cartagena and the Spanish encampment. Again, sailing around Cuba, the *Hell's Fury* made its way south.

Navigator Harv-Dog had an inkling of the location of the encampment. He had sailed that way as a youth aboard a merchant ship. Now, they needed to find the site of a vessel sunk several years ago in shallow waters, depositing its precious cargo throughout the coral rock incrustations. All that was required was to take it for themselves and be rich beyond measure from a true pirate hoard.

Rounding Cuba one morning, Redbone stood proud upon the quarterdeck, surveyed the vast ocean, and turned his attention east. There he spotted sails disappearing around the tip of Isla de la Juventud. Hopefully, they belonged to a merchant ship bringing cargo to native villages for trade. Nonetheless, it was best to keep a wary eye open; none could suspect when or if these sails would turn south to intersect with their ship. Instead of a merchant, the sails might belong to a pirate raider, fiercer than themselves. None would escape the battle to the death.

Hearing a commotion near the poop deck, Redbone turned to see Robbie adjusting himself to get comfortable. Walking over to his old shipmate, he asked, "Ye, have a bit of a problem getting comfortable, Robbie, do ye?"

"Aye, Captain, this cage is wearing on my bones; it is."

"It was not my intention to bring ye aboard to have you put in a cage; ye had done this yerself, man!"

"Redbone, come on, man, we are pirates after all; why should this surprise you in any way?"

"Each day, I awake with the knowledge that me ship could be captured, set ablaze, and all my crew hanged. Not to mention storms that plague these regions; we could be blown off course onto a rocky shore and drown. Robbie, ye have served me by weaning out any treasonous members of me crew that lay hidden, much like ye rocky coral that appears without warning."

"If what you say be true, man, then please set your old shipmate free and call us even."

Redbone erupted with laughter as he considered the humorous proposal. "Tell you what, Robbie. Ye lead us to the treasure as promised, and ye will not taste me steel in yer body. Now man, do ye not forget at any moment I might become dissatisfied with yer company and order your cage tossed overboard, with ye inside!"

"That would be a sad day indeed."

"Before ye deceived your old shipmate, ye should have considered the likes of who it is ye be betraying, ye fool. I thought more of ye, Robbie!" Their conversation was over; Redbone walked away and stood on the poop deck. Calling out to one of his crew, Redbone ordered Mr. Arnette to climb up into the crow's nest and look out for approaching sails. Seeing the white fabric on the horizon earlier made him nervous.

Not far off, his first mate oversaw a group of sailors repairing a metal anchor ring. "Mr. Schmidt, come here, man."

Mr. Schmidt looked up and joined Redbone. "You wanted to see me, Captain?"

"Aye, Mr. Schmidt. I'm not sure what we be expecting, but order the gun crew to the stations and remain there until I give the word otherwise."

"Captain, are you expecting a fight, sir? I have not seen any other ship for some time now."

"No, but it best to be prepared for a fight. Have the necessary powder kegs and shots ready. One never knows, man. I have seen sails about our port side. Ye have yer orders; see to it, sir."

"Aye, aye, Captain, at once!"

Occasionally eyeing his crew from his perch, Redbone surveyed the horizon for any sign of trouble and remained on alert until the evening hour. That night, no candles were lit. The men were fed and ordered back to their stations below deck. The danger seemed to pass, and the duties aboard the ship continued. Over the following days, the voyage remained uneventful. Harv-Dog steered the boat south.

Finally, the land was sighted toward evening on the twentieth day of their expedition. Now more than ever, the men stayed on their toes, looking for Spanish ships. The difficulty arrived when they looked for a suitable spot for their vessel to anchor. According to the sailing charts, an island off the Cartagena coast, Isla de Tierra Bomba, was the best choice to anchor.

Harv-Dog coxswained the ship into the narrow waterway, and they set anchor in a deserted part of the island with no lanterns or torches to light their way. Redbone reappeared at Robbie's cage, saying, "Now, be the time to tell me everything ye know about this encampment."

There was no sound from inside, so Redbone quickly opened the cage, grabbed Robbie's collar, and shook him. Robbie's dead body fell forward. "Curse ye man, what have ye done to yerself?"

Redbone noticed a sticky substance on the deck.

Looking down, he saw that he was standing in blood. Looking back into the cage, he saw a small blade beside the body; it must have been hidden in Robbie's boot. Redbone grabbed the man's arm. His suspicions were verified; Robbie had taken the coward's way out and cut his wrist, no doubt understanding his value was over when the crew spotted land.

The punishments Redbone had imagined for Robbie's betrayal were now moot. It was time to consider the future. His strategy was simple enough. Under darkness, every able man would cast off in small rowboats and paddle over to the main shore. The armament's strength was unknown; the crew must scout it out.

"Mr. Schmidt, come here, man."

"Aye, Captain; what is it, sir?"

"Look in yonder cage; it be the remains of Robbie, the coward. Order the men to discard the body overboard for shark food."

"At once, Captain."

"Tell me, are the men ready to depart? There be but a few hours left until daybreak."

"Yes, each man has been issued a musket and sword. The longboats are lowered and ready to set off."

"Very well. Today, man, ye shall see more spilled blood, I'm afraid, not taking into account the blood splatter ye be standing in, sir."

"We shall be victorious, Captain, I have no doubt."

"On second thought, order the cabin boys to discard Robbie's body while we're away and have them clean up this mess."

"Aye, Captain."

"Meet me at the longboats; do not dawdle, man."

As Redbone walked over to the taffrails and descended into a longboat, he could hear his first mate shouting orders. A few moments later, Schmidt crawled down the ladder and joined Redbone as the rest of the crew followed. The four boats silently pushed off. Redbone and his crew gazed at the small harbor lights of the port town. There were small lanterns on the beach. Everyone suspected it to be the location of the Spanish treasure encampment. Redbone directed their boats toward an isolated stretch of beach with a rocky shoreline, where he saw no sign of life.

Landing, however, was tricky. The tide was going out, and their boats crashed into the coral and became stuck. No time to waste, each man jumped out and heaved hard to bring their boats to shore, knocked about by the crashing waves. Relentless in their resolve, the pirate crew finally brought their rowboats in safely and collapsed onto the wet sand. Redbone watched as his men rested and recovered. He called out to Hunter, his trusted scout and assassin.

Like the rest of the crew, Hunter looked much like a washed-up creature from the deep. Nevertheless, Redbone needed to understand the strength of his enemy. He ordered the man to seek out the Spanish encampment and ascertain their fighting capabilities. Hunter and his group departed, and Redbone ordered the remaining pirates to get the longboats under the green foliage to hide their presence in case a watchful eye caught sight of their group and reported them to the military authorities.

After the boats were secured, everyone collapsed wherever they could find shelter. Hours passed, and Hunter and his party finally returned by the evening meal. Redbone listened to Hunter's report with great intent. The Spanish camp had a select group of soldiers guarding a storehouse. No more than twenty men. It would be easy pickings.

The plan was set into motion. Redbone ordered Hunter and his men to rest before the assault. Soon, under cover of darkness, they would raid the camp, take the treasure, and escape. Putting Cartagena behind them, they would sail away rich men.

That was the dream, and it all sounded easy, but when reality meets desire, truth often wins. That day, the attack was flawless. Every man, both pirate and Spaniard, performed his duties as expected—except one, a young lieutenant who fought off three pirates at once. Redbone, impressed with the young man's fighting skills, cocked his revolver and pointed at his heart. The Spanish soldiers were ill-equipped to fend off the attack and faced the pirates with gold fever; they abandoned the lieutenant and ran for their lives.

"Arrrr, ye be a good fighter. Ye must understand that it's not easy to fight off the Iron Born, but ye lad has shown a good account of ye self. Indeed, I have seen you fight off three of me men. Now, enough of these charades, man, throw down yer weapon or die!"

"*Señor,* you're too late; all the gold and treasure have been shipped back to Spain."

"No, not possible. Tell me, man, ye be telling a lie to Captain Redbone, are ye not?"

"No, sorry, *Señor,* please help yourself to the storehouse. You'll find the door unlocked."

Redbone threw the door open and looked about. The shelves inside were empty. Aside from one empty chest, all the treasure was utterly gone. The reality infuriated Redbone. Walking back outside, Redbone, with fire in his eyes, ignored the weapon in the officer's hand, walked up, and grabbed the Spaniard by his neck. "Tell me, man, how long it be since the Spanish armada set sail?"

Choking out a response, "Perhaps, a parley is what's needed, Captain. You, *Señor,* a pirate, will appreciate my situation. I cannot tell you the direction of the Spanish ships because it would mean being shot by my superiors as a traitor. I would have to surrender my commission and become a pirate myself!"

"Arrrr, be it as it may, boy, tell me what ye wants to know, or else yer life won't be worth spit! You'll die with yer principles and nothing more." Looking into the desperate captain's eyes, a few mere seconds left to decide his fate, Mauricio Barros responded, "As you wish, *Señor*. I'll tell you everything you want to know. Besides, I'm not truly Spanish; I'm Portuguese. That treasure belongs to King Dom Pedro II. Release your grip, *Señor;* I'll tell you what you want to know but on one condition. You take me with you!"

"Arrrr, so ye want to become an Iron Born pirate, do ye?"

"Is that your title? No matter what. My career is ending; I might as well be a pirate; it's the only option left for me, *Señor!"*

Releasing his grip, Redbone said, "Very well, tell me quick. In which direction did these fatted geese sail?"

Mauricio was still holding his sword. He began to draw their location in the sand with two distinct lines that separated. Looking up, he announced, "One ship called the *Nuestra Señora de la Concepción*, with a complement of fifty guns, has sailed directly to Havana. The other, *Santisima Sacramento*, also has fifty guns. It travels to Portobelo, Panama, where your fellow pirate, John Coxon, invaded some years earlier."

"Tell me, man, why sail to Portobelo?"

"To relieve the militia there and bring the remaining treasure back to Spain."

"How long ago did these ships sail?"

"They both departed yesterday morning. Treasure laden, they'd both make slow progress."

"To the longboats, ye men of Iron, we must capture the *Santisima Sacramento* before she reaches Portobelo."

"What of me, *Señor?* You promised that I could join your crew?"

Redbone pointed his pistol at Mauricio's heart; he

scoffed and answered, "Tell me, lad, what type of turncoat you be? If ye swear an oath to the Iron Born and survive the ritual of the Bloody Hag, will ye be devoted to your pirate brothers by mere words or a sincere heart, believing in one single cause? Look now at me wrist. Have ye ever seen marks as these?"

"Heavens no, *Señor.*"

"It be the mark of true believers. Are you willing to be marred in such a way as this?"

"Capitán, you must understand I had no choice in wearing this uniform. It was the wish of my father that I enlist in the Spanish army. It was never my intention growing up, but you must understand tradition. My father was once a naval officer, and he hoped that I would walk in his footsteps instead of my own."

"Ye be a fair swordsman, but that will only get ye so far. If ye wish to join the Iron Born brotherhood, you'll take the dance, but now we haven't the time. Disarm yerself and hand over yer sword. Rip the uniform off and come with us!"

There was a pause, a brief respite when Mauricio's life flashed before his eyes. A minute later, handing over his sword, he said, "I am ever grateful for you not shooting me, *Señor."* Ripping the jacket from his body, sending brass buttons flying everywhere, Mauricio stood shirtless.

"Come lad, follow me."

The two quickly ran toward the longboats. Mauricio watched as the pirates appeared out from the bushes. Taking a final glance behind him, he knew it was too late for regret. He made his choice and followed his new captain to the waiting boats. The tide was coming in, making it easier to leave the beach. Taking his place at an offered spot, Mauricio grabbed ahold of an oar and dug deep into the water as the boat parted an approaching wave and sliced through it to open water.

Redbone was first up the ladder at the ship, shouting orders to get underway. The longboats were emptied and hauled onto the ship. As the anchor was pulled up from the sandy bottom and the boat prepared to leave, everyone had a job to do except the scallywag Mauricio, who knew little of being a sailor and even less of becoming a pirate. Instead, he tried his best to stay out of everyone's way.

Still, as Mauricio watched the ship leave the small island of Isla de Tierra Bomba, he glanced back toward Cartagena. What remained of the camp to house the treasure was already emptied; there was nothing to guard. Why had his squad been asked to stay diligently on guard when there was nothing to protect? He and his commander didn't always see eye to eye, and to Mauricio, it was simply a way to keep him away from his home base and make him miserable. He had orders to stay until he was relieved sometime the following year.

Now a pirate, soon to bear the mark, a strange symbol that all must wear. To Mauricio, the real question was, what would he do when this ship of pirates clashed with the Spanish navy? What part would he play in the coming battle to the death? Would he forget his promises to both sides and choose only one to follow? Would it cost him everything in the end?

Chapter 15

SEVERAL DAYS LATER, smoke billowed in the noonday sky. Two ships clashed in battle. The sounds of booming cannon fire echoed in the distance. Still some ways away, The *Hell's Fury* slowed her approach. When the Iron Born arrived on the scene, Redbone ordered his spyglass be brought to him. Lifting the round object to his eye, he observed the black pirate flag displayed on one of the ships and the Spanish Royal seal on the other. Redbone's immediate consideration was to wait to see who won. Of course, there was always the chance that they both would sink to the bottom of the sea. It rarely happens, but one never knows.

"Captain, should we strike our colors and get into the fight?" Mr. Schmidt asked.

"Nay, Mr. Schmidt, do not be in a hurry to clash steel and iron. We will wait; a spectacle is being played before us as if two gladiators were in the arena and one was about to die. Do you not find this thrilling beyond measure? Abisai, come here, lad."

"Aye, aye, Captain, sir, what is it?"

"Aye, go to yonder cabin and bring me the cognac, and be quick about it."

"Captain, is it wise to drink at this time, sir? Wouldn't it be wiser to wait until the battle ends and we discover who's victorious?" Schmidt asked.

"Nay, better yet, Mr. Schmidt, an equal share of rum

for every man. Every man who's not engaged in duties aboard the ship. Keep a watch on Harv-Dog; the man can drink!"

"Redbone, I still don't believe it's wise at this time. Shouldn't we be on our toes? Prepared for a fight? Within an instant, a thing could change, and we must return fire to stay alive."

"Arrrr, Schmidt, you be right as rain, man, ye do. But no, all of us could die and be blasted out of the water any time now. It's best to laugh in the face of the devil, especially when he comes knocking on the door. Ye heard me orders, be quick about it, sir."

Regardless of Schmidt's feelings about the subject, mugs were handed out and filled to overflowing as the crew aboard the *Hell's Fury* eagerly watched the goings-on. It soon became apparent that the pirates had superior fighting skills and maneuvers.

As the Iron Born crew watched from afar, mooring lines were thrown between the ships, and the two behemoths were drawn close to one another for a frontal assault. Men swung across the great divide, musket fire erupted, and close hand-to-hand combat began. Eager to get into the fight, Redbone shouted curses to the men dying as they splashed into the water.

Slowly, the tide of the fight turned, and Redbone shouted for his crew to come close as he explained how he planned to enter the battle by boarding the pirate ship. Still unknown was how they would perform and what was expected during the skirmish.

Looking through his spyglass toward the bloody scene, Redbone spotted bodies floating in the blue sea, turning a dark red. Both sides were taking a licking. Both sought to keep the booty for themselves, although for different reasons, one king and country, the other loot. Too busy staying alive, no one on the other ships noticed the *Hell's Fury* floating a distance away, ready to engage the winner. Still, the skirmish raged on for several hours. More cannons fired from the ship's batteries. Both ships were sustaining irreparable damage.

The *Hell's Fury* crew could only watch, cheering on the victor, whom it seemed was their fellow pirates. Still, the very pirates currently winning the day would soon give up the prize they had won. The freshly rested men of the Iron Born, some half-drunk, would swoop down upon the unsuspecting pirates and rob them of their ill-gotten gain.

The *Hell's Fury* prowled about, much like a lion preparing for an attack and maneuvering for the best advantage. As they circled the carnage, their sails, partly lowered, carried enough wind to reposition themselves if needed.

Fires broke out on both ships, although the sounds of musket fire abated. Redbone watched with great interest, spyglass to his eye, itching to join the fight.

But still, he waited. The view constantly changed as *Hell's Fury* sailed in a circular pattern. A group of men fought near the bow, engaged in swordplay. The Spanish seemed to lose; fewer men fought to save their ship.

Soon the Spanish flag was lowered, the death toll of a once-proud ship. A final barrage of small arms fire erupted. All fell silent. As Redbone spied out the victors, he saw pirates running across the gap carrying treasure and booty.

There was distant shouting as several men were hung up on the yardarm. Their bodies swung side to side. No less than eight men were being hanged all at once, no doubt the Spanish *Capitán* and his officers. Still, men continued scurrying across the two ships, carrying everything of value. Sometime later, the mooring lines were cut, and the sinking *Santisima Sacramento*, with its fifty-gun complement, was left to sink beneath the waves.

Whatever pirate ship this was, it would have

sustained damage during the fight. Redbone hoped so, anyway. He planned to take on a crippled ship, not one whose strength was at full measure.

"Capitán." The scallywag Mauricio appeared next to him. He hadn't shaved since leaving the Spanish Navy. His pirate clothing consisted of hand-me-downs from Redbone's wardrobe. And he now bore fresh marks from the Hag on his wrists. "Can I borrow your spyglass for a moment? Many of the men aboard the *Santisima Sacramento* were friends of mine. It's a shame to see them hanging on the yardarm like meat hanging at a butcher's shop."

"Aye, I understand; many of me shipmates have perished over the years, but with a bit of a difference. I am glad they are gone. Here, take me, spyglass."

Redbone walked away. Already he had seen through the spyglass the captain of the other ship staring at them, watching to see their intent. The moment had come for him to orchestrate the battle plans to take the booty from the other pirates. The other ship would assume that a fellow pirate, loyal to the brotherhood way of life, would steer clear of the captured prize.

Redbone's bounty was the highest—not for capture but for his head on a spike. When today's battle ended, he'd be not only wanted by his fellow pirates but by all the countries who hoped to profit in the Caribbean waters as well. But the Iron Born was loyal to no one except themselves, especially since having a reward for their capture.

After administering all the damage to its enemy, the other pirate ship unfurled its sails and began to depart.

A smile appeared on Redbone's face. He turned to Harv-Dog and said, "Ye thinks they will make off with our booty intact?"

"Aye, Captain, it seems to be their intentions, does it not?"

Redbone turned back and yelled, "Hoist the black flag."

Mr. Bisset quickly went into action, unfurled the giant flag, and hung it over the stern, snapping the cleats into place.

Now, ye will meet the Iron Born. Sadly, the result will be much like the Spanish ye slaughtered! Redbone thought. Turning to address his first mate and crew, he shouted, "Drop the sails, boys; it's time to give this pigeon a chase!" Redbone called the master gunner, "Mr. Arness, come here!"

Running up to the quarterdeck, Arness responded, "Aye, Captain?"

"Get down below. Do not open the hatches yet but wait until I give the order. Load the cannons on the port and starboard sides of the ship and make them ready to fire. I suspect to see them fire a barrage from our port side before long. Make haste, sir; we haven't much time."

More often than not, it always seemed a deadly game of cat and mouse, these games to win the prize. Although the *Hell's Fury* crew held all the cards, it still didn't mean they would come out victorious. If the two parties could agree, they could perhaps spare one another unnecessary bloodshed.

As their pirate ship gained speed, Redbone anticipated the battle ahead. He stood next to his navigator, and his men waited at their cannon stations below. His guerrillas on deck were ready to board the pirate ship. Every man was healthy and primed for war. Taking his spyglass, Redbone glanced at the escaping ship and watched the pirate captain glassing them.

Redbone wanted the stolen Spanish treasure. He needed it to pay his men. Their marred wrists confirmed their loyalty, but why continue an unprofitable quest if they weren't getting booty? There was no other reason to risk their lives to the hangmen's nooses.

The pirate ship looked familiar, but from what he could see of the pirate captain through his spyglass, the captain was not. Perhaps a junior officer made captain, and the original captain marooned on some God-forsaken island someplace? For now, all that mattered was that treasure.

Redbone's pirate ship soon gained speed on the crippled ship. The other ship sailed a straight course without maneuvering to escape as if suspecting a meeting of the minds. Smoke from down below decks still billowed out into the tropical sky, leaving a trail a blind man could follow.

Unpredictably, the black pirate flag was lowered, and, in its place, a white flag was quickly and deliberately unfurled. Seeing this change, Redbone whispered, "Aye, ye want to parley, do ye now?"

Redbone lowered his spyglass and looked at his navigator. "Mr. Sneed, maintain course, steady as she goes." Walking toward the railing, Redbone looked down at his first mate and shouted, "Mr. Schmidt, a change, sir! The pirates want to parley. Prepare us a longboat."

"A parley, Captain? Wouldn't it wiser to blast them out of the water and simply take the treasure?"

"Arrrr, the ship be crippled. If ye blast the ship further, she's liable to sink in deep water. Ye see for yerself the billowing smoke. Already there be danger of her capsizing! If they have any hope of saving themselves or us of saving the treasure, then a parley is in order, man. See to it at once."

Redbone heard someone behind him and turned to see Mr. Bissett. "Arrrr, what ye say, man?"

"Captain, the black flag, should we take it down?"

"No, ye be best to let it fly. We would not cowardly conceal ourselves as fellow pirates. Be proud to exhibit the flag; leave it, man."

"Aye, Captain, as you wish."

Gaining speed on the crippled vessel, Redbone shouted the command to lower the sails. Gratefully, calm seas prevailed, and as the *Hell's Fury* came alongside, she could see and smell the ship's burning fires and dark smoke down below decks.

By what miracle they survived, an encounter with the Spanish navy was still to be determined, but here they were, barely afloat and suffering badly. Already it seemed to Redbone that a large portion of their crew was missing. Whoever played the role of the captain had put these men in danger; the final result was the unnecessary loss of limbs and lives.

The two ships came alongside one another; the longboats were lowered, and the pirate crewman crawled down rope ladders into the boats and untied the lines. Each crew member grabbed an oar, and the two small craft rowed toward one another. When they met, Redbone eyed the younger pirate captain to see if he'd seen him before. Redbone waited for the man to speak.

"I wish to thank you, sir, for coming to our aid. You can see our predicament. It's sad to say; I never expected such a fight from the Spanish!"

"Aye, it be so when in the pirating business!"

"So, tell me, Captain, how long before my men can transfer ourselves aboard your ship?"

"Transfer yer men aboard the *Hell's Fury*, ye must be mad, sir!"

"Whatever do you mean, sir?"

"Tell me, lad, and be honest, have we met before? You seem familiar to me!"

"Yes, Redbone, we have met. However, it wasn't under pleasant circumstances. Back in Tortuga, we were ordered to surrender our master gunners or suffer death at your hands. At the time, I was no more than a quartermaster. I watched the whole affair unfold. My captain cursed you to damnation that day, but it didn't affect the outcome."

"Aye, see, we had no choice. Tortuga's pirate clan offered us no help, especially the governor, whose reputation preceded him in crude double-cross dealings. What's most troublesome is that ye stole what isn't yours to keep, lad. Ye see, we have been in chase of yer Spanish ship since she left Cartagena. There be no help to ye lad, I'm afraid! Now, if ye be so kind as to surrender the booty, ye can be on yer way."

"That's absurd, Redbone. My men fought to get that treasure, and we will not so easily give it up without a fight, you yellow pirate turncoat!"

"Arrrr, I be afraid ye'd see it that way, lad." Redbone, lifting his hand in the air, gave the prearranged signal, and the entire bay of cannon hatches shot open. The heavy irons were shoved outwards, pointing their barrels directly at the other pirate ship. Seeing the display of firepower, what could the young pirate captain do except surrender the booty? That was the logical choice, but things don't always go as planned, and before Redbone knew it, several other cannons were pointing their barrels back at the *Hell's Fury*.

"Aye, it seems a daring move, indeed, Captain," Redbone announced. "Now out with it, lad. What be yer name?"

"My name is Edward Teach."

"Aye, it seems a bit of a stalemate between two gentlemen, it does. Today, I have lost; ye hold the upper hand. There will be other days you'll be victorious, but today is not that day! To spare you further damage and the sinking of ye entire ship, I'm offering ye a compromise."

"A compromise, you say, Captain?"

"That be correct, it is! Now hear ye my proposal. Surrender two-thirds the treasure, and ye can sail away, unharmed, with enough to repair yer ship and pay yer men."

"I've seen your ruthlessness, myself, Redbone; tell me, how do I know you'll keep your word and not take all the treasure for yourself?"

"Ye don't! Decide now; me men have itchy fingers on the barrel."

Sickened by the idea of handing over the treasure, this Edward Teach also realized that all his crew dying wouldn't profit him either. The young captain spat in his hand and stuck it toward Redbone. He, in turn, did the same, and the two men shook on the bargain.

After ordering his men back to the sinking ship, Edward was followed by Captain Redbone and his men in tow. Redbone had called more longboats to follow to gather the treasure. Still, crew members were at their stations if this Edward Teach changed his mind. As an expression of kindness, Redbone ordered several of his men to help put out the pirate ship's fires.

In the end, soured by the loss, this Mr. Teach and his crew could only watch as the *Hell's Fury* sailed away carrying much richer men than before.

That night, with full goblets of rum, every man was given a share of the treasure. Some men were made rich by their position and status, while others soon gambled away their winnings. Redbone and Mr. Schmidt took a more significant portion of the treasure, but it wasn't enough to retire their position. To them, the formation of the Iron Born was worth more than coins or precious gold and gems. Weeks spent in Port Royal amongst their pirate brothers seemed a welcomed relief. Their stay was temporary, as every member of the Iron Born crew knew that soon they would embark on another adventure for more treasure. The odd thing was the announcement from Harv-Dog that he was retiring his buccaneering ways and returning to England. None was more surprised than Redbone, who thought he knew the man well. Harv-Dog had hidden from everyone that a fortune-teller he'd encountered in Port Royal had warned him that he would die painfully upon his next pirate voyage. That was it; he'd had enough; no more pirating ways. Besides, he had a childhood sweetheart back in Bristol whom he could not wait to visit.

As the *Hell's Fury* prepared to leave, all the crew wished Harv-Dog the best. As they slowly departed Port Royal, Redbone caught a final glimpse of the man he had relied upon for navigational skills and advice on matters that required the most finesse and honesty. Hoping for a happy life, he said his goodbyes.

Even when they were not aboard their ship, The Iron Born were easily identified. As the Iron Born gained popularity, so would those wanting to hunt the pirate band. One only needs to roll up their sleeves to expose the symbol that marred them forever.

Chapter 16

As THE YEARS WENT BY and the reputation of the Iron Born Pirates grew, their impending doom became more evident to Redbone. He understood that having no country's banner to sail under meant the eventual end of the feared pirate brotherhood.

All the while, the thought of retiring and living the life of a wealthy nobleman had been Redbone's hidden dream. All that was required was to retrieve the treasure he'd stolen from his former pirate captain De Vries. Although being a pirate captain was only allotted to the most successful privateers, the job was temporary at best. But Redbone was cunning and mistrusting and never diminished in cruelty. In the end, if the *Hell's Fury* captain was not successful, another captain could be chosen from a list of pirates waiting in the wings. So far, Redbone had met all challengers with his cutlass.

On one particular day, while sailing from Port Royal to San Juan, the man from the crow's nest broke the passing silence. "Ship off the starboard bow!" The crew hurried to starboard to have a look. There was what appeared to be a three-mast ship sailing away from their position. As if the curtain had just lifted on a well-choreographed play, all the characters, knowing their roles, went into action, directed by the notorious first mate Mr. Schmidt.

The commotion aboard the ship paused briefly when

Captain Redbone himself appeared on deck, dressed in his colorful red jacket. Its large pockets were outlined with stitching made from fine gold thread, with matching gold buttons, all in a row. His black boots gleamed from polish. A thick leather belt crossed his shoulder, with several muskets hanging free. His favorite weapon, his gold-handled cutlass, hung at his side. His tricorn sat atop his head, hanging past his shoulders, his black, powdered wig. Taking his place on the quarterdeck, he walked to the taffrail, lifted his spyglass, and stared at the prize.

"Full sail, Mr. Schmidt," he called. "We wouldn't want our little goose to escape, man. Quickly, tell the lads atop to hurry with the mainsails."

"Aye, aye, Captain." Mr. Schmidt felt disgusted and angry as he watched the latest addition to the Iron Born crew struggle with a sail. Turning to a senior crewman, he yelled, "Mr. Barnaby, see to it, sir. Go up top and give this lad a lesson on how to unfurl a sail, damn it, man."

"Right away, Mr. Schmidt."

While the first mate was busy getting the ship underway, Captain Redbone appeared next to the temporary navigator since Harv-dog's retirement.

"Steady as she goes, Mr. Bisset. We would not want our little guppy to get away."

"Captain, we need more sail, sir."

"That be taken care of as we speak. Turn her into the wind, man. Ye claim to be a navigator once in your career sailing these waters. Now prove yourself, or else ye find a new position aboard ship is that of cleaning out chamber pots."

"It shall be done, sir." Suddenly changing course, the giant ship pitched over to her side as her sails caught hold of the hidden power within the passing airstream. Gripping the wheel tightly, Bisset spun it several times, causing the ship to lift as it gained speed. Now on a course set to run down the boat ahead of them, the navigator turned to Redbone. "On numerous times past, the *Hell's Fury* has proven herself capable of giving chase. Why, sir, the mysterious ship will be ours in no time."

Mr. Schmidt appeared next to Redbone. "Captain, it took a little doing, but finally, we're under full sail. Tell me, do you believe the ship to be a Dutch merchant or perhaps a French brigantine?"

"We shall overtake this ship and see what profit can be given us for our efforts. Truly, I wouldn't expect too much in the way of profit, as I counted its sails to be square-rigged on the foremast and a gaff-rigged mainsail with square rig above it, obviously a brigantine by all standards."

"Now isn't the time to bring this up, but I must tell you that the crew has been grumbling. There hasn't been much profit as of late, and I overheard Zackery Lowe and Pierre le Grand saying there was a need for a new captain that could make them rich rather than chase down these accursed merchant ships with little or no profit."

"Oh, I see."

"Captain, these men bear the mark of the Iron Blood brotherhood. It's the only reason I find myself being lenient to their complaints. Otherwise, sir, they'd be shark food for their disrespect."

"No, Mr. Schmidt, it is true that I have a short temper regarding complaints from me crew. Still, let's see what profit this ship brings. Lately, I have struggled with returning to the Spanish Main, searching for a treasure galleon heavily laden with gold. Although the risk of such an adventure will put us in mortal danger, perhaps it's a risk I'm willing to take. Still, it remains to be seen."

"Aye, aye, sir."

"Mr. Schmidt, strike our colors, man. Let the cowards see who it is on their heels, sir."

"As you wish, Captain."

"A little closer, we'll fire a round broadside to halt

their foolish attempt to get away from us. Now see to it."

The merchant ship's tactics to outrun the *Hell's Fury* were outmaneuvered at every turn. Soon the French flag was unmistakable, flying off the transom. An order from Redbone to fire a salvo across their bow meant that all hope of escape was futile. Especially after the captain of the French ship saw the dreaded black flag bearing the design of the goblet and crossed swords. With horrid certainty, the French captain knew who was giving chase. His best course of action was to cease their efforts to get away and instead lower their sails. Perhaps the pirate captain, seeing their surrender, would offer some leniency. The captain worried for his two passengers aboard: the French noblewoman Jacqueline de Bellegarde and her handmaid. The noblewoman had obtained passage to sail to Fort-de-France on Martinique to meet her fiancé, Charles Comte d' Houdetot, an army brigadier.

Capitaine Henri Francois d' Aguesseau of the French ship *Dauphin Dansant* knew these pirates would soon arrive to take whatever they deemed valuable, and there was no way to stop them. He fired a salvo at the approaching pirate ship and hoped to land a few shots that would cripple and slow its approach. With her accompaniment of eight cannons, the smaller brigantine was no match against the pirates' giant barque sailing ship.

Giving orders to his crew, Capitaine Aguesseau directed the four cannons on his ship's port side to fire at the oncoming boat. Still too far away to be effective, the four rounds shot toward their mark but landed helplessly in the water. After the cannons were let loose, the French Capitaine ordered the ship's navigator to continue changing course to divert a barrage of cannon fire from the pirates.

Back in her cabin, Jacqueline could hear the

commotion above deck during the ship's desperate attempt to flee the approaching pirates. As the boat swayed from side to side, both women became ill. Jacqueline and her handmaid remained on their knees, praying for rescue. Though there was no time to consider their human frailties, Jacqueline prayed louder to avoid the seasickness.

Then as if on cue, the eruption of distant cannons sounded, and two distinct sounds of cannonballs whistled past their bow, landing in the water with mighty splashes. As the French ship's crew reloaded the cannons, they waited for the order to fire. Still, the pirates aboard the *Hell's Fury* hadn't returned fire, which Capitaine Aguesseau found curious.

Perhaps now—yes—the pirate scum is close enough, Capitaine Aguesseau thought. "Fire!" he screamed. The ship rocked as the blast of cannon fire erupted below decks, and as he and his crew watched with anticipation, two of the four cannonballs hit their mark. One hit the bow, and the other hit the forecastle, tearing into the ship's superstructure—a blast of timber splinters landed in the water as a direct result. Still, the vessel kept coming.

It was apparent to Capitaine Aguesseau that these pirates didn't want to sink them or damage the *Dauphin Dansant*. No, they had other plans. They desired to board the French ship and take her as a prize. Most of his crew would die fighting. His staff of only thirty men could not match the pirates, who no doubt were at least ninety men, if not more.

What choices did he have? His first loyalty belonged to his passengers and then his crew. Although now, what little chance did any of them have at surviving this encounter? Seeing the dreaded Iron Born flag flying off the transom, he knew that these particular pirates were the cruelest of them all.

Of course, the murder of young men was one reason he retired from service in the French navy. He had hunted pirates such as these throughout his career, and the outcome was always the same, hanging, no matter the age. Seeing a young cabin boy hanging on the gallows has become too much.

Knowing his crew would not receive mercy, Capitaine Aguesseau pondered what to do. Surrender without a fight? To fight or flee? Perhaps fleeing was his only option. Thinking about the women, he knew their fate.

Although showing cowardice went against his grain, Capitaine Aguesseau knew that surrendering meant they would die to the last man. The master gunner waited for his order to fire. The pirate ship was clearly in range as it continued on its course to intercept.

Meanwhile, the first mate, back aboard the *Hell's Fury*, appeared, saying, "Captain Redbone, sir. The gun crew is standing by awaiting your orders to fire upon the French ship; why you haven't given the order already is anyone's guess."

"Aye indeed, Mr. Schmidt, I have been considering our situation and the men aboard the *Hell's Fury*. Something is disturbing about the number of scallywags we have signed on and the fact that we have no more room to house our pirates. Our ship can only care for a crew of a hundred and twenty; we have surpassed this amount and currently have a crew of over one hundred forty men. I want to capture this French brigantine. Together the two ships will be quite a formidable fighting force, making it easier to attack and claim any prize we seek.

"It's making sense to me now; I understand your reasoning. Take the French prize and make it our own. Tell me, sir, what of the crew of the French ship? Assuredly, we have too many sailors and cannot afford to take on more crewmen."

"No, obviously not! Tell me, Mr. Schmidt, are ye not familiar with the term cutthroat?"

"Yes, I grasp your meaning, Captain. As you wish, Sir."

"Tell the master gunner to keep the gun crew at the ready as we come alongside, just in case they decide to fire upon us. By nightfall, this prize shall be ours."

"A brilliant plan, if I say so myself, Captain." With nothing else to be said, Mr. Schmidt walked away to prepare the Iron Born clan for the upcoming raid.

As the *Hell's Fury* drew closer to the French brigantine, she still hadn't fired her cannon or given any defensive response. Instead, the ship tried various tactical maneuvers to evade the approaching pirate vessel, all of which amounted to nothing.

Redbone eyed the proceedings from his perch. Glancing down at the main deck, he saw his fiercest crew members standing ready to board the French ship. Looking forward through his spyglass, he saw what he desired most. A white flag was hanging off the transom of the brigantine. The French Capitaine wanted to parley. Seeing this, Redbone called out to Mr. Schmid. "Have ye crew stand down. It seems these French want to have a word."

"Men, you heard the captain. Stand at the ready."

Moans of displeasure echoed throughout the crew as they stood in place and didn't move.

As Redbone watched, the smaller French brigantine lowered her sails and slowed her pace. Nevertheless, all the ship's gun ports remained open, ready to fire. The *Hell's Fury* pulled alongside, and both captains met at the gunwales.

The French Capitaine yelled from his ship, "I can see the Iron Born flag hanging off your stern, Capitaine. I wish to have a word with you before any of my men are lost. I beg us to parley, Monsieur. Assuredly, you are a reasonable man and can see that there is no need for bloodshed."

"Hear me now," shouted Redbone, "off your port side is an uninhabited island. Steer your ship there and set anchor. We shall have a parley once both our ships have come to a complete rest."

"Very well, Capitaine, as you wish."

Redbone gave the order to have the sails trimmed and stowed. Three men ran toward the bow. The calm seas and a gentle wind allowed the two ships to slow beside each other.

Once the two ships stopped, held tight by their anchor chains, Mr. Schmidt was ordered to join Redbone on the quarterdeck; he wished for a word in private. Redbone instructed Schmidt to tell Hunter and his group of assassins to meet him in his cabin for a particular assignment.

"At once, Captain," the large man replied and left Redbone at his station.

Taking one last look at his prize, Redbone whispered, "Aye, soon, you small guppy, you'll be one of us." Returning to his cabin, he poured a glass of rum and downed it quickly, then filled his glass a second time. He heard a knock on his door, and Hunter and seven other pirates entered.

"Hunter, I be having a special assignment for ye. I needs ten of yer best swimmers. All of ye will be equipped with swords and knives. You, Mr. Hunter, will lead the attack once the two ships have set anchors. Yer men will sneak out the ship's starboard side, through the gun port at station twelve, and swim over and take control of the French ship. Meantime, their captain will be invited over to share a glass of cognac. When the deed is done, and you have set a lit lantern over the bow, then I meself will deal with the captain."

"Aye, Captain Redbone, the French ship is as good

as yours," Hunter replied, and he and his men left the Redbone's cabin to prepare for the assault.

Meanwhile, aboard the *Dauphin Dansant*, Capitaine Aguesseau considered the pirate's acceptance to parley suspicious. However, what choice did he have? Concern for the two ladies aboard his ship had influenced his decision to avoid firing his cannons. Again, he hoped to spare his men from certain death. A parley gave some hope that they would remain alive.

As the French crew busied themselves with the upcoming meeting, there was a knock on Capitaine Aguesseau's door. Jacqueline de Bellegarde and her handmaid stood there when he opened it.

"Excuse me, Capitaine Aguesseau; please don't tell me that you intend to surrender to these pirates?"

"I beg your pardon, Mademoiselle de Bellegarde, this is not the time to discuss battle tactics with a lady. I'm trying to keep everyone alive, and I cannot be bothered by your concerns."

"How rude, Capitaine. I have never been treated with such disrespect. I promise you, Monsieur, you shall hear from my fiancé, Charles. Once he hears of your mistreatment of his beloved, he will strike you down where you stand."

"You foolish woman, do you not realize who's anchored off our starboard? It's the Iron Born pirates. Assuredly you have heard of their deeds and how ruthless these men are, not just in reputation but in their thirst for blood and cruelty above all other pirates sailing these waters. We will be lucky to survive this encounter with our lives. Now pardon me, I have a meeting with their Capitaine."

Jacqueline stepped aside with nothing more to say, allowing Capitaine Aguesseau to leave his cabin. Two crew members stood at the taffrail; a small dingy was already lowered into the water, awaiting his arrival. As

Aguesseau got inside the small boat, a strange feeling overcame him. Would he ever see his crew again? As the small party rowed away, Lady Jacqueline and her maidservant watched with fear and desperation.

Chapter 17

When the small party arrived at the pirate ship, a ladder was lowered to the waterline. Telling his men to stay in the boat, Aguesseau ascended. There to meet him was one of the largest men he'd ever seen—not only tall but with massive muscles and a heaving chest—a man not to be crossed.

"Come this way, Captain Redbone wants a word," was Mr. Schmidt's harsh demand.

Following the giant to the captain's cabin, Aguesseau couldn't help but notice the sneers and vile stares from the pirate crew. It was as if they were caged animals waiting for word from their master to attack and devour his French carcass.

The first mate knocked on the door of Redbone's cabin. After some time, hearing the command to enter, they entered.

"Come in, Captain; ye have a seat; I want to discuss thee details of yer surrender."

"My surrender, Monsieur?"

"Aye, yes, but before we get to that, I would like to offer ye a glass of rum to ease yore conscience, so to speak."

"I'm not sure this is the time for alcohol, and my conscience is not your concern, Monsieur. My hope in having this parley was to come to an understanding between two sea captains and avoid innocent bloodshed."

"Innocent blood, ye say, tell me whether such a thing exists. As a babe, perhaps one is innocent, but soon a soul is corrupted and stained in this harsh world we inhabit!"

"Capitaine Redbone, I'm not here to discuss one's theory on life but to try to save my men and the two ladies aboard my ship."

A sudden outburst of musket fire and screams of dying men echoed between the two ships. Turning to his captive, Redbone said, "That is where ye are wrong, Captain."

Suddenly, the reality of what was happening aboard his ship rocked Aguesseau. He understood that he had been fooled into believing that Redbone would honor their agreement. "Wha…what is happening to my men aboard my ship, you son of a whore? You tricked me into believing that you would honor the parley as gentlemen. I must return to my ship at once!"

Walking over to the window to look, Redbone waited for a sign. It wasn't long before he saw the lit lantern hanging off the bow of the French ship. He turned to the unsuspecting captain. "No, I be afraid ye don't see me meaning. Ye see, when I discussed the 'innocent' earlier, I was only referring to those first precious moments when a child is born into this world." Redbone positioned himself within a few inches of his captive. Without warning, he drew a small dagger and repeatedly thrust it into the captain's heart before he had a chance to defend himself.

A look of surprise glazed over the man's face as he stumbled forward, dying. Aguesseau stared with vile hatred toward his killer, holding onto the ship's beam. As the last remnants of life disappeared from the man, Redbone poured himself a cognac. Taking a long drink, he turned to the dying man. "Understand me, *Monsieur,* the swashbucklers aboard this vessel do not parley with anyone. We take what we want, and today it is yer ship we want! To hell with yore crew; they shall all meet yore fate except the two ladies ye mention. I have other plans for them!"

Aguesseau, falling to the floor dead, could no longer hear Redbone's boasting.

"Mr. Schmidt, a word."

Standing by outside the door, the first mate opened it to see the dead French captain on the floor. "You called me Captain?"

"Yes, Mr. Schmidt, have ye men assembled on thee deck. I want to examine our new ship."

"What of the dead, sir?"

"You know what's to be done. Complete a thorough search for a doctor, navigator, or any man of talent that can be useful. As for any survivors, assemble them on deck. Tell me, the men who brought thee, captain?"

"They surrendered without a fight."

"No honor in a coward's death, then. What of the two women that our dead Frenchman spoke of?"

"All are assembled above deck, sir, awaiting your command."

"Arrrr, that be good news indeed; now call the two cabin boys here at once to clean up this mess. I shall join ye in a few moments. Prepare thee Bloody Hag for ye ritual. I feel that one or two will be begging to join thee brotherhood. Of course, with two ships in our control, this will be much easier than before."

"I understand, Captain." With his orders laid out, Mr. Schmidt disappeared. Returning to the dead Frenchman, Redbone removed anything of value, including an expensive gold watch and a small snuff box ornately carved from ivory. Opening the box, he withdrew some snuff, placed it between his thumb and index finger, and snuffed it into the nasal cavity, instantly delivering a quick nicotine hit. When the two cabin boys arrived, the dead Frenchman had already been stripped naked and was lying outside the captain's door.

Abisai turned to Brendon and said, "We'd better hurry with this." Brendon nodded his head.

No strangers to seeing corpses, they had grabbed the man's arms and legs and begun to pull the body away when a harsh voice yelled out from beyond the partly opened door. "Lads, return at once and mop thee floor inside me cabin; it smells of Frenchman. Afterward, you will find some clothing lying in my chair, take these items and wash them clean. Now hurry away with ye." Redbone appeared at the cabin door, dressed in his most elegant garb, and walked past the two youths.

Abisai whispered, "No, sir, I wouldn't want to meet that man in a dark alley."

"What? Our Captain Redbone. No, you're mistaken; he's our leader; what better man to lead the Iron Born brotherhood?" Brandon paused. "I've heard whispers saying there needs to be a change in leadership."

"Quiet, man. What you say, I wouldn't want anyone to hear you speak those words aloud."

"I'm just telling you what I've heard from the cook. It's not me suggesting that we change captains. Besides, I like Redbone; he's always been kind to me; I can't wait to take the oath, can you? I believe you turn of age next month."

"Yes, I know, the ritual of the bloody dance with the Hag,"

"Aren't you scared?"

"Who wouldn't be? I have seen brave men dance with the iron maiden and die. They had great strength, but it wasn't enough."

"You'll do fine, Abisai. Besides, no one here knows of the time you killed that reef shark trying to eat your younger sister, all of this with only a knife. No, you're the bravest boy I know!"

ON DECK, Redbone casually examined the sight before him. All of the captives knelt on deck. The two ladies the deceased French captain spoke about were dressed in colorful finery, along with four remaining crew members.

"Captain, these sad leftovers before you, sir, are the lone survivors," Schmidt announced. "The small group includes one navigator, one acting cook who performs as the ship's doctor, and two worthless merchantmen of no value."

"Very well, Mr. Schmidt. Ye know what to do with the merchantmen. In all me days, I have discovered that merchantmen have no stomach for looting and piracy. Thee same could be said about tits on a boar, sir, worthless in any case."

A simple nod to his first mate, and Mr. Schmidt withdrew his sword and ran it through the first man without hesitation. Just as quickly, he drew his sword in a single stroke. Afterward, the man let out an ear-piercing scream and fell on his face dying. Schmidt turned to the other man with his red-coated saber still in his hand.

Desperately, the man cried out, "Capitaine Redbone, sir. Throughout the Caribbean waters, it is well known that your crew is the most feared of all pirates. It is why I beg you to allow me to take my chances at becoming a member of your crew rather than die a cowardly dog like my late friend Tumas. I'm not a simple merchantman as you believe; I have acted as a spy and played a significant role in the occupation of Madrid, where I reported back to my commanders about the town's defenses, putting my life in mortal danger."

"Arrrr, fine, as ye wish, this evening ye shall dance with the Hag." Turning to the rest of the *Dauphin Dansant's* crew, Redbone proclaimed, "Are ye willing to become a member of me crew, or do you find it better to dance with me first mate Mr. Schmidt, whose ax has an unquenchable thirst for blood?"

"Aye, aye, Captain, it is better to die as fighting men than suffer the same fate as Tumas," the cook yelled out for all to hear. The other crew members nodded in agreement.

Mr. Schmidt turned and shouted, "Lads, looks like we shall be having an Iron Blood ceremony."

The crew began chanting, "A dance with the Hag, A dance with the Hag, to test their metal. If not worthy and the man's life ends, then the Devil can have what remains!"

The pirate crew went to work disposing of the dead sailor's body and taking the remaining crew members down below to be housed until the ceremony. Redbone approached the two women. He stopped in front of the more finely dressed woman and said, "Tonight, ma'am, ye shall be me dinner guest, and afterward, ye shall warm me bed." It was evident to him who was the lady and who played the part of the servant.

"Excuse me, Monsieur, but you mistake me for a whore or some other loose woman. I refuse to dine with you and will take my chances inside your prison cell rather than give myself to your wanton desires. Besides, I'm already engaged and have no intention of being with a man before my wedding day; this I have sworn to God himself."

Turning to his first mate, Redbone said, "Ye hovering angel, then?"

"Aye, aye, as you wish, Captain."

"Monsieur, I demand to know what this hovering angel is that you speak of," said Jacqueline de Bellegarde.

"It be a simple matter, really. Ye are to be taken to me cabin and stripped of all your clothing. Afterward, your legs will be tied together, and you will be deposited out me window and hang there until you submit to me wishes."

"I shall never give myself to you, cowardly dog."

"Ma'am, if that be the case, and ye chose death over a romantic evening with such a notable pirate as meself, then so be it. I shall cut the line that holds yer earthly remains aloft and deposit them into thee sea for yonder sharks to feed. The choice is entirely yers alone. You see, over the years, I have fought to win over a woman's heart and have their body as me own, but with all the kicking and screaming that one must endure, by the time their will is exhausted, I be too bloody tired to enjoy what reward I have coming to me. No, the choice is totally up to you but know this, I will not hesitate to cut yer lifeline."

"Tell me, what of my young handmaid, Adrienne?"

"I suppose that be up to ye, although she seems to need dieting to thin her roundness. Regardless, aboard this ship, she will find true love in the arms of me crew members. What finer gentleman could she hope to acquire than an Iron Born pirate? Why she'd be the envy of all the ladies at court when they asked her about her romantic escapades? Aye, no doubt she would become most popular among the ladies."

"I have but one other question; what happens to Adrienne if I die while hanging from the rope?"

Stepping forward and kneeling, Redbone shouted, "If ye choose to die rather than give yerself to me, then yore handmaid would enjoy the company of all me men, from the oldest to the very youngest aboard this ship. Afterward, no value to anyone, she would be tossed overboard where the fishes could dine on her remains."

Looking at her handmaid, Jacqueline didn't want to be responsible for the horrid rape by all the pirates because she refused to sleep with the captain; it didn't seem right. But she felt within her heart that she could never sleep with another man while engaged to Charles Comte d' Houdetot. *Oh, Charles, what choice do I have? Will you ever forgive me?*

"Tell me your answer, Ma'am, or else I make the decision meself," Redbone warned.

Taking another glance at Adrienne, whose look of terror said it all, Jacqueline knew what she had to do.

She observed the pirate captain. His looks were not at all disgusting, and perhaps he could have been a proper suitor in another life. But apart from this, Jacqueline was a virgin.

"Tell me, wench, I grow tired of your games."

There is something to be said about showing yourself strong in the face of danger. What man couldn't resist the attraction of a woman's alluring propositions? Now in the hands of these ruthless men, Jacqueline decided to bargain her future. Betting all to fate, Jacqueline stood to her feet and addressed both captain and crew. "Throughout the Caribbean, none is feared more than the Iron Born. All of you men have built a reputation as the most ruthless pirates. Yet, there is a code of conduct between you men bearing the mark that we, the innocent, must admire. It is well known that you never leave yours behind. This undying fortitude is rare amongst your pirate brothers. It is the very reason I implore you to show mercy for my handmaiden and me. I realize that what I'm asking for is unique, but I wish to strike a bargain."

Suddenly, all around the deck, the pirate crew members sounded out, "A bargain, the lady wishes to bargain, Captain!"

"I see that she does. What about it, men? Ye know yerselves that our kind doesn't bargain. We take what we desire and kill those that stand in our way. Ours is a proud tradition of piracy that goes back to ancient times when those poor men starving to feed their families sought a better way of life and refused to bend the knee to the wealthy few who have more than they should. No, me fellow Iron Born, we do not bargain!"

"Bargain, the lady wishes to bargain," came the

shouts, louder than the first time. Looking at his crew, it quickly became apparent that the men would not relent in their demands. He turned back and stared at the woman. "What bargain is it that ye seek? Hurry now with yer words. My passions are rising, and I grow anxious for female company."

"Captain Redbone, sir, soon you and your fellow pirates will perform your ritual to send off your crewmen that perished; afterward, these men who wish to join your crew and become Iron Born pirates will dance with your Bloody Hag. Allow me to suffer the hovering angel for no more than six bells. If I survive the encounter, you will release my handmaid and me unharmed and deposit us both at the nearest port available; what do you say, Captain?"

Looking over his crew and seeing the smiles plastered on their faces, Redbone felt he had little choice in the matter. He knew that if he didn't agree to the lady's terms, it would bring him closer to the end of his career as a captain.

"Arrrr, have the lady prepared at once! Inform Mr. Bisset I need his services." Stepping closer, Redbone remarked, "Mademoiselle, you shall find Mr. Bisset to your liking. Both you and he have much in common. He is a man who has a flair for pretty things in this life, much like yourself. He is the man that shall undress you and attach ropes to your naked body. Know this: if you are noble and deserve to survive this test, it will be because ye hung on the end of a rope, not for a mere six bells but eight. If ye can endure such an achievement, then ye shall have your freedom, but if not, I shall take your innocence from you." Having nothing else to say, Redbone disappeared and prepared the *Dauphin Dansant* to join his pirate arsenal.

A young man appeared, carrying a long rope. He was dressed in colorful silks and a white powdered wig.

"Mademoiselle, please come with me at once." Mr. Bisset repeatedly apologized, saying, "Oh my heavens, how dreadful that you must endure the hovering angel. Few ladies ever survive such an encounter. It's horrible, you know, how they bang against the ship. After a few hours, their resolve fades. Yes, of course, some hearty souls resist to the end. The sad outcome, you'll see for yourself, those deep gashes in the windowsill."

"That's horrible," Adrienne remarked.

"Nothing less than I would expect from this scoundrel, Redbone," Jacqueline cried out.

As the party arrived at the captain's cabin, two boys were leaving carrying a mop bucket: the water inside was a deep red. The unmistakable smell of death lingered in and around the cabin door. As they passed, the hopeless expressions on the boys' faces spoke volumes.

Walking inside, Mr. Bisset proclaimed, "Here we are, ladies, please, let us hurry and prepare ourselves for the ritual. It will soon be six bells, and what better time to begin counting down the hours than to hear the night watchman announce each hour that you must endure this dreaded testing of your virtue? You will be able to hear the commotion aboard the ship as we send off our fellow Iron Born that have passed and then begin the ritual for the scallywags wanting to join our little merry band. Please hurry now and allow me to help you undress, Mademoiselle."

"No, Monsieur, I can manage to undress by myself. If I need any help, it will come from my handmaid."

"As you wish, but please hurry soon. Redbone will arrive and check on you, and I, for one, would not want to disappoint that man."

It took nearly ten minutes before Jacqueline was utterly naked. As she removed the stockings on her feet, Mr. Bisset refused to allow it, saying, "Please leave those on; it will help prevent the rope burn." Suddenly, the announcement that Jacqueline dreaded most had arrived—the sound of the watchman saying, "Six bells and all is well!"

Gratefully, Mr. Bisset did not seem the least bit interested in examining her body, and with his help, Jacqueline found herself crawling out the captain's window. She gripped the windowsill before descending and saw the window frame's deep cuts from the last victims' humiliations. Standing completely naked, being modest, she did her best to keep covered. Quickly, she understood Mr. Bisset's kindness in allowing her to keep her stocking on her legs. Otherwise, the rope would have instantly burned her skin.

Finally, she reached the end of the rope and looked upward. She saw the panic on Adrienne's face. She began the ceremony of the hovering angel. Knowing there was a time limit to this torture helped her hang onto the rope rather than surrender to despair. Perhaps she could endure this ritual and save her and her handmaid's lives. A commotion from the captain's cabin made her look up. Redbone stared down at her.

"Mademoiselle, I hope that ye are comfortable. There has never been another time in your life that ye have faced such danger." He grabbed the rope and jerked it side to side. "Aye, Mr. Bisset has done his job well. We wouldn't want ye come loose and fall into the deep now, would we?"

Jacqueline chose her words wisely. The man staring down at her naked body had the final say on whether she lived or died. It was not the time to show arrogance or pride. Instead, Jacqueline cried, "I shall come through this test victorious. Please, as a gentleman, keep my handmaid safe from harm."

"There be no need to worry. Currently, I have Adrienne busy cleaning me cabin. There is something about a woman's touch that I admire regarding cleanliness. No, you must remain strong if not for yerself, then for your handmaid. However, I would not be a gentleman if I did not inform ye that there are rough seas ahead. Sailing the Caribbean, the weather can change at a moment's notice. Ye should feel grateful that I be looking out for ye. Now ye have been warned what to expect!"

"Thank you, Captain Redbone. Please, won't you reconsider this ridiculous trial? Bring me back inside, and I'm sure that we can come to some understanding."

Redbone found something humorous in her statement and began laughing loudly. A moment later, he said, "Mademoiselle, already ye have the key to your freedom. All that's required is a few nights of passion with yours truly, and afterward, I shall set ye free meself on any island ye choose, both you and your handmaid."

"No, sorry, Captain, it is not within me to give myself over to you without a fight. It is the character that you pirates admire most; I understand. I will show that I am strong in the face of danger. Surrendering without a fight is not within me."

"True, very true, Mademoiselle. I hope ye change your mind, but for now, I be willing to wait, as time will not allow me to argue any further. I have a funeral to attend. A few of my men died while taking your ship. You will hear the grand affair from your roost. Please make yourself comfortable. I shall check on ye a few hours. I have positioned Mr. Bisset here in my cabin to listen for your cries of surrender. When the time comes, he will inform me of your request. Afterward, ye will be brought upward into a place of shelter from the cold and into the arms of warmth and passion."

Jacqueline remained steadfast in her resolve not to surrender her womanly virtue, and with nothing else to say, she focused on surviving her ordeal. She quickly became uncomfortably cold, but she also learned that she could pull her body up by grabbing the rope, giving some relief from the blood pooling down at her head. She then needed the privy, but this small hurdle was quickly dealt with.

She began to laugh as she thought of the irony that this ship belonged to one of the most feared pirate groups ever created, and she was now pissing upon it. She imagined Redbone shouting out curses, and she laughed again in defiance.

Of course, this situation was dire, a matter of life and death. These cutthroats were ruthless and could throw her and her handmaiden overboard at any moment. But still, if only once in her life would she show herself strong, this was the precise time to do it. It seemed that all the pirates aboard agreed to take up her cause, no doubt to the disliking of their captain. Nonetheless, here she hung, like a piece of meat at the end of a rope.

The ropes cut her delicate hands, and she quickly grew tired. Lifting her entire weight became tiresome, and she had to let herself fall after some time. Above her, men shouted to one another, a commotion of sorts. Redbone began shouting out something about the men he'd lost in the battle, how they, the Iron Born, died bravely for their shipmates. As the shouts rumbled above, Jacqueline could feel the rope holding her aloft cut into her flesh.

She struggled to lift herself again but could only raise herself a short way up. As time passed, she noticed above her that the clouds were darkening, and the ship was beginning to rock more heavily from side to side. Below her, the waves became choppy and splashed against the transom.

As Jacqueline held on to the single rope for dear life, Adrienne called her from the window. "Mademoiselle, tell me, how are you?" The desperate question needed no answer, as anyone finding themselves in this situation would attest. Taking a long breath, she said nothing.

Mr. Bisset appeared next to her maid. "Mademoiselle, were you able to hear the ship's announcement? It is now past eight bells. Stay strong and be encouraged; you can do this."

But could she? Hanging there, banging against the back of the ship, was not an easy task. She thought of her fiancé and whispered, "Charles, where are you now? Did you not realize the danger in allowing me to sail these waters? Did you think how pirates could capture me—the most desperate of all pirates, the Iron Born? Curse you, Charles, that I find myself here because of your desire to have me in Fort-de-France on Martinique."

She became increasingly angry as she realized the total weight of her test. *Two hours it's only been two hours! How can I ever hope to endure such a trial for eight hours?* She screamed aloud curses, although her shouting was muffled by the sounds of the wind, which was howling ever more forcefully now. It felt good to release the pent-up anger, even if it was only heard by herself.

The darkness of night appeared as if a curtain had fallen, erasing the daylight as a storm approached. Lanterns came alive in the captain's cabin, the soft glow reminding her of her childhood when she and her family would take outings to the coastline. She could still imagine her mother cooking in the small kitchen. The memory soothed her, giving her a moment's respite from the misery of the cold that robbed her flesh of warmth.

As she hung on that rope and rocked back and forth, she noticed that the waves traveled the length of the ship, appearing near the transom and rising to an alarming height. Above her, the festivities were nothing short of spectacular. It seemed that one of the scallywags had survived the bloody ceremony and was being hailed as a new crew member, although another had died from blood loss, as evidenced by the howls and boos from the crew.

A short time later, a wave splashed her, and she saw the hopeful buccaneer's corpse drift past. His eyes stared coldly up at her as if he were searching for the afterlife door. He slowly floated past and disappeared from view.

A cold numbness covered her bare skin, blood pooling in her head as she hung upside down. Her long hair had come unfurled and occasionally dipped into the water. Who could have devised such an act of cowardice? This pirate, Redbone, must be the creator. Still, one had to see the brilliance in his scheme. Who could hang for such a long period and hope to survive the ordeal? In the end, how would she fare? Would she give in to the man's desires, or become a hovering angel departing into the afterlife, much like the poor soul who drifted past her a short time ago?

Above her, a man's voice called out, "Mademoiselle, were you able to hear the ship's announcement? It is now past ten bells. Stay strong and be encouraged; you can do this."

"Ten bells, what happened to nine?" She never heard the announcement of nine bells. Now, more than ever, her situation was becoming alarming. No longer could she think clearly. She realized she was no longer fighting to stay erect. Somehow, while reminiscing, she had surrendered to the weight of her hanging body, much like a piece of meat from the butcher shop—and she no longer cared. The strength to pull herself upward had left her, and the waves broke just a few feet below her head. Her hair occasionally dipped into the cold water, but she no longer fought against it.

Her body was numb, but hunger pangs assailed her. She thought about Charles and asked the question most troubling. *Could Charles forgive her for the betrayal?* If his pledges of love were genuine, they could survive this test. Another question. *Is it that important whether or not she waits for her wedding night, or should she give herself to this pirate? It is her body to give away as she wishes. What marriage bed would there be if she died at the rope's end?*

She could no longer hang on to this accursed rope. She had fought with all her might and lost in the end. She would surrender her hopes for a happy marriage to the man she loved most. *Charles, please forgive me. I don't wish to die.* Jacqueline stared up at the open window. Not in her wildest dreams had she ever expected to end up in this predicament. It must be the will of God, no other. With one final look into the dark and murky sky, Jacqueline asked for forgiveness for what she must do.

"I surrender, I surrender all. Bring me up, please, in God's name, and may he forgive me for what I'm about to do!"

Chapter 18

SPENDING TIME IN the company of pirates for over three weeks was an experience Jacqueline never wished to repeat. She'd been reduced to nothing but a bed whore, and this pirate captain drank too much and snored. Although she was not privy to his business dealings, there was something in the works: something that involved her and Adrienne.

It was a well-known practice of pirates to hold captives for ransom and barter their lives for money. She would fetch a shiny penny, a French aristocrat, but what if dear sweet Charles couldn't or wouldn't pay their price? Would she be forever a whore to this pirate?

The idea seemed incredible, but she prayed daily for their safe return and rescue.

The ship made a stop in Petit-Goâve during the night. A small boat paddled into shore. The five men inside returned to the ship some six hours later. Overhearing them discussing plans with Redbone, Jacqueline made out one word: ransom.

Redbone seemed quite pleased with his plans and drank himself to sleep that night. It was the first time he had kept his dirty hands from her body in almost a week, a welcome relief. She longed to return home and be with her family. The thoughts of being married to her fiancé were fading with each passing day. Charles would know that this captain, no gentleman by any standards, had raped her continually—although one could not precisely say rape. Not anymore. This captain has treated her kindly, not forcing her to commit acts that she would deem unpleasant.

In time, her opinion toward these cutthroat pirates softened. They had treated her and Adrienne rather well. Adrienne was proposed to on more than one occasion. Although she refused to accept any offers, she confided in Jacqueline that she had become enamored with the first mate, Mr. Schmidt. His tall stature and muscular body were eye-catching, and Adrienne did her best to get close to the man. A known killer and ruthless pirate, his reputation attracted Adrienne to him like a bee to honey. And he had offered his cabin to the ladies, a kind gesture from a ruthless killer.

As the ship anchored in an inlet near Petit-Goâve, a small boat again left the vessel to return some hours later. A lone pirate came to Redbone's cabin and delivered a message. The pirate captain read it and smiled.

"What is it, Capitaine?" asked Jaqueline.

"Mademoiselle, it seems that yer fiancé has agreed to pay the ransom for yer safe return to Fort-de-France."

Jacqueline only stared at him. She did not smile or seem happy at the news. "What is it, madam? Why I could swear, ye'd be happy to hear the news."

"Capitaine Redbone, you, sir, have wreaked havoc on my virtue and left me a life with little hope for a happy marriage. No, sir, you have had your way with me, and now you hope to discard me as if I'm nothing but garbage. Tell me, sir, do you truly believe a man will want to marry me now?"

"It be true, we both have engaged in an exchange of sexual passions that none would deem unpleasant, but still, lass, ye be forgetting that the man ye have been sleeping with is captain of this ship. What happens aboard the *Hell's Fury* is no one's concern except me own. I have a plan, but to make it believable, it will be both unpleasant and hurtful. But I believe it will carry the day, and in the end, no one the wiser except the men aboard the *Fury*."

"Capitaine, tell me your plan. I'm excited to hear how you will save my virtue as a lady."

SEVERAL DAYS LATER, two parties met on an isolated beach at a prearranged location. Captain Redbone, his first mate, and two other men, plus the French noblewoman Jacqueline de Bellegarde and her handmaid, met an attachment of soldiers from Fort-de-France. Charles Comte d' Houdetot led the military officers.

Two pirates dragged the ladies through the white sandy beach and stopped halfway. Redbone held onto Jacqueline's arm while Mr. Schmidt, brandishing his shining ax, stood behind the party in case any trickery was tried.

Still some distance away, Charles shouted, "Jacqueline, my beloved, are you well, my dear? Tell me, have these brigands mistreated you?"

Charles, hearing no reply, got closer and strained to listen. There was no response. "Captain Redbone, you scoundrel, what have you done to my fiancé?" Coming closer, he again asked, "Jacqueline, tell me, are you hurt?" He saw that a shawl covered Jacqueline's eyes, and she was gagged from speaking. Charles's worries mounted, and he became angry.

Staring at Redbone, Charles noticed that this man, too, wore a scarf across his face and gave no response.

Turning back to his men carrying a heavy chest of pieces of eight, Charles shouted, "Here, take this Redbone; I'm sorry to say you won't be spending it anytime soon. As soon as I'm able, I will order a British man-of-war to hunt you down; you'll pay dearly for what you've done."

Redbone did not need to count the loot; he knew that

Charles was an honorable man and would never risk cheating them of their money, not if it meant the life of his intended. Mr. Schmidt walked over, picked up the heavy chest, and returned behind Redbone.

Redbone approached Charles, dragging Jacqueline by her arm. "Arrrr, here be ye lady, and curse the wench to hell. In all me years, I have never met such a wildcat. Why she shreds me, sorely. Behold me face and see me scars, man." Removing the scarf from his face, Charles could see nail marks and scars across Redbone's face. The damage looked dreadful. "Take yer wench before I forget meself and remove me musket and shoot the bitch!"

Stunned, Charles never expected to see such deep cuts on the pirate's face, especially not from the tender-hearted lady he had known and proposed to just a short time ago. Now safely in the arms of her beloved's embrace, Jacqueline began to cry bitterly. Charles started to console her, wrapping his arms around the woman he loved. As the pirates began to leave, Jacqueline removed her scarf. In horror, Charles gasped; an instant later, seeing the damage caused to her face, he too began to cry. Her split lip and black eyes, the swelling across her delicate nose, meant only one thing, her virtue was still intact, and she paid a high price to keep her virginity.

"My dear, I'm so sorry you had to experience all of this; believe me, if I could erase the memories, I would do so."

"Charles, do you love me?"

"Why, my dear, would you ask such a question?"

"Please answer me, Charles. I realize I'm no longer pleasant to look upon, but please, Charles, answer me now. Do you still love me?"

"With all my heart, I love you."

"If that's true, my love, let's not delay and become husband and wife this very day."

"What are you saying, my dear, marry one another today? How? Where?"

"It is simple enough. The captain of the ship you sailed upon can marry us. Why Charles, I cannot wait another moment to become your wife. If you refuse my offer, then I cannot remain your fiancée. I will seek passage back to my home and live as a spinster!"

"Oh, my dear, I'm afraid that will never be; I love you too much. I will make the necessary arrangements with our captain if you desire to marry this day. My only wish would be that mother could be here to witness our union."

"Charles, marry me this day, and when we return home, we'll have a proper wedding. But for now, I love you too much to live one more minute apart!"

"Very well, my love, please let us go far away from this place and the memory of that bastard pirate and his men."

"Yes, Charles, let's leave it all behind!"

If only Jacqueline could leave behind the memory of what had happened to her. None would ever comprehend, although many would remain suspicious of the child born to the reunited couple through the years. Was his father Charles or the pirate Captain Redbone? Both had brown hair and were tall in stature. Only Jacqueline knew for sure; it was a secret she would keep for the rest of her life.

As they left the island, Charles's last words were to the pirate captain. "Redbone, I swear by heaven and earth that one day I will see your head swinging on the yardarm of his majesty's ship, both you and your first mate and the entire crew of the bloodthirsty Iron Born Pirates!"

As the small group of pirates walked away, back toward their ship, Redbone responded to Charles's outburst under his breath by saying, "Me Iron Born brothers, it's bottles of rum for ye. Bravest of them all. Braver than the rest, we blood pirates shall never rest as long as there be booty. All other pirates fail to be as courageous as us; both their cutlass and blunderbuss fail to be!"

Arrrrr, the end of Iron Born pirates, or is it?

About the Author

Timothy Patrick Means was raised on the sunny beaches of Southern California. As a young boy, his love of pirates began while spending summers swimming and playing in the ocean without care.

Learning that becoming a pirate was not a viable career in the late 20th century, he landed a job in Aerospace, working for McDonnell Douglas. He worked there on military aircraft and, most exciting of all, rockets! He worked on all types of space hardware, including the space station, Space Shuttle, and the Delta rocket.

Timothy is a father to four children and two stepchildren, and a grandfather to fourteen, giving away his heart to all. He has always loved writing and has written in many genres, letting his imagination soar.

He has published several books and has more in the works. The first three books in *The Bishops' Sacrifice Series* are available on Amazon and other book websites. *The Sterling Chronicles*, currently available through Amazon Vella, further explores the adventures of the mystery's psychic detective. Timothy plans to add more books regularly to his growing list of published works. You can learn more about Timothy and his latest works at https://timothypatrickmeans.com and on Facebook at https://www.facebook.com/tmaddog38

Printed in Great Britain
by Amazon

15165636R00140